Praise for

Debra Webb

"Debra Webb delivers page-turning,
gripping suspense and edgy, dark characters
to keep readers hanging on…"
—*Romantic Times* on *Her Hidden Truth*

"Debra Webb draws readers into an
enthralling suspense with terrific characters…"
—*Romantic Times* on *Physical Evidence*

"…sizzling passion and fast pacing…"
—*Romantic Times* on *Protective Custody*

"Debra Webb's fast-paced thriller
will make you shiver in passion and fear…"
—*Romantic Times* on *Personal Protector*

DEBRA WEBB

was born in Scottsboro, Alabama, to parents who taught her that anything is possible if you want it badly enough. She began writing at age nine. Eventually, she met and married the man of her dreams, and tried some other occupations, including selling vacuum cleaners, and working in a factory, a day-care center, a hospital and a department store. When her husband joined the military, they moved to Berlin, Germany, and Debra became a secretary in the commanding general's office. By 1985, they were back in the States, and finally moved to Tennessee, to a small town where everyone knows everyone else. With the support of her daughters, Debra took up writing again, looking to mystery and movies for inspiration. In 1998, her dream of writing for Harlequin came true. You can write to Debra with your comments at P.O. Box 64, Huntland, TN 37345 or visit her Web site at www.debrawebb.com to find out exciting news about her next book.

Debra Webb

STRIKING DISTANCE

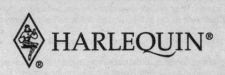 HARLEQUIN®

TORONTO • NEW YORK • LONDON
AMSTERDAM • PARIS • SYDNEY • HAMBURG
STOCKHOLM • ATHENS • TOKYO • MILAN • MADRID
PRAGUE • WARSAW • BUDAPEST • AUCKLAND

ISBN 0-373-83557-4

STRIKING DISTANCE

Special thanks to Denise O'Sullivan,
the absolute best editor on the planet.
Thanks so very much for your trust and
your encouragement. It was only with your
unerring guidance that this dream came true.

This book is dedicated to one of the finest men
I have had the personal and professional pleasure of
knowing. He is definitely one heck of a good man.
This one is for you, Ebb Deason.

CHAPTER ONE

NO MATTER THE LEGACY a man left behind, ultimately it was his death that defined him.

Chicago's Rosehill Cemetery was something of a tourist attraction with its medieval castle–like entrance of Joliet limestone and dozens of brooding mausoleums ranging in architectural styles from Egyptian to Gothic. The inhabitants, Civil War generals and soldiers as well as vice presidents, all laid in perpetual slumber in a place so blatantly filled with pomp and circumstance that even the soft tread of footsteps seemed an intrusion.

However well landscaped and adorned with lush shrubbery and graceful trees, this city of the dead with its foreboding Celtic cross and shimmering lake was still just a cemetery. Row after row of markers, whether mere headstones or more elaborate structures, represented lives that existed no longer.

His seeking gaze settled on one plot in particular where a woman stood quietly, probably reminiscing about the life long since laid to rest there.

The date of death engraved on the cold granite headstone indicated little about the man interred...but the name inscribed on that same glossy black surface said all that one needed to know.

James Colby.

Beloved husband and father.

Another epitaph should have been added: Ruthless butcher and marauder.

The great James Colby had been shot down and killed like the worthless bastard he was and not a minute too soon. But, even in death, his presence still lingered among the living. His essence kept alive…his work continued by a woman who was no better than he had been. Though she'd been warned, she persisted in her self-ordained, lofty endeavors. Just like her husband, nothing would stop her.

Except death.

And now her time was close at hand.

From his vantage point fifty meters away, well within striking distance, he read her every expression, watched her every movement through the crosshairs of his high-powered tactical scope. It was a face he had come to know intimately with the use of advanced technology and unending patience.

Looking weary and resigned the woman peered down at the elegant headstone as she no doubt struggled with the overwhelming silence around her…felt dizzy with the stifled senses of the dead and buried. The smell of damp earth would fill her nostrils with each breath she drew into her lungs, a sickening reminder that the rich, sodden soil perpetually cloaked her long-dead husband in its cold, relentless embrace.

Nothing could change the past.

Victoria Colby, he knew, had slowly come to realize that only she had the power to change the future. He'd waited a very long time for her to come to that understanding.

And yet she was powerless to deter him from his course.

She would die.

Soon.

The decision had been made long ago. His mission sanctioned even before he became a man.

He zeroed in to where her black heart beat beneath the tailored navy suit she wore. His finger curled around the trigger as his respiration ceased entirely. The bipod held the rifle steady, its precision aim a work of master craftsmanship.

He could kill her now…this instant…and nothing or no one could stop him.

Certainly not the crippled excuse for a man who stood a few meters to her left, watching, his senses so keen, his internal alarm so sensitive that he recognized some unknown threat even now. Smelled the danger in the very air. His rigid posture broadcasted a status of elevated alert.

But Lucas Camp had nothing to fear today.

The venerable Victoria Colby remained safe for the moment.

Oh, she would die.

But only one knew the day and the hour that death would come.

And it damn sure wasn't God.

CHAPTER TWO

VICTORIA COLBY KNELT before her late husband's headstone, uncaring that the waning October sun had yet to dry the morning's heavy dew from the grass. She traced the deeply gouged lines in the sleek surface that formed the letters of his name…the date of his passing. A heavy breath caught in her throat before it raggedly slipped past her trembling lips. How she missed him still.

Fifteen years had passed since she'd watched his body lowered into this grave. Since then the life she had once known had ground to a sudden and vicious halt. Without the help of her dedicated friends and colleagues at the Colby Agency, the private investigations firm her husband had nurtured like a child during his final days on this earth, she would surely not have survived his murder.

Her friends had gathered around her, united in strength and loyalty by the heinous tragedy, and held her up when she would otherwise have fallen. With their help she had risen from the ashes of devastation and forged ahead with her husband's dream, making the Colby Agency the very best in the business of private investigations. She had reached that goal, surpassed it, even. James would be very proud. The Colby Agency employed only the finest in the fields of investigation and security. The reputation she had garnered with the help of her outstanding staff was unparalleled.

As proud of that accomplishment as she was, fifteen years was a very long time to devote oneself to nothing but work. In a few months she would turn fifty. That milestone would be reached with nothing to show for her half century on this earth other than her esteemed agency. For some that might be enough, but not for her. She needed...wanted...

She glanced at the man who respectfully waited a short distance away. His presence made her all the more aware of how much more she wanted. *He* had been there for her through it all. Had waited patiently for his time to come.

Lucas Camp had served the United States government in one capacity or another for his entire adult life. Most of that dedicated duty had been spent working covert operations that only the president and God knew about. Not once had he hesitated, not even when his own life was at grave risk, when assigned a mission. It was that same man's selflessness that had saved James Colby's life in Vietnam and had shored up her resolve on too many occasions to name when she had felt ready to give up...to crumble beneath the weight of seemingly perpetual agonies. He had showered her with an unending source of friendship and kindness, of encouragement and belief in her ability to go on.

For some time now she had known that Lucas was in love with her. Admittedly, what she felt for him could be called nothing else. She knew without reservation that James would want her to be happy, would want no less for her than the kind of man Lucas Camp epitomized.

And still she had hesitated to allow their close relationship to evolve naturally.

The past had haunted her for far too long.

Victoria stared down at her left hand and the narrow gold band that had resided there for twenty-seven years. It was time she moved forward with her personal life. She slipped the band from her finger, held it tightly for one more moment, then pressed it gently into the soft soil at the base of the headstone. "Thank you for all that you gave me, James," she whispered. "You'll always be in my heart."

She swiped away a lone tear that trekked down her cheek and drew in a deep breath of much-needed resolve. It was time to move on, to look to the future rather than the past. She braced a hand on the cool surface of the granite and pushed to her feet.

She had waited long enough.

So had Lucas.

If only she knew the right words to say to thank him for his patience and unending devotion. But there were no words to accurately describe her feelings. Actions spoke louder than words. She'd asked him to bring her here today to show him her intentions.

She smiled when he joined her. "Thank you for giving me a moment."

Those gray eyes searched hers with a kind of uncertainty she would never have associated with the man she knew so well. "You're sure about this?" He glanced at her left hand and its bare ring finger.

Victoria nodded. "Yes. It's time I paid attention to what's important *now*."

An emotion she couldn't quite define replaced the uncertainty in his eyes. The ferocity of it made her pulse rush with anticipation. "We'll take this slow, Victoria. One step at a time. There's no need to hurry."

Warmth spread through her at his words. He'd stood vigil so very long and still he wouldn't make a single move without considering her feelings first and foremost.

"We'll take it slow in the beginning," she allowed, wanting him to hear in her voice the warmth that his nearness generated inside her.

A tiny smile quirked the corners of his mouth. "You're the boss." He gently folded his arm around her. "Let me take you to lunch," he suggested, that ever-watchful gaze doing a quick, covert—but not quite covert enough—area sweep. "The wind is brisk out here, don't you think?"

She kept her smile firmly in place and resisted the urge to look around the cemetery, brutally squashed the little shiver that threatened to scurry up her spine. Something had put Lucas on guard. He wanted to get her out of here in a hurry but without alarming her in any way. He didn't want to ruin the moment that he knew had been a long time in coming for her—for them.

She trusted his instincts too much to ignore his assessment. Though she hated even the suggestion of running from a threat, she wasn't a fool. Fate had been cruel to her, she'd lost her child and her husband in the space of three years. There had been a time when death would have been a blessed relief. Even now, at times, she wondered how she had survived the utter devastation. If the threat involved only her, she might choose to ignore it…but that was not the case. She'd come too close to losing Lucas only a few months ago on that godforsaken island to think for one second that he was as untouchable as he'd like her to believe.

She could not lose him…not now when she'd only just fully realized how very much she needed him.

She would do whatever it took to keep him safe and away from the evil that had destroyed her life once.

Leberman, the soulless devil, would not win this time.

Though she had never been able to prove it, she knew Errol Leberman was responsible for her husband's death. She couldn't be positive he was the one who had taken her son, but in her heart she knew it was a strong possibility. He had done all within his power for twenty long years to destroy her. Just a few short months ago he'd almost succeeded.

The ruthless bastard had lured first Lucas, then her, to St. Gabriel Island. Lucas had been badly hurt…and she'd known that she could not let Leberman win.

He had to be stopped.

Permanently.

CHAPTER THREE

LUCAS ALWAYS ENJOYED his time with Victoria, but today he'd been distracted. She had noticed, and to some degree there had been nothing he could do about that. She read him too well.

"You're sure that's all that's bothering you?" she asked again as she closed the door of her office behind them. He hadn't felt she was secure until he'd gotten her back into this building, this office. His concern at the cemetery as well as at the quiet, out-of-the-way restaurant where they'd dined had apparently been obvious.

Her own suspicions had been raised and she didn't intend to let it go. No one could accuse Victoria Colby of being anything less than persistent. As she awaited his response she shouldered out of her jacket and hung it on the coat tree in the corner, unknowingly providing him with an opportunity to simply look at her in a rare, unguarded state.

He suddenly wished he could see her dark hair loose. He knew it would be long, though she always kept it in a serviceable, upswept arrangement. The silver highlights enhanced the depth of the woman. As she turned to face him once more, he stole yet another moment to admire her effortless beauty. Great personal loss had etched her porcelain skin with fine lines, yet failed to detract from the gentle, sophisticated elegance.

He had been in love with Victoria from the moment he first laid eyes on her thirty years ago. But she had been the fiancé of his best friend and colleague, later to become his wife. As much as Lucas loved her…wanted her…he would, even now, undo the past, resurrect her husband and son in a heartbeat to make her happy, if only he possessed the power. But he could not, of course. He could, however, love her and protect her until the day he took his dying breath.

That he *would* do.

He produced the expected smile and stuck to his original story that would tie in to his immediate plans. "It's nothing, really. Casey has gotten it into his head that I need a vacation and, well—" he shrugged, using all the tactics he had learned over the years in the spy business to hide what he didn't want her to see "—you know how I am about work. I can't see myself taking off that kind of time. But Casey is the boss and he keeps insisting." He heaved a sigh. "I have a feeling he isn't going to take no for an answer. This little trip away from D.C. won't be enough to appease him."

Victoria looked thoughtful for a moment. "I've been getting the same hassle around here," she said, her brow furrowing. "Everyone but me thinks I need a vacation. I suppose even I realize it's past time I took some time off." It was her turn to shrug. The gesture drew his eyes to her slender but proud shoulders and the white silk blouse she wore. The contrast of the delicate, feminine fabric to the strong, tough-as-nails woman beneath only served to widen his smile into the genuine article. "Maybe I should," she went on as she looked directly at him, a new kind of sparkle in those brown eyes. "Maybe *we* should." Her expression turned inquisitive, the barest hint of a smile curled the corners of her lips. "What're you grinning about?"

He held her gaze for a couple of beats, weighing her words and the emotion that looked very much like desire he'd noticed there. "Is that an invitation, Victoria?" he ventured, ignoring her question for the moment. His heartbeat accelerated, sending a surge of heat through his body. He wanted this. Wanted it very much. But it had to be her choice…her decision.

She unconsciously rubbed her left hand, missing the ring she'd worn for more than half of her life. "Yes," she said succinctly. "It is."

Scarcely breathing for fear he would somehow break this spell, Lucas took her hands in his and considered how she'd tucked that precious gold wedding band into the ground next to her husband's headstone. That act had taken a great deal of courage, and he respected what it surely meant. She was ready to move on. But he would not push the issue. He had waited a lifetime for this woman, a few weeks longer wouldn't hurt. But her safety was another issue altogether.

He was getting closer.

Lucas had sensed his presence today at the cemetery. During lunch he'd excused himself briefly to meet with his security team leader in the restaurant's bar. His suspicions had been confirmed.

The man, who they assumed at this point to be a hired assassin, had taken up a position about fifty meters from Victoria. He'd been armed with a special police-style rifle, complete with tactical scope and bipod. At one point, one of the two specialists assigned to Victoria's secret security detail had almost engaged the target. Lucas had warned his men that the assassin was to be kept alive if at all possible. But he'd gotten damned close today. The only thing that had kept Lucas's man from taking out the assassin was the fact that he'd visually verified the weapon's positive three-position thumb safety was still locked. The shooter had had no intention of killing Victoria today.

He'd simply been watching.

Lucas could only assume that he was standing by for final authorization to complete the mission. He'd had at least three opportunities so far and hadn't acted. But there would come a time when he would, that was a certainty. Lucas had to take countermeasures before that happened. Somehow, while keeping Victoria safe and allowing the assassin to stay on their trail temporarily, he had to get someone close to this guy. It was the only way he could hope to catch the real threat: Leberman.

Victoria would never be safe as long as Leberman was alive. If he had hired this assassin as Lucas suspected, there might be a chance of tracking this hired killer right back to the bastard's hiding place. Which was the only reason they hadn't taken out the shooter already. They needed him to get to Leberman.

"Then we have plans to make," Lucas offered as he dispensed with the other troubling thoughts and focused on her invitation. "Where would you like to go?"

She searched his face, looking for some hint of what was on his mind. Suspicion still nagged at her, he knew. "Shall I have Mildred bring us coffee while we discuss the possibilities?"

The prospect of planning their joint vacation pleased her, and he hated like hell to disappoint her. They were so close. He groaned and glanced at his watch. "I have another meeting in thirty minutes. I could try and reschedule or—" he pretended to mull the idea over "—why don't you think about the destination possibilities and then we'll discuss the options over dinner tonight?"

"That would be lovely."

He squeezed her hands once more before letting go. "I'll see you at eight, then."

She nodded, her hopeful expression wilting just a little.

He would make this up to her.

Victoria watched Lucas leave her office, the ever-present limp only adding to his distinguished demeanor. He looked so handsome today. The gray shirt emphasized his eyes.

The elegant charcoal suit fit his lean frame perfectly. Their time at lunch had been more relaxed than any they'd shared since before the incident on St. Gabriel Island. It had felt good to simply be, with no talk of Leberman or the past.

She wanted it that way from now on.

He wanted it, too. She knew he did.

The only thing she couldn't figure out was why he insisted on lying to her.

CHAPTER FOUR

LUCAS LEANED against the examination table in the small treatment room and waited for the others to arrive.

The door opened, and a nurse with a cheery expression peeked in at him. "Mr. Camp, would you like some water or coffee?"

"No, thanks."

She shot him a cheeky smile and disappeared, allowing the door to close with a slow whoosh behind her.

He couldn't risk detection of this meeting. Complete secrecy was crucial. If Leberman or any of his people—and he could only assume that the assassin might be one of several—saw Lucas with Victoria's most-trusted investigators, they would know he was on to them. He didn't want that to happen any sooner than necessary. Nor could he risk that any part of the Colby Agency offices were bugged. It was a long shot since the offices were swept for foreign electronics on a regular basis, but one he wasn't willing to chance. As long as Leberman thought they were one step behind, he wouldn't get nervous and perhaps do something rash, like giving the final execution order.

The door opened again and Ian Michaels entered the room followed closely by Simon Ruhl. They were the kind of spit-and-polish guys who epitomized the term *spy*. But Lucas knew the gritty, less glamorous side of the business. He couldn't be deputy director of Mission Recovery without having been exposed to the worst that man was capable of. The highly trained Specialists in Mission Recovery were only called in when all else failed.

Ian acknowledged Lucas with a mere nod while Simon commented, "Nice place for a meeting."

This wouldn't be the first time Lucas had used a physician's office for a clandestine meeting, but it had been a long time. Not since his surgery after bringing down the traitor who'd almost destroyed Mission Recovery before Casey came on the scene as director. Had it been four years already? At any rate, this physician was an old friend from his military days. His Chicago clinic, situated mere blocks from the Colby Agency's location just off the Magnificent Mile, was a perfect front for conducting covert ops.

"You have any trouble with the transportation?" His lips twitched when he noted the slightest flinch in Ian's carefully controlled exterior.

"Not if you discount the siren," Ian commented dryly.

Though Lucas had walked into the office like any paying patient, Ian and Simon had arrived by ambulance and were hustled in through the rear emergency entrance. Anyone watching Lucas enter the clinic would never know that two Colby agents had arrived via the back door.

"So, what's going on, Lucas?" Simon was the first to call the meeting to order. Ian remained occupied with sizing up Lucas and his intentions. The man was good at that. Could tell more by watching his prey for mere minutes than from listening to hours of interrogation. Victoria had bragged to Lucas long ago about Ian. He was good at the business of peeling away the outer layers and getting to the bottom of things.

"I told you two weeks ago that I suspected Victoria was being watched." He spread his hands in a speculative gesture. "I couldn't be sure of the source of the problem— still can't be absolutely certain. But we now have reason to believe that this man may be connected to Leberman. He may be on the verge of making a move."

Silence reigned briefly while the two men absorbed the ramifications of that bit of information. Anyone who had been with the Colby Agency for any length of time knew about Leberman. The bastard had made it his life's mission to destroy Victoria Colby and all that she stood for. Lucas was certain he'd killed James Colby as well as the boy, Victoria's only child. But even that wasn't enough for the devil. He just kept coming back for more. Playing his sick games and then going back into hiding. He hybernated for years…until it was safe to surface again. Then he'd strike.

But this time was going to be different. This time Leberman was going to die.

"We don't have any real evidence to support our assessment, of course," Lucas went on pushing the disturbing memories away, "but I'm certain enough to take the appropriate action. I've put a security detail in place."

"We've reviewed every case that might carry enough significance to warrant this sort of vengeance," Simon informed him, bringing him up to speed on their end and lending even more credence to Lucas's conclusion. "There simply isn't anyone out there related to a Colby Agency case who we have reason to suspect at this time."

Lucas stroked his chin as he considered how to broach the next step. Neither of these gentlemen was going to like his strategy, and their cooperation was essential.

"What is it you're not telling us?" Ian cut to the chase.

Lucas almost smiled. Two minutes and the guy had nailed him to the floor. Judging by the fierce glare he had trained on Lucas at that moment there was no way around giving him a straight answer.

"The man watching Victoria may be a professional assassin hired by Leberman. I believe his mission is to complete what Leberman started on that island."

The air thickened with a new level of tension. All three were well aware of the events that had unfolded on St. Gabriel Island in a matter of hours. Events that had been years in the planning. The tiny island off the coast of Georgia had proven the perfect stage for his devious plans.

"Then she is no longer safe in any public setting," Ian suggested.

"I would have to agree with you." Evading the issue would be pointless. "To be frank, he's had ample opportunity already, but has chosen not to take the shot. My conclusion would be that he's keeping surveillance and waiting for final authorization from Leberman."

"But you can't be certain that Leberman is the one behind this," Simon countered. "You don't have any actual proof. No factual intelligence."

"No." Lucas looked from one to the other, reading the skepticism they wanted to cling to. No one wanted to believe Leberman was back, least of all Lucas. "Everything I have is speculation. But we all know he's the most logical candidate."

"Why haven't you taken out the assassin already?" Ian pressed as his own sense of anticipation obviously moved to the next level. To his way of thinking that would have been the most strategic move. Hell, it made perfect sense, but Lucas had his reasons.

This would be the tricky part. "We all know that Victoria will not hide from this once she's briefed on the situation. Nothing any of us could say would change her mind. And we also know that she will never be safe as long as Leberman is alive—"

"We've had this conversation already," Simon noted matter-of-factly. His agitation was somewhat more evident than Ian's. Tension radiated in every aspect of his posture.

"We have," Lucas agreed. "My stand on the matter has

not changed. We need to get Leberman. If this assassin can lead us to him, we have to take the risk.''

"The risk you speak of," Ian interjected calmly, his subdued tone more lethal than if he'd shouted the words, "involves Victoria's life, correct?"

Their gazes locked for two beats. "Correct."

"And you are willing to take this risk?" Ian pushed for finite clarification.

"It's our only option."

The two Colby agents exchanged a look.

Simon spoke up first. "Lucas, I'm confident that Victoria's best interests are your primary concern. I know you'll do whatever is necessary to protect her, but you must know that we can't simply pretend this isn't happening. We have to take some sort of action."

"The only action that will make a difference requires Victoria's cooperation, which will compromise our efforts." He divided his attention between the two somber-faced men. "I have an alternate approach in mind. First I have to persuade her to take a vacation with me. I've plotted a destination. She'll be completely cocooned by my team of Specialists until we can reel this guy in. I won't allow anything to happen to her, you can rest assured of that."

"You'll keep us informed of every step," Simon persisted.

"I'll keep the two of you informed." Lucas gestured from one to the other. "I don't want anyone else to know the plan. *No one,* is that understood?"

"Are you implying there might be a traitor inside the Colby Agency?" Ian inquired, one brow raised slightly higher than the other his only outward indication of surprise.

"I'm not implying anything," Lucas asserted. "I'm simply not taking any risks. No one but the four members assigned to her security will know exactly where she is. And even those four won't know where they're going and for what reason until they get there. If there is a breach in security it won't be on my end."

"If you spirit her away to safety," Simon countered, "how is that going to affect the situation with the assassin and his leading you to Leberman?"

Another dicey maneuver. "I'm going to send someone undercover to get close to him."

"Since complete anonymity is essential, who will you utilize for that assignment?" Ian wanted to know, his tone reflective of his uncommitted stance on the matter.

"I'm going to use someone who isn't affiliated with my people at Mission Recovery or the Colby Agency. Someone completely out of the game."

"You think that's wise considering who we're up against?" Simon prodded, his arms folded over his chest. He clearly didn't like this any more than Ian did. For that matter neither did Lucas.

"This agent is a recruit fresh from the CIA's training facility. Our Forward Research group has been tracking her progress since before she entered the program. She's good. Damn good. She has a degree in psychology, which could prove useful. And she has no stake in the matter either way."

"What makes you think she'll go for this assignment?" Simon looked even more suspicious of the whole strategy. It did sound like a suicide mission, even Lucas had to admit it.

"If she's got half the fire burning in her belly to impress the brass as it appears, she'll go for it."

"But is she good enough to do the job?" Ian voiced the remaining variable.

Lucas smiled as he thought of the hotshot he'd observed steamrolling her peers, female *and* male alike. He'd been waiting for the right kind of opportunity to bring her on-board. "Oh, yeah. She's good enough."

"She'll try to get close to this guy in hopes that he'll lead her to Leberman, is that it?" Simon relaxed, but only marginally.

"She'll get close to him, and then when Victoria vanishes he won't have any choice but to contact Leberman for additional instructions." Lucas hoped like hell it would be that easy.

Five seconds lapsed into thirty as the two men closest to Victoria at the Colby Agency considered his proposal.

"I can see how this might work." Simon was the first to edge toward commitment.

"And what about you, Ian? Do I have your support?" Lucas couldn't move forward without both these men on board. Timing and synchronized reactions were everything. There couldn't be a single glitch.

"I have no reason to doubt your loyalty to Victoria," he said in response, without actually answering at all. "I do, however, have reservations as to the plan you've outlined, but I can't conceive of a better strategy." His gaze locked fully with Lucas's. "As you say, Leberman must be stopped. It's past time we got this done."

"All right, then. I'll set things in motion on my end. The only thing I need on yours is full cooperation and complete secrecy."

"You have that unconditionally," Ian said with that quiet intensity that would unnerve most men.

Lucas nodded. "I'll keep you posted."

With the preliminary plans out of the way there was nothing further to discuss. "We'll ensure status quo at the office until we hear from you," Simon offered in parting.

"I don't want Victoria to suspect anything," Lucas re-iterated as they moved toward the door. "She's already picked up on my uneasiness."

"We understand." This from Ian. He paused before following Simon into the corridor. "Just one more thing." He looked directly at Lucas. "I have no doubt that you will do all in your power to protect Victoria from this assassin."

"I will," Lucas assured him.

"If," Ian qualified in that low, deadly tone, "you take this risk and fail, it will be the last thing you do."

Their gazes held for a beat of screaming silence.

"If," Lucas allowed grimly, "I fail, you can use my gun to do the job."

CHAPTER FIVE

TASHA NORTH TOSSED her bag into her car and yanked off the confining double-breasted suit coat that had felt like a straitjacket all day. This stuffy attire was just one more thing she hated about her new job. She flung the inside-out garment into the back seat and dropped behind the wheel of her Volkswagen Beetle. She breathed a sigh of pure, unadulterated relief. Whenever she settled into the white leather seat of her little yellow Bug she felt normal... almost.

Jerking the pins loose from her hair, she shook the blond shoulder-length mass free and pushed her sunglasses into place. She cranked and revved the engine. Thank God it was Friday. She couldn't wait to get out of here.

Tires squealing she rocketed out of her designated parking slot and zoomed toward the exit of the mammoth parking garage. At the security checkpoint she slowed for the guard to ID her, gave him a big, friendly smile, which he returned sheepishly, and then proceeded forward.

Once off Langley property she floored the accelerator and headed home.

Frustration pounded in her brain. She hadn't joined the elite CIA to sit behind a desk. All day long she did the same thing: reviewed intelligence reports, looking for tidbits others had missed. Oh, she'd found an item here and there, especially the past couple of days. But that wasn't how she'd seen herself fitting into the agency she'd been in awe of all these years. At any rate, when she'd graduated from training, her superiors had insisted that her battery of assessment tests had determined that this was the best assignment for optimum use of her skills.

In her opinion that was a load of crap.

So what if she had a near-photographic memory and felt like cyberspace was her second home or that she could hack into the Pentagon's computer system as easily as checking her e-mail? Would they never forget that little incident?

She rolled her eyes as she merged onto the expressway. She'd only done it once. Good grief, she'd been seventeen. Kids did stupid stuff like that. She was more sensible now, played by the rules, thought before she acted... Well, most of the time, anyway.

But at seventeen she'd been impetuous. Still, once the hoopla had settled down, especially the part about no charges being filed, and her parents had stopped having cardiac episodes, she'd actually gotten a little excited about having stepped knee-deep in national security shit. A CIA recruiter had come to see her at high school. It had all been very secretive. Her first covert briefing. He'd told her how impressed he was with her skill and how he'd personally kept her out of trouble. Had said that he'd be watching as she moved through her college career. Then, with a mysterious "I'll be in touch," he'd disappeared just like the spy she dreamed of being. And just as he'd promised, on graduation day he'd shown up at the university to recruit her.

And what had they done?

They'd stuck her behind a metal desk reading boring reports all day every day.

Oh, the training program had been great. She'd loved it, kicked ass and taken names, coming out top in her class.

Those intensive weeks had been exhilarating...had felt like the CIA she'd dreamed of joining.

This—she glared at the skirt and low-heeled pumps she

wore—was not. She looked just like her mother for heaven's sake.

Tasha took a breath. Okay, okay. She knew the deal. Paying her dues wasn't the end of the world. Impatience had always been her most glaring flaw. She was almost twenty-three. It was past time she'd learned how to take the waiting in stride.

"Grow up, Tasha," she grumbled. "You have to earn your way in the real world." How many times had her father told her that theatrics didn't pay off? "Patience is a virtue," he'd say at least once a day while she was growing up. Be that as it may, in high school she'd gotten noticed by proving she could do what no one else could—like cracking the Pentagon's cyber security.

Another sigh heaved from her chest. This wasn't high school. Being slick and cagey and, as bad as she hated to admit it, irreverently arrogant wasn't going to put her at the top of the food chain when her superiors, those rating her ability, were all replicas of her dear old dad. She had to be patient. Had to prove her worth behind a desk before she graduated to field operations. Hadn't she learned a good deal about the human psyche in college? A degree in psychology taught her one thing if nothing else—meet the expectations of the humans in charge and life was much easier.

She could do it. Five days a week, eight hours a day, for a while longer. Her time would come…eventually. All she had to do was play it cool and bide her time. She reached to turn up the volume on the CD player just as the sound of her cell phone ringing drew her hand in another direction. Groping around in her bag she fished out the phone and flipped it open.

"North."

"Tasha, this is Martin."

Her respiration came to a screeching halt before accelerating into double duty. Her recruiter. A major player amid the powers-that-be at the Agency. Could this be the call she'd hoped for? "Martin, how's it going?" she asked when she had reclaimed her voice, then moistened her lips in nervous anticipation. Why would he be calling now? She hadn't heard from him for nearly three months…not since surviving training…and being shackled to that damned desk. She'd all but given up.

"We have to talk. Can you meet me right now?"

A frown worried her brow as she considered the urgency in his tone. What was up with that? "Sure. Where?"

"Take the next exit. There's a gas station on the right once you've cleared the overpass. I'll be waiting."

Her frown deepening, she closed her phone and tossed it in the general vicinity of her bag.

What the hell was going on?

She slowed for the upcoming exit ramp and took it as instructed.

But…she glanced at the discarded phone, then back at the expressway she'd veered from…how did he know where she was?

Tracking device. She'd heard rumors that all new agents were injected with the latest technology. A device so small that it could be installed with nothing more than a subcutaneous pin prick. With all the immunizations required in training, she could have been injected with anything and not known the difference.

She shrugged it off. Just part of the business. If they wanted to keep tabs on her comings and goings she didn't mind. Anything for the job.

She stopped at the end of the exit ramp, then made a sharp left.

The highway that cut beneath the overpass was one of those takes-you-nowhere kind that sprawled off into the woods in either direction. To her surprise there was a gas station up ahead. It looked deserted. As she eased into the parking lot her assumption was confirmed. Not simply closed but out of business.

On the far side of the lot Martin waited, leaning against his shiny black Jaguar. Smiling in spite of the buzz of warning going off in her head, Tasha pulled up next to him and climbed out. This was Martin. The man who'd held the door to the CIA open for her. He'd assured her that he had his eye on her and would see that her future turned out the right way.

Maybe he had news along those lines for her now. A jolt of irritation shot through her. He'd better have good news. She was sick of all talk and no action.

"I'm glad you came," he said as he removed his dark glasses. "We need to talk."

She nodded, slipped off her eyewear and tossed the designer sunglasses onto the dash of her car. He was right. They did need to talk. If he didn't have an offer for her now, he'd better get things in motion. She'd had about all the nine-to-five grind she could tolerate. Moving closer, she propped a hip on the rear quarter panel of his sleek automobile. "I hope you've got good news for me."

He studied her for a moment, then asked the last question she'd expected to hear, "You have the codes, don't you?"

The hair on the back of her neck stood on end. "Codes?" Her posture stiffened before she could stop it. He noticed. Dammit. "I don't know what you mean."

"They're watching you." He surveyed the wooded area around them. "They know."

"Who knows?" She straightened, adopted a fight-or-flight stance and did a little surveying of her own.

He reached into an interior pocket of his high-priced suit jacket and pulled out a 9mm handgun. "Take this. You may need it."

She stared at the nickel-plated weapon before accepting

it. "How do you know?" She'd reported the breach the moment she stumbled upon it while reviewing endless boring text. Someone, inside the agency, had hidden the codes in the documents. She had no idea how or why, she'd simply done her job. But, as Martin said, she had, in fact, uncovered some sort of code. Her supervisor had appeared agitated that she'd made such a discovery. And it wasn't like she could forget what she'd seen. Once she viewed data—any data, written, visual, whatever—it was in her brain for all time.

"I always know what's going on with my special students."

He'd been an excellent mentor. She'd counted on him. Trusted him…but somehow this felt off. The psych evaluators who'd assessed her prior to advancing into the CIA's training program had called the little sixth sense she possessed elevated precognitive reception. Well, whatever the hell it was, her little precog receptors were humming like mad.

"Is there something else I should know?" Was he only here to warn her to be careful? She resisted the urge to shake her head. It just didn't make sense.

"You'll need—" The rest of his words were cut off by screaming tires and a roaring engine.

Tasha dove for the ground, hitting the asphalt hard and rolling behind his car just as a hail of gunfire erupted.

Martin followed suit, their movements like a well-choreographed dance.

She shifted into a crouch and prepared to return fire when the world suddenly went dark.

HER HEAD ACHED.

Tasha slowly opened her eyes and surveyed the room around her. Plain white walls. No furniture other than the chair in which she sat.

Where the hell was she? She blinked and even that small movement cost her. The ache in her head sliced through her skull like a machete.

Her hands were secured behind her back. She twisted her wrists, the flesh there burning from the tightness of the ropes.

Martin.

Her heart skipped a beat.

Had he been shot?

The code.

Surely this wasn't about that code...she didn't even know what it related to.

The door across the ten-by-ten room suddenly opened, and a man dressed in black combat gear walked in. He closed the door behind him and leaned against it.

"Hello, Agent North."

She looked up at him from beneath her lashes and told him her position in no uncertain terms. "I don't know what you want. You're wasting your time."

He tugged at first one leather glove and then the other, pulling them firmly into place. "You think so?"

She laughed softly, anticipation already rushing to steady her spinning head. Let him take his best shot. "I know so."

"We'll just see about that."

He started toward her, and Tasha did as she had been trained.

She shut down all nonessential functions.

Closed him out.

Closed *everything* out.

CHAPTER SIX

THEY'D COVERED HER HEAD and tied her hands behind her back again. Tasha stayed very still, absorbing the details around her as best she could in her current state of near numbness. The vehicle—a cargo van maybe—she'd been shoved into glided smoothly toward its destination. City streets, well maintained. No back road. Not yet. Wherever they were taking her she had a pretty good idea they planned to execute her and dump the body.

She hadn't given either of the men who'd interrogated her what they wanted. She was of no further use to them. Those words echoed through her throbbing skull as she allowed her senses to awaken more fully, inch by slow inch. The bruised ribs and split lip were the least of her worries. Unless she finagled an escape she was dead.

Just in case she managed a getaway, she had studied each face she'd encountered very carefully. Had even gotten a DNA sample under her nails when she scratched one of them. She almost smiled when she thought of the head butt she'd pulled off, taking one guy down. She hoped his nose was broken.

Well, at least she'd put up a good fight and she hadn't given them the code.

That was something.

Though an alien emotion, what felt like fear, moved through her. She had to admit that the thought of dying so young lacked any appeal whatsoever.

The vehicle rocked slightly as it slowed, then stopped

briefly. She listened intently. No traffic sounds. A left turn. Then a right. They were likely nearing their final destination now. Her heart rate quickened.

The vehicle bumped over a rise and then stopped. Parking lot, she surmised. The sound of metal sliding over metal and a rush of cool air told her the cargo door had been opened.

It was now or never. She had to make a move.

When she would have pushed herself up, brutal hands shoved her forcefully from behind, sending her hurtling out of the vehicle.

She landed hard. Her skin, wherever exposed, identified asphalt beneath her. Struggling frantically, she maneuvered into an upright position, her legs folded painfully under her. If she could only get up…

Those hands pushed her back down.

She braced for the impact of a bullet.

Silence.

Footsteps retreating.

Tires squealed as the vehicle spun away.

Stunned as much by the shock of being left alive as by the pain now making itself known in a big way, for one long moment Tasha could only sit there, bewildered.

The sound of clapping jerked her out of her state of dazed confusion.

She stumbled to her feet, battling with the bindings on her wrists. Within seconds she was free, the knots oddly easy to escape. Not like before.

"Bravo, Agent North."

She jerked the cloth sack from her head and glared in the direction of the voice. *Martin.* Her mentor. Her recruiter. The man she trusted above all others.

"What the…"

Her words drifted off as realization seeped into her muddled gray matter. She'd been set up. He hadn't needed a tracking device...he'd planned this.

"You son of a bitch," she snarled as she charged toward him.

He held up both hands to halt her attack. The streetlamp on the outer perimeter of the abandoned parking lot provided sufficient light for her to see his features. "Now, don't go taking it out on the messenger."

"What the hell was this?" She swiped at the blood leaking from her split lip, wincing at the burn.

"Just a small—" he held his forefinger and thumb close together "—*final* test," he assured her with a knowing nod.

"Test?" she roared. "You people played enough mind games on us during training. I've been out of training for three months! What else do I have to do to prove my loyalty?"

He sighed and braced one elbow on the other arm so that he could rest his chin in his hand as he'd often done when pacing before the class. "You see, Tasha," he offered quietly, his easygoing tone making her want to slug him, "there are a chosen few who get special notice. For those, like you, we have exclusive plans. But, there's always one final test. And that test can only be administered *after* you have access to negotiable information, otherwise it's pointless. You, of course, passed with flying colors."

Some of the fire went out of her fury. But she was still as mad as hell. "What does this mean?"

He smiled. "It means, my dear Tasha, that you are on your way. Very soon you'll be brought into that exclusive club."

She narrowed her gaze, her suspicion mounting. "How soon?" She wanted more than an empty promise. She'd had that.

"Soon." He surveyed her haggard appearance. "Now go home, take a long hot bath and enjoy your weekend."

Before she could demand any other information, he got into his Jag and drove away.

"Bastard," she muttered as she staggered to her own waiting, considerably more modest vehicle.

She'd lost one of her shoes, so she kicked the other one away before climbing behind the wheel of her Bug. Her panty hose were shredded, and one knee was skinned. She dragged off the ragged nylon and tossed it out the window. Only one button held her blouse together. But at least she still had all her teeth, she mused, sliding her tongue over her undamaged pearly whites.

A quick glance in the mirror and she grimaced. She looked like hell. Well, as long as it got her where she wanted to be. No pain, no gain, right?

She started the engine and pointed the car toward home. Damn she was beat.

Literally.

Half an hour later she braked to a stop at the curb outside her small Crystal City duplex. Swearing profusely she eased out of the car. Every muscle in her body screamed in protest of each move. Fat lot of good three nights per week of martial arts had done her. With her hands tied behind her back she'd scarcely landed a single blow.

Appeasing herself with the memory that Martin had said *soon*, she padded barefoot up the steps and to the front door. Soon she would join an exclusive club. She knew what that meant—field operations. Smiling, she reached to insert the key into the lock. She stilled. A chill raced over her skin. Her pulse tripped into the rush zone.

Something wasn't right.

It was past midnight and damned dark. Most of her yuppy neighbors were in bed already. Like her they all worked too many hours to bother with pets, so the whole neighborhood was dead silent. They were all good little robots, spinning their wheels in their white-collar world by day and playing nice, tidy little home owners by night.

Boring…boring. Not the life she'd planned for herself.

Hopefully that was almost over for her.

At the moment *over* might very well have an altogether different meaning.

Cautiously, not making a sound, she moved around the side of her house. Her unit was the last one on the block, which gave her quick access to the rear of the property without passing a neighbor's window. Keeping close to the brick wall, she edged around to the back.

She flattened against the wall next to her back door and listened intently. No sound came from inside, but the goose bumps raised across her skin warned her that things were not as they should be.

During training she'd met a few other recruits who had this elevated sense of alert. Advanced precognitive warning system, whatever the shrinks wanted to call it. She'd always had it…had banked on it more times than she cared to recall. Whenever her gut clenched and her flesh pebbled she paid attention.

She eased a little farther across the rear of the house until she reached her bedroom window. A smile slid across her lips when she found it open an inch or two and with one broken pane. The bastard. He'd climbed through her window. Just who the hell did he think he was? He'd likely been damned disappointed that she didn't even own a VCR much less a DVD. She preferred making her own entertainment.

Another thought struck her on the heels of that one. This was too easy. Not right. She considered her options and decided that going in was the best route. She'd be prepared for whatever waited inside. And she knew someone was there…she could feel it.

In less than ten seconds she was in the room with

scarcely any effort and without having made the slightest noise to warn her prey.

The bedroom was dark but Tasha didn't need any light. She knew her way around her own home.

She reached into the tissue box on the bedside table and snagged her weapon. A .38 that she'd purchased the day she graduated from college. A girl had to have her protection. Besides, she'd thought she was going into the spy business. Didn't every spy carry a weapon? Fleetingly she thought of the 9mm Martin had lent her for about five seconds. It probably had been loaded with blanks, just like the ones that had sent her diving for cover when the van came barreling into the gas station's parking lot. She gritted her teeth against a new surge of fury. This sure as hell better not be another one of his games.

She frowned. The .38 felt wrong. She weighed it in her hand…too light. She crouched down and felt under the edge of the bedside table for her backup piece. A sinking feeling kicked in. This business of game playing had gone too far. A burglar would have taken the gun, not just the bullets.

She eased across the bedroom and through the open door. She had memorized each spot where her floor creaked and avoided those areas as she made her way down the short hall that connected the five rooms of her home like spokes on a square wheel. The bathroom was clear…the kitchen was, too, except for three nights' worth of dirty dishes. She didn't have to see them to know they were there, her memory provided a vivid image. Nothing in the guest room.

With each breath expertly controlled to avoid audible detection, she locked her right elbow and leveled her .38. She kept her left hand slightly behind her, the .32 grasped firmly there. She didn't want to give away her backup piece just yet. Giving herself a mental three count she entered the living room, her gaze sweeping left to right until she visually engaged the dark outline of the target framed in the meager light from the streetlamp outside the window.

On the sofa. Looked tall. Male probably.

The barrel of her .38 zeroed in on his torso. "Don't move or you're dead."

"Do you mind if I turn on a light? I prefer to look a person in the eye when conversing."

A new kind of wariness slid over her, and she squinted to make out the details of his face, which was impossible. "Who the hell are you?"

"I'm reaching for the light," he informed her as one arm moved toward the table next to him.

The lamp switched on and she blinked to adjust to the brightness. The warm glow from the sixty-watt bulb spilled over the intruder who looked to be about fifty or so. Graying hair...eyes the color of a winter's frost. Business suit, designer quality. His hands were propped on a cane in front of him. Briefcase sat at his feet.

Resisting the urge to frown, she cocked her weapon. "You'd better start talking, old man, before I decide to shoot first and ask questions later."

He opened his left hand and showed her his palm and the brass rounds gleaming there. "You might find that difficult without these."

She leveled the .32 in her left hand on him then. "I don't think it'll be difficult at all." She tossed the useless .38 aside.

He smiled, approval gleaming in his eyes. "You are good."

"I don't know who the hell you are," she growled, "but I can tell you that I've had a really bad day. So bad in fact that I could shoot you right now and blame it on post-traumatic stress and probably get away with it."

"Sit," he ordered. "And we'll talk."

That sounded a little too damned familiar. Talking had

done nothing but get her in trouble today. Still watching him warily, she moved to the closest chair, which put her directly across the antique-trunk-turned-coffee-table from him. She eyed his cane skeptically and let him see her dubiousness. "How the hell did you manage to climb through my window?" she asked bluntly. Beating around the proverbial bush had never been her style.

He smirked. "Who said I climbed through the window?"

Her gaze narrowed then cut to the front door. Sure enough the lever was turned to the unlock position. She'd known the whole window thing was too easy...staged.

"I only opened the window to make you think I'd climbed through," he explained unnecessarily. But then he did that on purpose, wanted to rub it in.

"Okay, so you have my attention now. What's this about? I've endured about all the head games I intend to play today. And you don't look like the type who has to force the ladies to do his bidding. So what do you want?" Despite being over the hill and using a cane, the guy was attractive, in a smart-ass sort of way, definitely distinguished looking.

That last jab won her a genuine smile. Her heart fluttered. When he smiled, wow! Those gray eyes sparkled with mischief and something deeper...something curiously fascinating. She scolded herself. That was just the kind of thinking that usually got her into trouble. This stranger had broken into her home and had unloaded her weapon. He could be armed. She surveyed him again. Probably was. Besides, she wasn't supposed to notice how cute he was. He wasn't a frigging stray dog looking for a home. In fact, she'd bet he was about as far from domesticated as one could get. Another concept crept into her thoughts. Had Martin's schemes moved to a new level?

"My name is Lucas Camp. I'm here because I need you for a mission."

Whatever he'd said after his name was lost on her. "Lucas Camp?" She lowered her weapon. "You're a legend."

Another of those charming smiles. "Some would disagree with you on that."

What the hell was a superspook like Lucas doing in her living room? "Former Military Intelligence turned CIA," she said aloud, recalling all the rumors she'd heard about the legendary Lucas Camp. "Then the story gets a little murky. Everyone knows you're out there, but no one knows any more than that. You're the best of the best. No one can touch you." She'd never say it out loud but he represented all that she wanted to be. Made Martin look like a pussy. Well, okay, maybe not a pussy, but she was a little pissed at him right now.

"Unless I choose to allow them access," Lucas said with a pointed look at her.

Her breath caught in her chest. He was allowing *her* access. This was Lucas Camp—in her home—talking to her. Her eyes rounded and she passed the back of her hand over her burning lip. "Would you like something to drink? Water? Beer?" Dammit, he probably preferred coffee and she didn't even own a coffeemaker. She winced again at her stinging lip.

"No, thanks, Ms. North. As I said, I'm here to discuss a mission with you."

She felt her eyes go even wider. A mission? Had he said that before? "With me?"

He nodded. The amused expression he wore told her she was making a complete idiot of herself. Time to pull it together and act like a professional. She'd survived CIA training after all. And today's *final* test. She was no lightweight. She squared her shoulders and looked him directly in the eyes. "What kind of mission?" She sounded strong, professional. Just when she would have given herself a mental pat on the back she remembered how she looked—

like hell for sure. While she tugged at her blouse to keep it closed he reached into his briefcase, withdrew a PDA, entered a code and offered the device to her. "The profile is pretty sketchy, but this is what we have."

She reviewed the meager contents, scrolling forward one screen at a time on the palm-size computer. John Doe, estimated age thirty, approximate height and weight six-two, a hundred and ninety pounds. Living somewhere in Chicago, specific address unknown. She surveyed the shot someone had taken from a considerable distance, probably zeroing in with a mega zoom lens. Blondish hair, similar to her own. Blue eyes. Chiseled good looks.

She looked up at Lucas and asked, "You don't know who this guy is?" Which was a dumb question since he was listed as John Doe. Duh.

Lucas shook his head. "Not a clue. We believe he's an assassin."

Now that got her full attention. "Who's his target? The president?" Another rush of adrenaline seared through her veins. This might just be her lucky day.

"Nothing politically related or that high profiled," he told her without going into specifics, which was par for the course. Intel was doled out on a need-to-know basis only.

"What part do you need me to play in this mission?" She emphasized the word need. No matter how he downplayed the scenario, this had to be big or Lucas wouldn't be involved. Maybe not Whitehouse big, but big in any case.

"We need to know who this guy is and, more important, we need to reach out and touch the man who hired him." Lucas pointed to the PDA. "The next face you see is the one we're looking for."

Tasha studied the final image on the screen with new curiosity. This one was older. Gray hair, gray-blue eyes. Five-ten, a hundred and sixty pounds. This one looked almost harmless. She flipped back a screen or two. Now this one—she studied the younger man's grim features—looked deadly. "So, you want me to get to know the assassin. In hopes he'll lead me to the man who hired him." Her gaze connected with Lucas's. "Is that it?"

Lucas nodded, then quirked one brow a fraction higher than the other. "That is, if you think you're up to it. The personal requirements might be steep. To get as close as you need to..." He allowed the unfinished statement to linger in the air a moment before he continued. "We'll be watching from a distance, but not close enough to keep you safe. You'll be on your own."

Another charge of excitement went through her. "I'm up to anything you can throw my way." She knew what he was worried about, and she could handle it. Her training had included intensive profiles to see if she could tolerate mental as well as physical abuse of all kinds. All results indicated she would hold up under pressure exceedingly well. She licked her busted lip for emphasis. She would die before she'd break. Fooling a polygraph as well as tactics to fight the effects of certain drugs were all a part of her vast repertoire. "Sounds almost too easy," she admitted.

"We don't know anything about this assassin," Lucas said grimly. "We have to assume he's extremely dangerous. There's no way to guess how many people he's killed in his career or what his MO is. If the man who hired him is who we believe he is, then you can rest assured that our assassin is highly trained and well experienced."

She could read between the lines. This was a mission that contained a definite "suicide" element. Getting close to the target and staying alive would entail a great deal of skill and more than a little luck.

"What's in this for me?" she wanted to know, undeterred. They might as well get to the heart of the matter.

"If I'm going to risk life and limb for you, what will *you* do for me?"

Lucas looked pleased that she'd asked. "You succeed in this mission and you'll come to work for me with the best of the best."

Struggling with the desire to do a victory whoop, she clamped down hard on her outward reactions. *Stay cool, don't let him see that you know this is an opportunity of a lifetime.* A route through all the BS and straight to the kind of work she longed to do. It was rumored that the elusive Lucas Camp headed some sort of elite top secret organization. A club far more exclusive than anything under the CIA umbrella.

"And if I fail?"

"Then it won't matter," he said flatly. "Because you'll be dead."

That was the answer she'd expected. If she got close to this guy and he suspected for one nanosecond that she was a spy, she'd be history. Tasha shrugged. "So, I won't fail." She looked straight into the knowing eyes of one of the most powerful men on the planet and watched for the slightest flicker of deceit. "Just one more question, Mr. Camp, why me?"

"Because you're good." No hesitation, not even a glimmer of deception. "Too good to be stuck behind some desk." A smile curled one corner of his mouth. "Too good to be working for the CIA period."

She inclined her head and pushed for a little more. "What's so bad about the CIA? The whole world is convinced that the CIA has ultimate power and prestige." That much was true. But those with the real power were few and far between, that was the part they never showed in the movies.

Lucas chuckled. "Agent North, my organization is what the CIA wishes it were."

His statement validated the rumors she'd heard. "When do I go to work?"

"Tomorrow. A cab will pick you up early and take you to the airport. Someone will be waiting at O'Hare to take you to your temporary quarters. This assignment may last a few days or a few weeks. I can't be sure at this point. Don't take anything from home. We'll furnish everything you need."

She knew a moment's uneasiness, but only a moment. "What about my work at Langley?" If this didn't pan out and she miraculously survived...

"Time off has been cleared with your immediate superior. He doesn't know why and doesn't need to. Once this mission is over, you can decide if you want to take me up on my offer or go back to your job with the Agency."

Sounded fair enough. "All right." This was the opportunity she'd waited for, a chance to prove what she was made of. "Once I'm in Chicago where do I start?"

"Our boy hangs out most weekends in a club downtown called the Metro Link."

She'd read that in the sketchy personal info on the PDA.

"You'll need to commit to memory the meager intel we have on this guy."

"Already did." She passed the PDA back to him. "How come there's nothing on the guy who hired him except a visual image?" That part struck her as odd. Lucas certainly sounded as if he knew more about the guy than what he looked like.

"Intel will be provided as necessary." He dropped the PDA into his briefcase as he stood. "I think you understand what to do from here."

Nothing she hadn't expected. "How do I let you know once I've made contact with the target?" she asked as she followed him to the door.

"I'll be in touch with you when the time comes."

Translation: Lucas Camp would be watching.

"By the way." He hesitated before going out the door. "Just in case you were wondering, Agent Bauer's nose *isn't* broken."

Before she could ask how the hell he knew about Martin's little test and her performance he'd disappeared into the night.

Just like a ghost.

CHAPTER SEVEN

VICTORIA STARED at her reflection in the mirror for a long time that night, the brush clasped in her hand as she stroked her long, dark hair. The silver streaks gleamed in the light, reminding her of just how old she really was. So much time had passed...and nothing in her personal life had changed. Beethoven's "Moonlight" Sonata played softly in the background. The music usually relaxed her, but it wasn't working so well tonight.

She sighed and laid the brush on the vanity table next to her bottles of perfumes and cosmetics, all lined in a neat row awaiting her attention. There was moisturizer for her skin, anti-aging cream for the fine lines that marred her eyes and mouth. And, of course, the skin firmer for less delicate parts of the anatomy. Everything that one could need to remain youthful looking.

Maybe she should have started using the products long ago. Then perhaps she would not look quite so old. But nothing she applied to her skin would change the way she felt inside.

Ancient would be the best description.

Age had never really bothered her until now. She looked down at the bare ring finger of her left hand, and for a moment her chest tightened with anxiety. She'd made a new commitment today. One that in no way lessened the old one, but rather, forged a new path for her to move forward. Looking back was definitely not good for her peace of mind. James was gone. It was well past time to move on. Lucas was alive and ready to move into the future with her.

She peered at the weary face in the mirror. But was she really ready for that journey? Her right hand moved to her chest, settling over her heart. On a conscious, cognitive level she felt ready. It was her heart that hesitated, that worried about starting over.

Victoria stood and moved away from the vanity table. She paused in front of the full-length mirror mounted on the wall near her walk-in closet. She was almost fifty. What did Lucas see when he looked at her?

Tugging the silk belt free she shrugged out of the robe, allowing it to puddle around her feet. She studied her nude body then. Her skin was still slightly flushed from her long, hot soak in the tub. Her dark hair, even with the silver streaks, contrasted sharply against her pale flesh. She'd never really noticed that before. Would the contrast please Lucas? Or did it only make her look pale and haggard?

Pushing that worrisome detail aside, she moved on to other features. Her breasts were still reasonably firm and high, not that they'd ever been that large, but they were presentable, she supposed. Her husband had never complained, but then, that had been a very long time ago.

Her waist narrowed nicely and her hips flared just enough, though she couldn't quite claim a flat tummy. Time and gravity had taken its toll there as well as behind, she noted as she turned slightly. Her legs were fairly toned, mostly from the treadmill she used every morning.

She wondered what kind of women Lucas had been involved with in the past. Though he'd never been married she felt certain there had been numerous lovers, after all he was a very handsome man with endless charm. A smile relaxed across her lips and affection twinkled in her brown eyes. Did her eyes glitter that way when she smiled at Lucas? She sighed, anxiety gnawing at her insides. Just something else to wonder about. She would know soon enough.

Locating panties and a nightgown, she dressed for bed, then turned off the lights except the one on her bedside table and crawled beneath the covers. She didn't have to bother with turning off the music, it was on a timer. An hour from now it would end on a graceful note and, if she were lucky, she would be fast asleep. The day had been long and tiring. Going to the cemetery always affected her that way. She thought of the way she'd buried her wedding band and took a moment to search her heart now for regret or guilt but found none. She stared up at the ceiling and wondered at the lack of the emotions she'd fully expected to experience. Fifteen years was certainly long enough to grieve. She needed to move on. Living in the past had taken a heavy toll on her in the past few months.

It wasn't really moving into a relationship with Lucas that weighed so heavily upon her, she felt reasonably sure. James would want her to be happy, there was no question there. It was her son.

He'd been gone for eighteen years. His twenty-fifth birthday would have been last month.

Her heart felt like a load of bricks in her chest as she sat upright and struggled for breath. Tears burned her eyes even now, after all those years. If only she could have had closure. The not knowing was the worst. She could only imagine the horrors her child had suffered before his death. Oh, she'd tried to pretend that some kind family had found and raised him. A couple who had been desperate because they couldn't have a child of their own. But that wasn't likely. She didn't need an FBI profiler to tell her the score. She was all too well aware of what happened to most children who vanished into thin air.

She closed her eyes and forced away the thought of Leberman. Both she and James had been certain he had had something to do with Jimmy's disappearance, but they'd never been able to find any proof. And as the years had dragged on that possibility had diminished. Leberman wanted to hurt them. If he'd been the one to take their child, wouldn't he have used him to wield the ultimate pain? Another part of her was utterly convinced that Leberman was indeed the culprit. But she would never be certain.

They'd searched the lake for weeks. James had hired special diving teams even after the authorities had given up. He and Lucas had worked personally with those men. If he'd somehow ended up in the water, surely they would have found something…anything. But there was always the possibility that he was out there…beneath the glassy surface of that lake near the house she'd once called home. She shuddered at the thought.

She hadn't been able to stay in that house after James had died. It was a splendid home. They'd planned its design together, had enjoyed every moment of the work involved in bringing it to life. The place was beautiful still…but she couldn't go back there. Too many memories. Yet she hadn't been able to part with the property, either. Too much of James was there, and then one of the FBI agents working her son's case had told her that sometimes when stolen children grew older, assuming they survived, they found their way back home…to the last home they'd known with their families. So she'd kept the house. The agency used it as a safe house or for the occasional VIP since it wasn't that far outside the city. But she never went there…never.

She didn't like thinking about it. The memories were too painful.

Victoria threw the covers back and climbed from the bed that had felt like heaven on earth a few minutes ago but now closed in on her like a prison. She padded to the kitchen and peered into the refrigerator to see what looked good. She wasn't really hungry, but she'd do anything to take her mind off the past. Lucas crossed her mind briefly, but she dismissed the idea. Too late for coffee and conversation…too soon for anything else. Food would have to suffice. Carrots, salad fixings. She made a face. Not in the mood. Yogurt. Not tonight.

Ice cream. Now that was more like it.

She pulled the freezer door open and reached inside, spotting her favorite flavor right off the bat. Her hand stalled halfway to its destination. A box of chocolate ice cream sat next to her vanilla. The bright yellow smiley faces drawing and holding her attention.

Why would there be chocolate?

She never ate chocolate. It gave her hives.

She frowned, but then remembered that her housekeeper sometimes brought along snacks on cleaning day…but she was on a diet. The carrots and celery in the vegetable bin were hers.

Victoria picked up the full quart of forbidden indulgence and studied it. The cold from the open freezer door, from the package, leeched through her skin, settling deep inside her. She shivered…tried to think why this carton's presence should disturb her. She hadn't seen those smiley faces for years….

Jimmy had loved chocolate anything…ice cream…milk. Especially the kind that came in this carton.

Just as Beethoven's sonata reached a crescendo the box slipped from her limp fingers.

She backed away from the refrigerator.

Her head moving from side to side, she told herself it couldn't have anything to do with him.

She should call Freda and see if she had brought it…if she'd gone off her diet—

The security alarm wailed, jerking Victoria from the unsettling thoughts.

Confusion pulled her in different directions before she

gathered her wits. She should turn the music off. Pick up the box of ice cream that lay on the floor. Needed her robe…

Shaking off the confusion, she rushed to the keypad near the front door. She'd set the alarm before her bath. It was habit…she scarcely remembered the act. The display flashed a warning that a failure had occurred in area fifteen.

The den. Grabbing the closest object for protection, which turned out to be a long-handled umbrella from its stand, she moved quietly toward the den, the siren wailing in the background, drowning out Beethoven. She wasn't really afraid. The community security guard would arrive almost immediately. As if to punctuate that thought the telephone rang. She ignored it. If she didn't answer, the authorities would arrive post haste, as well. Any burglar worth his salt would know that and run like hell. She huffed under her breath, any burglar worth his salt wouldn't have tripped the alarm in the first place.

The den stood in complete darkness. It was past midnight and any moonlight there might be was blocked by the trees shading this side of the house. She stood very still, listening, watching, but sensed no movement…no presence. Holding her breath, she reached for the wall switch by the door and flipped on the lights.

The problem wasn't immediately evident. All looked as it should be. The sheer panel hanging between her drapes suddenly shifted. A new kind of tension climbed up Victoria's spine. Moving cautiously, listening for any sound besides the insistent alarm and the rushing piano notes, she edged toward the window. Another slight shift of the sheer fabric. Every muscle tensed for battle, she jerked the panel back. The window was open only four or five inches. Just enough to allow a breeze to drift into the room. Just enough to break the connection of the security contact.

She exhaled the breath she'd been holding and peered

down at the open sash. How had that happened? It had to have been closed when she set the alarm, otherwise she'd have gotten a default message. When she would have reached to push the sash down she saw a small black, mangled object, not much larger than a quarter on the sill. She leaned closer and visually inspected the object. Knowing better than to touch it and contaminate any evidence it might offer, she stood back and considered the possibilities.

She always kept the windows locked. Always. Unlocking it from the outside without breaking the glass would be impossible. Plus, this was a gated community, it wasn't as if vandalism or burglaries were commonplace. Had someone intended to open her window earlier, before she came home, and somehow failed? That didn't make sense. How would they have gotten in with the alarm set?

Pounding on the front door startled her from her thoughts. Surprised that security had arrived even more quickly than she'd anticipated, Victoria disarmed the security system as she passed the keypad on the way to her front door. Perhaps the police had arrived, as well.

"Mrs. Colby!"

She hurried to the door and peered through the peephole. Better to be safe than sorry. She drew back at what she saw. "Identify yourself, sir," she demanded. This was no policeman. At least, not one in uniform. Nor was it the grounds security who donned clearly marked blue uniforms.

"Mrs. Colby, my name is John Logan. I work for Lucas. I need to know that you're all right."

He worked for Lucas? She remembered the name John Logan from that nightmare on St. Gabriel. She looked again. Her breath caught as she recognized the young man this time. What was he doing here?

She unlocked the door and jerked it open. "Is Lucas here? Has something happened?"

John Logan looked worried...or maybe upset. "No, ma'am, he's not here, but he's on his way."

A frown furrowed across her brow. "Why are *you* here?"

"Ma'am, if you'll let me come inside so I can ensure that the house is secure, Lucas will explain everything when he arrives."

Irritation wiggled its way up her backbone as a scenario formed in her mind. Oh, he would explain all right. She'd known he'd been keeping something from her. She just hadn't expected it to include John Logan.

"Come in, Mr. Logan," she said with a welcoming, utterly fake smile pushed firmly into place. "Look around all you'd like. There's an open window in my den. That's what triggered the alarm."

"Yes, ma'am." He nodded and walked right past her in the direction of her den.

Her mouth dropped open as she realized that he knew the layout of her home. But then, why was she surprised? Lucas always was thorough.

The golf cart security used to buzz around the small exclusive community came to a bone-jarring halt in her drive. Beyond that blue lights flickered, drawing her attention farther down the street. She knew without taking a second look that the SUV on the police cruiser's tail was Lucas's.

She left the door open and went in search of her robe. Dignity was required when exerting power over one's own domain. Lucas was about to find out just how much *indignation* she could rally.

"JUST HOW LONG were you going to wait before you told me?"

Lucas thought about that for a moment but one glance at Victoria told him he'd be better off just to tell her the truth rather than some concocted story. "Until we were safely away on our vacation."

She blinked, fiddled with her robe a bit more, then looked up at him again. "So this man, this assassin, has been following me for two weeks."

Lucas nodded. "At least. We're trying to identify who he's working for."

She looked heavenward and made a disgusted sound. "Please, Lucas, spare me the supposition. You don't need evidence. You know it's *him.*"

He sighed. It was after 3:00 a.m. They were both tired. Pursuing this discussion was pointless, but she wasn't finished punishing him just yet. "Yes, Victoria, I believe it's him. But I have to be certain."

"How are you planning to pinpoint his involvement?" Her expression boasted her considerable doubt. "You know how he is. He can stay underground for months—years even. He could be anywhere, posing as anyone, providing this assassin with his instructions over the Internet."

That was all true. She knew it and so did he. "I'm moving someone into position to get close to this assassin as we speak," he explained. "Once you and I have disappeared, he'll have no choice but to report to Leberman, leading our source straight to him." Lucas couldn't help glancing around the room even though he knew his own man had swept the entire house for surveillance bugs. Still, it was habit.

Victoria stood, abruptly announcing she'd heard enough. She was furious and he couldn't blame her.

Lucas supported his weight on his cane as he got to his feet. Damn he was exhausted. "Logan has removed the device from your windowsill and locked the window. The house has been swept for bugs and any other sort of foreign gadget or substance. Are you sure you'll feel comfortable here the rest of the night?"

He would like nothing better than to take her back to his hotel with him. But she would refuse. He knew her answer before he asked. He didn't really like her being here after what happened tonight, but his men would be watching.

The intruder had obviously gotten in while Victoria was at the office today. He'd disarmed her security, since she said she always set it before leaving for work, and then planted the device that contained a small explosive charge— just enough to push the unlocked window up at a later time, breaking the security mechanism's contact. Then he'd reset her alarm and left. Lucas assumed that the small explosive had been coated with a substance that deteriorated when subjected to air. The slow deterioration, likely calculated to the very minute, had allowed for the timing of the explosion and thus the security breach. Ingenious. Lucas knew before he looked there would be no prints. This intruder was a professional.

It was *him*.

The assassin who feared no one—not even Lucas and his men. Lucas wasn't stupid. He felt certain the guy was well aware his men had noticed his presence. And still he stalked Victoria. Fearlessly.

The idea that he could have left more explosives in the house tied Lucas's gut in knots. There was no end to the damage he could have done—poison and any number of other booby traps. He should have had someone watching the house at all times…but he hadn't even considered that avenue. His only concern had been keeping Victoria safe in real time. He'd failed to properly evaluate the threat. He was too close to this…not thinking clearly. It wouldn't happen again.

"No, thank you, Lucas," she said finally, the annoyance she'd felt at his deception visibly draining away. "I'll be fine here. Besides—" she gestured to the door "—your capable men are right outside."

That reminded him. Ian and Simon were still waiting outside with John Logan and Vincent Ferrelli. Lucas imagined the two of them would be dressed down next. Victoria had already told them in no uncertain terms that she would speak to them *later*.

Lucas nodded his understanding of her decision to stay home. As he had known, Victoria Colby would not run from any sort of threat. "We'll talk again later this morning. We still haven't reached a decision on where we'll take our vacation."

One brow winged higher than the other. "Do you really expect me to believe that you haven't made that decision already?"

He tugged at his collar. Even without a tie binding his neck she could make him squirm. "We can discuss it over lunch." He wanted her a lot calmer and more cooperative than she was right now before they made any decisions.

Damn, this was too close.

He hoped like hell Tasha could move in on their guy in a hurry. She'd be settled into her apartment by noon today. Maverick and Ramon, two more of his specialists, would serve as her backup, and bring her up to speed. She had to get next to this guy. Lucas needed something...anything to go on. He was counting on her to move quickly. He just hoped it didn't get her killed.

He swallowed hard. If it did, it would be entirely his doing. She was young and reckless. Far too reckless to fully comprehend the level of danger involved. But he'd needed her, and Lucas had never failed to take whatever risk required to accomplish his mission. For the first time in his career, he wondered if he had done the right thing.

Victoria squeezed his arm. "I'm okay, Lucas. Really."

He snapped back to the present. She'd mistaken his preoccupation for concern. And he was concerned. About a number of things. "That's all that matters," he said as much for his own benefit as hers. Keeping her safe was all that really mattered. He leaned down and brushed a kiss to her cheek. "Good night, Victoria."

He didn't want to leave her. She looked so vulnerable in that white silk robe with her dark hair falling down around her shoulders. He'd never seen her like that and it was all he could do not to stare in awe.

Allowing her one last smile, he turned away and started for the door.

"Oh, dear God," she gasped.

He turned back to her, performed a quick visual inspection. Had she only now realized she was injured in some way? "What?"

"In all the excitement I completely forgot," she murmured. Her frightened gaze collided with his and she gestured vaguely toward the kitchen. "I don't eat chocolate ice cream."

CHAPTER EIGHT

THE INSISTENT THROB of the music from the Metro Link nightclub kept a rhythmic pace with her confident stride as Tasha made her way to the entrance. Black thigh-high leather boots and skintight, cheek-baring silk shorts gave the illusion of legs that went on forever. Legs toned from all those five-mile runs, making every guy she passed stop and stare.

The strappy halter top showcased her flat belly and the contour of her spine, covering nothing except her breasts, and even then the gossamer-thin, lacy fabric scarcely left much to the imagination. A small leather bag, hardly large enough to hold some cash, a couple of loose cigarettes and her car keys, hung from a long, delicate gold chain that draped over her shoulder. The bag bounced against her hip with every step she took. An ankle-length jacket that was as sheer as air and designed from black netting so thin and fragile that it felt like a midnight fog against her skin completed the daring ensemble.

She possessed all the bait and weapons required for a manhunt.

At the main entrance she paused for the bouncer to wave his security wand around her body. She opened her purse to show her keys when the wand passed over it and hummed a warning.

She smiled wickedly at him. "Baby, you don't have to worry about me," she crooned. "The only thing I'm packing is a raging desire to find just the right guy."

His slick bald head stilled, his eyes level with her waist when the wand hummed another warning at the top of her right boot. He looked up at her, one eyebrow cocked in question.

"It's just my cell phone," she insisted. She reached into her boot and tugged out the slim communicator that had triggered the metal detector. "See." She waved it in front of his face before slipping it back into her boot. "Anything else you need to see?"

He straightened, glanced at the crowd lining up behind her and then back at her. He wanted to see more. No doubt. The gleam in his eyes gave away his every thought.

"Come on, man, we don't got all night," his co-worker groused. He waited impatiently, the official Metro Link stamp in his hand. A veteran on the job, she surmised. One who wouldn't be impressed by a half-naked woman and a sexy come-on line.

The guy with the wand waved her through. "Have a nice night," he offered, his tone chock-full of innuendo.

She leaned close to him and whispered, "Believe me, baby, I will."

"Let's go," the other guy grumped.

Tasha squared her shoulders and gave him a look that said, Buddy, you need to get laid, and held out her hand. He glared at her then smacked the stamp in place. An eerie ML glowed on her skin between her wrist and knuckles. She flashed him a "bite me" smile and moved on.

Heavy-metal music blasted from the surround-sound system as she strode into the crowded club. The maximum occupancy posted was five hundred, and she'd bet Martin's Jag that they'd long passed that limit. Patrons were jampacked into every available square foot. A long, sleek bar of black-and-mirrored glass flowed along one wall. Up front the crush of the crowd made it difficult to distinguish one couple from another on the dance floor. It more accurately resembled a sea of body parts, all connected some-how like a scene from a gruesome horror novel as they gyrated to the beat.

A laser light show splashed across a screen high above the band jamming on the stage. Booze and beer abounded like manna from heaven, and she quickly spotted a number of other less-than-legal stimulants. Leather, lace and tattoos. Smoke, heat and sex. Women with men and all variations in between. It was all out there. Just like Sodom and Go-morrah.

So this was his favorite haunt, she mused, scanning for her target. Tall, blond and deadly liked it trashy. Well, she could play any way necessary. Backup knew where she was at all times. The handy dandy tracking-monitoring device looked just like a skin patch, the kind people used for kick-ing the nicotine habit or for birth control. Skin colored and shaped like a small round bandage. Rafe "Maverick" Scott, one of the two men Lucas had assigned as her backup, had instructed her to place it under her left breast. The device would send out a constant signal providing her location as well as her cardio stats. If her heart rate esca-lated to panic level Maverick would come to her rescue.

But she wasn't going to need that kind of backup tonight.

She did a double take, her gaze landing on Mr. John Doe himself.

"Mmm-hmm," she muttered under her breath. "You are one amazing Y chromosome." For a killer, she added.

John Doe sat on a stool about center of the long bar, those ice-blue eyes scanning the dance floor like a hungry panther ready to pounce on his dinner.

Looking for a little action, big boy? Taking her time as she crossed the room, she took stock of his numerous phys-ical assets. Whoever had estimated his height and weight had done a stellar job. Those broad shoulders tested the seams of his black shirt. Powerful thighs filled out a well-worn pair of jeans. Black ankle boots, the kind made for walking and climbing, soft leather uppers, ribbed soles. For stealth and traction. Smart.

He wore a watch, but no other jewelry that she could readily see. The slight bulge at his left side about midway of his torso would indicate a shoulder holster. She wondered how he'd managed to get in here with a weapon. Official ID, perhaps? Just something else she'd need to check out.

The couple sitting next to him got up and headed for the dance floor, presenting the perfect opportunity for her. "The gods are watching over me tonight," she murmured.

She slid onto the stool next to J.D., John Doe just sounded too cliché. "Great band," she said when he glanced in her direction.

He didn't respond.

Okay. She crossed one leg over the over, offering up a length of thigh for his perusal. He never even looked her way. She leaned toward him. "What time it is?" she asked, ensuring she spoke loud enough for him to hear her.

He held up his wrist so that she could see the face of his watch. She splayed her fingers over his muscled forearm and drew it closer to her face. He tensed and pulled free even before she was ready to let go.

Not the reaction she'd hoped for, but a reaction nonetheless.

She leaned close again, ensuring that her shoulder rubbed against his. "Thanks. What's your name?"

Again nothing.

Five minutes passed with her sitting there gazing out over the mass of swaying, twitching bodies and him doing the same. Not one word was spoken.

Time for drastic measures.

She hopped off her stool, standing as close to him as

possible. "Hey!" she shouted at the bartender. "How about a beer?"

A long-necked bottle slid down the counter toward her. She snagged it and took a long draw. "Hmm," she purred as she wiped her chin. She sighed and plunked her bottle back onto the counter. She resisted the urge to wince. Although her lipstick did a great job of camouflaging her split lip, the alcohol still burned on contact.

She leaned against the bar and adjusted her position slightly so she could look her target directly in the eye…well, she could if he turned his head a mere five degrees and allowed her to. Jerk. What was this guy, gay or something?

Only one way to find out.

She pulled a cigarette out of her purse, a girl never knew when she'd need a conversation starter, and provocatively leaned in his direction. "Do you have a light?" she asked, peering up at him as if the world just might come to an end if he gave the wrong answer.

He looked at her, that piercing gaze cold enough to give her frostbite, then glared at her breasts for a fraction of a second. "No," he growled before looking away, clearly unimpressed.

Dammit.

Well, at least he'd spoken to her.

She tossed the cigarette onto the bar and propped fully against the counter, pressing her shoulder into his, as she drank her beer and contemplated her next move.

The beer was cold and refreshing once it got past her lip, but he was making her sweat. Usually she didn't have this much trouble getting a guy's attention. Surely three months sitting behind a desk at Langley in a two-piece suit hadn't thrown her off the game this badly. Giving herself grace, she hadn't actually ever attempted to bait a killer. It must be tricky, she mused. Rising to the challenge, she studied him out of the corner of her eye. His profile was strong, his jaw chiseled. A scar running from the corner of his mouth to the middle of his cheek served as a kind of permanent dimple. Otherwise, movie-star-quality features, but more rugged. She squinted for a better view. There was something in his hairline.

Another scar…

No.

Tattoo.

A number: 6…6…*shit*…

She stiffened.

He turned his head and pointed those laser-blue eyes directly at hers.

She opened her mouth but it took about three seconds for the words to come out. "Is that…?"

She couldn't say the rest. He knew what she meant. She saw it in his eyes. Damn. Was this guy for real? Focus, Tasha. Stay calm. She forced her heart rate to slow before that cowboy Maverick could come bursting through the door.

He was still staring at her.

"What do you want from me?"

An involuntary shiver raced over her skin at the sound of his voice. Or maybe she was just freaked out by the bizarre tattoo. But the deep, gravelly sound scraped over her flesh, leaving every single nerve ending raw and tingling.

"I…" She moistened her lips and grappled for the cocky attitude she'd waltzed in here with. "My name's Tasha. I just thought you were cute and that maybe we could—"

He looked her up and down. Not a fast and furious sweep, but a slow, methodical perusal…as if he were devouring every square inch of her with his eyes. She shivered again. Jesus, what was wrong with her?

When that unyielding blue gaze collided with hers once more, he said, "Go away."

Had this encounter tanked or what?

She mustered up a properly pissed-off look and the body language to go with it. "Maybe I don't want to. Maybe I like it right here." She guzzled the rest of her beer. "You know," she said, her gaze focused on the mirror behind the bar, but her voice just loud enough for him to hear, "I knew moving here would be a mistake. My first night on the town and I get the brush-off from the best-looking guy in the club." She turned toward him then, pressed even more intimately against him. "Why is that, do you think?"

He shifted just enough so that his face was about two inches from hers. "Maybe it has something to do with that big mouth."

She laughed softly and then sighed, allowing her breath to feather across his lips. "Well, now I know, don't I?"

He turned away as if he hadn't even noticed her seduction attempts. How the hell was she supposed to crack this guy?

Lucas's offer echoed in her ears... *succeed in this mission and you'll come to work for me with the best of the best.* Failure was not an option. The cell phone tucked into her boot vibrated. Maverick, no doubt.

She braced a hand against J.D. as she fished out her phone. He flinched. Great, he didn't even want her to touch him. "Yeah." She turned away from the exasperating man, straining to hear over the music.

"I take it we have contact."

Maverick's call would show up as a cell phone listed to her fake roommate, Patti. Under normal circumstances he would call if he didn't like what he saw on the monitor, if in distress she would say the right phrase or her inability to answer would equate to the same, and the cowboy would create a diversion, allowing her to escape whatever trouble she was in. But tonight's call was just to ensure contact had been made and to tie her to his monitoring link. Once he'd put a call through to her cell phone, as long as that phone was turned on he could trace her. Backup to the other apparatus, he'd told her. He liked playing it safe. She glanced at the brooding man at her side. "Definitely. I thought you were coming back to pick me up, Patti."

"Our friend is nearby," he said knowingly. "Very good."

"Yeah. Forget it, I'll figure out something." She hung up, closed her phone and tucked it back into her boot. She heaved a disgusted sigh. She couldn't be certain how this would go from here, but at least she'd made contact. That's all Lucas had wanted for tonight. But she wanted more. She wanted to prove how fast she could work...how deep she could go right from the start.

Her target suddenly stood.

Damn.

He tossed a couple of bills onto the counter, clearly preparing to split.

"You leaving already?" She shifted as close to him as possible. "We didn't even get to dance."

She looked up at him with all the sensual invitation she could muster. For two beats he stared right back at her without a word...without a reaction at all.

Abruptly he snagged her by the arm and moved away from the bar. Startled on one level but grateful on another, she allowed herself to be dragged around the fringes of the dance floor, zigzagging to avoid gyrating bodies. His fingers were like iron vises around her wrist. He didn't slow down until they had cleared an emergency exit and were standing in the alley behind the club. Fear trickled through her but she quelled it instantly. Somewhere in the back of her mind she wondered vaguely why no alarm went off when they pushed through the exit. The fire marshal needed to start doing his job. She suddenly hoped like hell Maverick was doing his.

"Decide you want to take me home with you?" she encouraged, blocking the internal alarm going off inside her head. She was playing with fire here. Pushing the limit…but at least she had his attention now. When she would have reached toward him he shoved her to her knees.

"You know what to do," he said savagely.

Oh, damn.

She took a breath, looked at his crotch and the sizeable bulge there, then peered up at him, careful not to let her uneasiness show. "You know, you're really cute and all, but I don't go down on a guy on a first date. Especially when I don't even know his name."

When she would have pushed to her feet he snagged her chin in a punishing grip forcing her back down. "I guess you don't know how to use that big mouth after all."

She glared right back into that icy gaze and countered, "Considering your attitude, I guess you'll never know."

His gaze held hers a second longer before he released her and started to walk away.

Tasha lunged to her feet and went after him. Dammit, she couldn't let him get away. "Wait a minute. I—"

"Shut up." He kept moving…didn't look back.

She hurried to keep up with his long strides. "Look, my roommate left me here. I really need a ride. Could you at least give me a ride?"

This could go either way…all she wanted at this point was to find out where he called home while in the Windy City. That was more than Lucas had asked for, but then, that was the point. Considering this guy's attitude, however, that might be all she could hope for period.

Glancing down his shoulder at her, his stride never slowing, he growled, "Call a taxi."

"Wait!" She stayed right on his heels. "Don't be a jerk. I just need a ride. Is that such a big deal?"

He stopped. A straining ray of light from a distant street-lamp filtered through the darkness where they stood, softly illuminating those Arctic eyes and highlighting the hard planes of his face.

She held her breath...all she needed was half a chance....

"A ride, nothing else."

"Nothing else," she promised.

He turned and started walking again. She followed. Two blocks later he clicked the remote on his keychain and the headlights of an SUV came on.

She climbed into the passenger seat while he slid behind the wheel. When she snapped her seat belt into place he asked, "What's the address?"

She gave him the address for her apartment and relaxed back against the seat as he pulled out onto the street. "Oh, no!" she groaned and smacked her forehead with the heel of her hand. "My roommate called me..." She looked over at him. "In the club, you know. She needs the apartment to herself tonight. I have to hang out somewhere else."

"A hotel, then." This he said, as usual, with no emotion and without even sparing her a glance.

She moistened her lips and reached way down deep for her whiniest voice. "But I don't have any money for a hotel. It took most everything I had to pay my share of the rent when I got here. Couldn't I just crash at your place for the night? I swear I won't be any trouble. I'll even sleep on the couch. I don't usually go home with strangers but I don't know anyone else in town and—"

He slammed on the brakes. The seat belt was all that kept her from an up-close encounter with the dash.

"Get out."

She glanced around the dark neighborhood. They'd already left the cluster of night spots behind. Rush Street and Division were safe enough, she knew from Maverick's briefing, but it was after midnight…who knew? Of course, she had backup, but this guy didn't know that. Mr. Coldhearted Snake apparently didn't give a rat's ass.

"Fine." She muttered a couple of fitting expletives as she jerked the seat belt loose and scrambled out, then slammed the door as hard as she could.

When she walked away she gave it everything she had, swaying her hips like a hooker on a desperate mission.

She might not have his home address, but she had his license plate number. That was something.

When he didn't immediately drive away, an uneasy feeling quivered up her spine. She resisted the urge to turn around and assess his intent. If he gunned the engine she'd hear him in time to dive to safety.

She forced herself to put one foot in front of the other and to pretend he wasn't even there, watching, waiting, for God knows what. The memory of that bizarre tattoo made her shiver again. There was something really wrong with this guy. Her sixth sense hadn't stopped vying for her attention since she walked up to that bar.

As if she didn't have enough trouble already, a drunk staggered from an alley a few yards ahead. A friend joined him five seconds later. Both watched her steady progress without making a move. She braced herself for a scuffle.

Was everything determined to turn out badly tonight?

The SUV rolled slowly forward.

She sensed the movement more than heard it.

Just before she reached the plot of sidewalk where the two winos waited, the SUV stopped next to her, and the passenger-side window powered down.

"Get in."

She folded her arms over her chest and turned a belligerent glare in his direction. "Are you sure? You know they have medication now for bipolar disorders."

"Get in."

Those cold eyes cut through the darkness with a warning. He wouldn't be pushed any further.

"All right." She opened the door and climbed back into the luxurious leather seat. "So," she ventured when he'd eased into forward motion once more. "You'll put me up tonight?" She resisted the urge to smile in victory. Why had she ever doubted herself?

He braked for a traffic light and swung that piercing gaze toward her. "If you're certain that's what you want."

She blinked...knew a foolish moment of panic. "Of course I'm sure. Is there some reason I shouldn't be?"

That relentless stare bored into her for several seconds more. "That depends."

The light changed and he shifted his attention to the task of driving.

She swallowed, wet her lips and considered whether or not she had made a serious mistake. "Depends on what?" she inquired nonchalantly, uncertain as to whether he would even bother to answer.

He didn't look at her...just kept driving. But his voice when he spoke was every bit as icy as she knew his eyes would be. "On why you picked me out in that club tonight." He relaxed into his seat, still not so much as glancing her way. "You see, I don't believe in coincidences. Everything happens for a reason. And—" he did look at her then...the fleeting stare chilled her to the bone "—I will know your reason."

CHAPTER NINE

"WE LOST HER."

Maverick stared at the handheld monitor, hoping like hell he'd pick up her signal again.

Nothing.

"Dammit."

"He could have a jamming device in his vehicle," Ramon offered from behind the wheel.

"Just keep driving," Maverick barked. Ramon had been in this business almost as long as he had, but that didn't give either one of them an edge at a time like this. If they couldn't pick up a signal on the tracking device or the cell, the bastard had to have a jammer on board. It was that simple. "We gotta find that son of a bitch."

He studied the electronic map of the vicinity where they'd last picked up the signal...where they'd last known Tasha North to be. She'd climbed into the SUV with the guy, and they'd lost her signal but had visual contact, so Maverick hadn't worried. Then, when she'd gotten out a couple minutes later, the signal had come through loud and clear once more. He shook his head and hissed another curse from between gritted teeth. The bastard had a jammer in his vehicle, all right. He knew all the ropes and wasn't taking any chances.

Able to maintain visual contact for a while, they'd followed him for several blocks. But, erring on the side of caution, they'd had to lag too far behind to keep up. He'd moved out of visual range...the signal hadn't returned.

Now she was gone.

Maverick called up on the screen a ten-mile radius relative to the last visual sighting. "We'll take this area one block at a time and hope we spot his SUV."

"And if we don't?" Ramon asked, his expression as disgusted and worried as Maverick's surely was.

"Then we report in."

He didn't have to say the rest. If they couldn't find her soon they'd have to let Lucas know…and start looking for her body.

CHAPTER TEN

"WHAT DID YOU LEARN?"

Lucas settled on Victoria's sofa in the very den where approximately twenty-four hours earlier the assassin had been setting his little booby trap. He leveled his attention on the woman waiting expectantly for his response. She looked as regal as ever; the coat dress, the color of ripe peaches, flattering to both her complexion and her figure. One would never know that she'd been through pure hell. She sat in the elegantly brocaded chair directly across from him as if a briefing related to her home's intrusion were an everyday affair.

"How are you holding up, Victoria?"

Though she looked prepared for anything, her shoulders square, her chin lifted high. He knew better. This couldn't be easy.

"Lucas, I need to know what you've learned. Please don't attempt to spare my feelings. It's far too late for that."

He set his cane aside and looked her straight in the eye. "He's been in your home, as you know. Planting the device that opened your window would have been impossible by any other means. He left no prints that we can find. Nor did he leave any other surprises."

She shifted slightly then. He resisted the urge to shake his head. No matter what she said she wasn't as ready for this as she wanted him to believe.

"So you'll keep my home under twenty-four-hour surveillance now."

It wasn't a question. She already knew the answer. Lucas had hoped to conceal the depth of his awareness regarding the assassin's movements, but that was impossible now. He would note the increased surveillance on the home. That couldn't be helped. But keeping his suspicions from the assassin that Leberman was behind this was imperative.

"Yes."

"He'll realize that we know, then," Victoria noted, reading Lucas's mind.

He nodded. He tried without success to keep the other worry from interfering with his concentration. They'd lost contact with Tasha at one this morning. If the bastard had killed her...

Lucas forced the idea away. Tasha was too good to go down this easy. He refused to believe she was dead...just yet.

Something changed in Victoria's eyes. Her expression went from firm and solemn to fragile and frightened. "What about the ice cream."

This was the part he'd dreaded the most. "Freda didn't bring the ice cream." He managed a smile. "She swears she's still on a diet."

Victoria nodded stiffly. "I thought as much."

Lucas leaned forward, braced his forearms on his knees. "Is there a possibility that you picked it up by accident. Didn't notice that one of the flavors was chocolate."

The weariness that settled over her expression then tied his insides into knots. "You know, I've considered that possibility over and over." She clasped her hands together in her lap. "I'm nearly certain I didn't...but then I can't be sure." She looked at Lucas. "I've even wondered if I'm losing my mind entirely. Having memory lapses maybe." She looked away and shook her head. "I just don't know."

"Yours are the only prints we found on the carton."

Her gaze met his once more, and the anxiety there almost undid him completely.

"But that doesn't really mean anything," he hastened to add. "Since he didn't leave his prints anywhere else, either."

He didn't want her to go through another moment of this. Couldn't bear it. "Victoria, I think it's time for us to make those plans. I'd like to get you away from the danger. I don't like how close he's gotten."

She appeared to consider his suggestion for a few moments, but before she could respond, Logan came to the door of the room. Lucas pushed to his feet and strode across the room to see what news Logan had brought. When he moved into the entry hall, farther away from Victoria, Lucas's tension ratcheted up a notch.

"I just received additional information on the brand of the ice cream."

His people were analyzing the chocolate ice cream from every standpoint, from taste to the manufacturer.

"I assume it's a local manufacturer."

The look in Logan's eyes set him even closer to the edge.

"It used be. But that brand hasn't been manufactured at all for more than ten years."

Chocolate. Little Jimmy Colby's favorite. Even the brand was the one Victoria remembered buying for her only child. But it had been off the market for ten years.

"So he's been keeping it all this time," Lucas suggested.

Logan nodded. "The age of the product would be consistent with that theory."

The memory of those hours on St. Gabriel Island when he'd been face-to-face with Leberman for the first time in nearly two decades came pouring into his mind. The bastard hadn't said much…had apparently gotten his jollies from merely watching Lucas squirm when faced with the realization that Victoria was somewhere on that island and he couldn't protect her. Lucas hadn't cared if the bastard killed him but he couldn't bear the idea of him hurting Victoria any more than he already had.

Something had been different.

For all those years Leberman had lain in wait. Then, out of the blue, he struck. He could have killed Lucas... possibly even Victoria. But he'd disappeared instead. He'd played them. Lured them into his trap, dangled the possibility of death, then disappeared, leaving someone else to finish the task. But that had been a ploy. Leberman had known the effort would fail. Everything that happened on that island had been a precursor. Some sort of test or preliminary tactic for the real thing. An appetizer to the main course, so to speak.

He'd killed James Colby fifteen years ago. Lucas was certain of that. Though Leberman had not claimed responsibility he'd left his calling card. James had been tortured relentlessly then shot twice, once in the back of the head execution-style, then once in the heart. The first shot had killed him...the second hadn't even been necessary. It had made a statement from the killer.

From Leberman.

Just as the ice cream did now.

He was here.

He'd devastated Victoria all those years ago. Could have devised a way to kill her a dozen times over since...he was far too cunning for anyone to believe otherwise. But he'd chosen not to strike. The little drama he'd set in motion on the island had been to prove something. Otherwise why would he have simply walked away, leaving both of them still alive? Lucas's gaze narrowed as he thought about that. The answer was suddenly so simple.

He'd played out that whole ridiculous scenario to make sure Victoria was ready for the next step. He'd waited all these years to make sure he could hurt her as deeply as he desired. She'd needed time to get over losing both her child and her husband…to finally get on with her life. He'd waited for her to fall in love again.

With Lucas.

It all made sense now.

Killing her years ago when she'd already lost so much that she'd wished for death anyway would have lacked the zenith he yearned for…the fulfillment he needed.

So he'd waited. Waited for her to feel again.

Waited for the ultimate moment.

When Lucas was prepared to make her his once and for all.

The weight of the epiphany crushed down against him.

The game this time would be for keeps. Lucas could feel it in every fiber of his being.

If the bastard had his way, both Victoria and Lucas would die.

Soon.

But first he would play, draw out his pleasure.

Lucas gritted his teeth against the fury that whipped through him…and that one obsession would be his doom.

Lucas would see to it.

Errol Leberman was dead already…he just didn't know it yet.

CHAPTER ELEVEN

TASHA JERKED AWAKE.

She sat up straight and took stock of her environment.

The room was dark.

She couldn't be sure how much time had passed but she was certain it should be daylight by now.

The perpetual darkness, along with the dank, musty smell confirmed her suspicions that she was in a cellar or basement. Someplace underground.

She lifted her right foot, crossed it over her knee, the metal on metal clanging a noisy reminder that she was shackled to the cot. Rubbing at her ankle where the metal chafed her skin, she stretched her neck first one way and then another. She had a hell of a crick in her neck and shoulder from sitting in such an awkward position while she dozed. Her side still hurt from the beating she'd taken during Martin's little exercise. But she'd slept, anyway.

She hadn't meant to sleep at all, but exhaustion had finally claimed her after hours of trying to get loose. He'd taken her boots and her tiny purse, leaving her with nothing to pick the lock or attempt to pry it open.

After feeling around on the cold concrete floor and stretching the chain as far as she could and finding nothing, she'd admitted defeat and plopped back down on the cot to wait. She'd decided to conserve her energy for kicking ass.

She set her jaw firmly when she considered the heartless bastard who'd locked her down here. When he showed up again she intended to let him have it, shackled or not. To punctuate her heated thought she jerked on the confining chain with all her might.

"Don't waste your time."

The deep voice cut through the darkness like a knife, piercing her defenses. She gasped in spite of herself. Dammit. She hated even the implication of weakness. Hated even worse that he could rattle her so easily. How had he sneaked up on her like that? She'd always been a very light sleeper.

Since Maverick hadn't shown up, she could assume that being underground had silenced the tiny electronic pulse her tracking device emitted. *He* had taken her cell phone and likely turned it off.

Just her luck he had a brain to go with the awesome bod. Renewed fury raged through her.

She rocketed to her feet and moved as far in the direction the sound of his voice had come from as the chain would allow. "Why the hell are you keeping me here like this?"

The silence thickened as she waited for an answer. Her heart banged painfully against her rib cage.

"To watch you."

She laughed, a dry, totally pissed-off sound. "Yeah, right. You can't even see me."

"Sure I can."

She drew back slightly. He was right in front of her. Her expression hardened with the anger sizzling inside her as she pushed all thought of playing it safe aside and leaned toward him. "Then read my lips." She mouthed a detailed description of what she thought of him.

He snagged her chin in one iron grasp. "So you don't think I'm cute after all?"

She stilled. He couldn't see her...reading her lips was impossible. Her eyes narrowed. Unless he was wearing night vision goggles. She reached for his head. He manacled her wrists but not before she touched his face and found no goggles. The idea that he actually could see that well in the dark startled her all over again.

"Why didn't you leave when I told you to get lost?"

She tried to analyze his tone but it proved impossible. He spoke firmly, harshly almost, but there was no underlying emotion. No anger…no concern…nothing.

"Well, we both know it wasn't because of your sparkling personality."

He jerked her closer still. So close that she could feel his breath on her face when he spoke once more. "What do you want?"

Tasha took a moment to shut down her emotions. So far she'd been pretty much going with the flow, but things were different now. He was dead serious. She couldn't screw up. Her reactions had to be calculated.

She peered up at him, though she couldn't see a damned thing in the dark, and relaxed in his hold. "I thought you were cute. I…I was attracted to you." Then she lifted her chin and glared belligerently since he, apparently, could see. "But that was before I found out what a jerk you are." She tried to wrestle her arms free from his hold. "What are you? Some kind of serial killer or something?"

"And what if I am?"

She stilled, allowing him to think that the idea startled her. Well, it did, sort of, but not enough for the drama queen performance she was laying on at the moment. "You're…you're not going to kill me, are you?"

He made a sound…a laugh, only too soft and with no humor whatsoever. "I don't know. Maybe."

Time to pump up the theatrics. She tried to pull free again. "Let me go!"

He released her, and she stumbled back a couple of steps. "Look, just let me go and I won't say a word. I don't even know your name."

"That's what they all say," he countered, his tone purposely sinister.

He wanted her afraid…he didn't like it that she wasn't scared of him. Tasha pondered that assessment briefly. He wanted to be in complete control. Testing the waters of her theory, she summoned the proper emotion and pleaded, "I swear I won't say anything!"

Another of those soft, humorless laughs, scarcely more than a breath. "With that mouth do you really expect me to believe you can keep a secret?"

She balled her fingers into fists and suppressed the urge to slug him. Jerk. "Just tell me what you want," she urged, going for a placating tone and forcing her muscles to relax from their battle-ready stance. She had to remember he could see. "I'll do anything you ask."

He moved closer…a step, maybe two, the movement soundless. But she didn't have to hear him, she felt him, as if they were somehow connected on some weird level. "But, if I'm a serial killer as you suggested, anything you do won't make a difference. You'll die anyway."

He liked the power…wanted her helpless. She was sure of it. Reacting as he would expect to the encroaching sound of his voice, she backed away, the chain rattled as she bumped into the cot. "Just my luck to hit on a psycho," she muttered, forcing a tremor into her voice. "But my luck has always sucked anyway." She had a hunch. It was a long shot, but what the hell. "My own mother ran out on me as a kid, but I managed to get by." She glared in his direction, lifting her chin with a hint of defiance. "Looks like fate had it in for me all along."

He moved again…close enough that she could have reached out and touched him.

She collapsed onto the cot in a show of defeat. "Just get it over with." She hugged herself and exhaled a shaky breath. "I don't want to play any sick games. I got enough of that crap from my old man before he cut out on me, too.''

''You just don't know when to shut up, do you?'' Before she could make an evasive maneuver he grabbed her by the shoulders and pulled her to her feet.

Surprisingly, she sensed anger in his tone, felt it in his punishing grip. She thought about that for the three seconds she dared permit the distraction. He didn't want to hear about her fictional childhood distress. Was there something like that in his past? Maybe she'd play up the whole ''beaten down'' strategy and see where it took her.

''Look,'' she said wearily, ''if you're going to kill me you'd better let me pee first otherwise I'm going to make a hell of a mess on your floor.''

He grabbed her right hand and pried it open. Before she could fathom his intent he placed a key in her palm. Startled all over again by his actions, she crouched down and unlocked the steel bracelet around her ankle. She rubbed the raw skin there and then straightened and offered him the key back. Could this guy be human after all?

''Does this mean you're not going to kill me?''

He didn't answer, just manacled her arm and dragged her across the room. The stairs were a little tricky in the dark, but he didn't seem to have any trouble.

She wondered how he could possibly have such excellent night vision. There were people like that she knew, but generally there was some physiological reason. He'd have one, as well.

When he opened the door at the top of the stairs, she blinked rapidly to allow her eyes to adjust to the light.

She studied the layout of the house as he led her through the kitchen and down a hallway. Back door in kitchen near sink. Three more doorways in the hall. One leading to what looked like a living room, the one they'd exited from the kitchen and the third one led to a bathroom. The stairs climbing to the second level started where the hall ended opposite the front door. No pictures on the walls. No other decorating touches.

At the bathroom door he stood aside. "Make it fast."

She sidled past him but hesitated before closing the door. "You mean you're not going to watch."

He folded his arms over his chest and leaned against the wall without responding.

Tasha closed the door and sagged with relief.

She exhaled some of the tension tightening her chest, but instead of relaxing, she quickly surveyed the small room for a means of escape. Not that she'd decided she needed to make a run for it yet...but just in case. She was pretty sure that if he'd intended to kill her he would have, whether she needed to relieve herself or not. Besides, she was trapped.

The only window was one of those small rectangular ones above the tub/shower combination. As slim as she was there was no way she was getting out that route.

Knowing he was waiting right outside, she pushed off the door and took care of nature's call.

As she flushed the toilet she couldn't help smiling. She'd done it. Gotten him to bring her to his lair. *Lucas Camp,* she mused, *wherever you are, I'm in.*

CHAPTER TWELVE

THEY'D DRIVEN AROUND most of the night.

And found nothing. Her signal had restarted briefly at one point, but not long enough for a lock on her location.

Maverick scrubbed a hand over his face and cursed himself for letting her get away.

He was her backup.

If she was dead...

Ramon was part of her backup, as well, but Maverick was the one in charge. In nearly two decades of this kind of work he'd never lost a team member. Not once. He didn't want to start with one so damned young.

An almost inaudible beep sounded in the silence of the truck.

He jerked to attention, his gaze going instantly to the monitor he still clutched in his hand.

The two previously flat lines he'd stared at for hours on end blinked into activity.

"We've got her back," he said in a rush, the words scarcely more than a relieved whisper.

Ramon sat up a little straighter behind the wheel. "Give me some directions, amigo."

He rattled off the necessary information, not once taking his eyes off the tiny pulsing lights that represented Tasha North's heart rate and location.

They were back in business.

He had to get word to Lucas.

CHAPTER THIRTEEN

TASHA MOISTENED A CLOTH and washed her face. She couldn't be sure how long he would give her in here alone, but she needed some time to get a better grip on her strained emotions. She might be tough but she was still only human. Playing this guy's game had been hard work.

There was something not quite right here, but she couldn't put her finger on it. If he'd been the stone-cold killer he appeared to be she'd be dead now. It didn't take a master's degree in psych to see it...and she had one.

She'd be lying to herself if she didn't admit that a small part of her wanted to get the hell out of here ASAP. But the professional in her needed to see this through. She was close—right where Lucas wanted her. If she could just stay alive she could bring this guy down.

Whether he was as bad as he wanted the world to believe had nothing to do with her mission. Lucas wanted her close to him so he could be stopped. She got the distinct impression that as soon as he had led them to the man who'd hired him, he would be terminated.

That thought gave her an uncharacteristic pause. The hesitation confused her...but it was there. She'd have to deal with it.

She shook off the thought. That was the number one rule in the spy business—never, ever let the enemy close enough to make it matter.

The door opened, and the enemy in question barged in.

"Did you forget how to knock?" she asked the face glaring at her in the mirror.

"You never answered my question."

Back to that again, huh?

She spun around on her bare heel, bracing herself against the sink and staring up at him. "I already told you that I hit on you because you were the cutest guy in the club. Deal with it." The images Lucas had captured of this guy didn't do him justice, especially his eyes. Nor had the dim lighting in that club last night. His eyes were...amazing.

Suppressing a shiver she started to give him her back. He stopped her with a hand on her shoulder. "What's this?" He tipped her chin up and looked first at her healing lip then at the fading bruise on her cheek.

Concealer and makeup had covered the evidence of the roughing up she'd taken night before last. The low lighting in the club had helped, as well. But with the makeup long gone and in the bright light of day, there was no hiding her battle scars.

"My roommate and I had a disagreement." She drew away from his touch. "It happens." She turned back to the mirror and grimaced at her reflection. She looked like hell. Nothing she could do about that since she had no cosmetics, not even a brush. She combed her fingers through her tousled hair. The net jacket that had looked so sexy last night reminded her of snagged pantyhose this morning. She peeled it off and stuffed it in the trash can next to the toilet, purposely bending from the waist to startle her *host*.

"And this?" He gestured to her right shoulderblade when she straightened once more. "Did your roommate take a knife to you as well?"

Dammit, she'd forgotten about that old battle scar. Her first scuffle with a would-be mugger once she'd moved out on her own in college. He might have drawn first blood, but he'd also been the only one lying on the ground when the police finally arrived.

"I guess I forgot to mention that between my successful attempts at running away from the system, I survived a couple of foster homes. Nobody really wanted to deal with a rebellious teenager, but they didn't want to lose the government check with my name on it." She shrugged as if it didn't matter. And it didn't, because she was only making this stuff up. But, like a good movie, it was based on true stories she'd heard while interning in a social services office. "People don't bother with troubled teens unless it's for one of two reasons." She looked him straight in the eye via the mirror, sensing that she would see a reaction. "For the money or the sex."

He flinched. She resisted the urge to pump her fist in the air and scream yes. She'd gotten to him...maybe just barely beneath the surface, but someplace under the skin all the same. She'd sensed a resistance in him before when she brought up the past. He definitely did not like going there. The first piece of the puzzle. She might not have the opportunity to dig more deeply, but she'd learn what she could until it was over.

She turned around, stared up into those cold, hard eyes once more. "What about you?" She touched his jaw, tracing the outline of an old scar that gave him a permanent dimple before he could evade her touch. Her gaze moved lower, to another scar where his shirt opened into a vee at his throat. She hadn't been able to see that one last night in the low lighting. A jagged little line a shade or two lighter than the rest of his skin.

Some unknown force driving her, she reached toward him with her other hand. Oddly he didn't move away. She released the next button of his shirt. And then another and another until it lay open to his waist where he'd tucked it into his jeans. Too caught up in the moment to note his reaction other than the fact that he allowed her to continue, she pulled the shirt free of his jeans, pushing the sides farther apart so that she could see more of his well-defined torso.

For one long moment she couldn't breathe. There were too many scars to count...some small, thin lines...others much more lethal looking. She wanted to ask him about them, but when she opened her mouth no words would come. Instead she touched one particularly brutal-looking scar so damn close to his heart she couldn't imagine how he'd survived the wound. She felt him tense beneath her fingertips, but, again, he didn't move away.

That extra instinct she possessed was screaming at her now, warning that she was about to dive headlong into dangerous territory...delve past some unseen boundary of no return, and still, she couldn't stop herself. She looked into those ice-blue eyes, letting him see every confusing emotion she felt at that moment.

''Still think I'm cute?''

Right now—this moment—was the turning point. Her response to him now would determine whether or not he allowed her full access. He refused to trust her, but some part of him wanted to believe that she was telling him the truth.

Her future depended upon this one defining second.

She went up on tiptoe, and even then, reaching that grim mouth was a task. He stood several inches taller than her. She brushed her lips lightly to his. Something electric zipped through her...startled her.

He pulled away...eyed her suspiciously.

Just when she felt certain he wouldn't respond, he grabbed her, whirled her around and pinned her against the wall with his big body. His mouth came down hard on hers. The kiss was punishing, savage. A mixture of desire and fear surged through her veins. She couldn't deny the attraction, but his touch was brutal.

She shoved at his chest. Every muscle her body encountered was like granite. Her lip burned, the wound reopening beneath his onslaught. The tang of blood had her pushing harder against him.

"Wait," she murmured breathlessly when he broke the seal of their lips just long enough to take a breath. She touched her lip, swiped at the trickle of blood. He watched her intently, his own breath ragged, but a good deal more controlled than hers.

Just then she remembered the monitor and made a conscious effort to slow her respiration…her heartbeat. If Maverick was still monitoring her activity, she didn't want him barging in.

"Not like that," she whispered. "Like this." She told herself it was a mistake, but that didn't stop her. She kissed him tenderly…slowly. He didn't move a muscle…held perfectly still. She kissed those firm lips until her own unexpected reaction forced her to break the contact. Not taking the time to evaluate her motives, she pressed her lips to the tiny scar on his cheek and then moved lower. Scar after scar she acknowledged with her lips…tracing each with her tongue. Her fingers fisted in the worn soft cotton of his shirt, and she fought the crazy need swirling inside her. This was work, she repeated mentally over and over. She dropped down to her knees, careful not to break the contact of her lips against his skin.

She was winning this battle. He braced his hands against the wall, his eyes closed and for the first time since she'd met him, the hard lines of his face softened just a fraction. But that was the only thing soft about him. Flirting with danger, she drew her tongue along the warm flesh just above his waistband. If she didn't stop now…she might have to finish this but every instinct told her that seduction was her only chance of reaching this guy.

Without warning, he grabbed her by the shoulders and pulled her to her feet. When her gaze collided with his, he looked totally unaffected. Anything he'd felt was long gone.

"I'll take you home now."

He released her and walked out of the room. Tasha let go a shaky breath and sagged against the wall to pull herself together. She was hot…damn hot and wet. She'd enjoyed that more than she should have—definitely more than he had, it seemed.

Damned fool, she railed at herself silently.

She knew better than to let that happen.

Staring at her reflection in the mirror, she just shook her head. The chance of a lifetime and she was going to screw it up playing amateur psychologist.

Whatever this guy's problem, it wasn't her job to save him. Her mission was to deliver him up to Lucas Camp for one thing and one thing only.

To die.

CHAPTER FOURTEEN

WHEN HE PULLED THE SUV next to the curb outside her apartment building, Tasha couldn't help thinking she'd had her chance and now it was over.

This wasn't the kind of guy to allow any sort of strings. She most likely would not see him again. But at least she knew where he lived, for the moment. She had his license plate number and a damned up-close description. But that's it. She knew absolutely nothing else about him.

"You didn't tell me your name," she said in the silence that ensued after he'd shifted into Park.

He turned toward her, his gaze cutting right through her like cold, hard steel. "Does it matter?"

She nodded, feeling startled by and wholly unprepared for the emotions he wrought in her.

"Seth."

"Seth," she echoed, thinking that it somehow fit. Some Egyptian slayer or something. "I like that."

He stared at her for a second that turned into ten before she started to squirm. There was something about his eyes...

She couldn't just get out now...she had to leave him with some reason to contact her again. She grabbed a pen from the console that separated them, then reached for his hand. He resisted at first, but eventually allowed her to draw it to her lap. She jotted her number on his palm.

He stared at his open hand for a moment then at her, but he didn't say he would or he wouldn't use the number.

"Bye, Seth."

She opened the door and climbed out, but his voice stopped her before she walked away.

"Just one thing."

She looked at him expectantly, her hand on the door ready to push it closed.

"Tell your roommate if she touches you again she's dead."

TASHA ENTERED THE BUILDING without allowing herself to think. She needed a long, hot bath. She needed to think... but first she had to get that final look she'd seen in his eyes out of her head.

He'd looked directly at her and issued that warning as if she belonged to him, and anyone else who touched her would be risking life and limb.

It didn't make sense.

On the elevator she stabbed the button for floor fourteen and leaned back against the wall. God, she was exhausted, mentally and physically.

The lift stopped on thirteen and she opened her eyes to see who would be boarding an upbound elevator with only one floor to go.

The doors slid open and Maverick waited in the corridor. "This way, North," he instructed.

Coming to immediate attention, she exited the elevator and followed the big cowboy down the quiet corridor. Though he didn't wear a hat, he had the boots and the attitude. She'd never been so glad to see anyone in her life. He was tall, broad-shouldered and had just a sprinkle of gray in his dark hair. Just enough to tell a girl he'd been around the block a time or two. She was glad to have him on her team.

At the fourth door on the right, he opened it and stepped back for her to enter the apartment before him.

"This whole floor is ours," he said in answer to her questioning look. "The escape route I showed you in your apartment upstairs will bring you here."

The escape route he spoke of was an oversize laundry chute accessed from her walk-in closet.

Inside the thirteenth-floor apartment, Maverick's partner, Ramon Vega, waited. He was much smaller in stature but quite confident and capable looking as well. His Latin heritage showed in his good looks, but he'd long since banished any accent from his dialect. He pressed a couple of buttons on a remote control and a wide-screen monitor came to life. Lucas Camp behind a desk blinked into vivid focus, his gaze zeroed in on her as if they were face-to-face in the same room.

"You look like hell, North," Lucas said by way of greeting.

She noticed the Webcam then and knew that, for all intents and purposes, they were face-to-face. She plopped down on a chair directly across from the screen and accompanying camera. "Feel like it, too."

"Tell me what you've got."

Before Tasha launched into a detailed report of the events since making contact with her target, she needed to get one thing out of the way.

"Something isn't right with this guy," she said, confusion lining her brow. She could feel it but couldn't quite label it.

"You mean something besides his being a sociopath?" Maverick ventured.

She nodded. "Yeah. Something besides that."

"Give us a profile on how he lives," Lucas said, setting the direction of the briefing. "Maverick has already told me where he lives and a brief summary of the neighborhood, but what did you see inside?"

"Not much at first. The lights were out when he took

me in and he locked me in the basement until this morning.''

Lucas frowned. ''Locked you in the basement?''

''Shackled me to a cot down there. The cot was bolted to the concrete floor. There was no way to escape. I had my doubts as to whether or not I'd see the light of day ever again.'' She sighed wearily. ''I can't be the first person he's held prisoner down there. His preparations were too well thought out.''

''That's why we couldn't get your signal back,'' Maverick concluded. ''I'm certain he had a jammer in his vehicle, but after that I couldn't be sure what happened. He stashed you underground, that explains it. You had me worried for a while.''

She nodded. She'd been a little worried herself. ''This morning he brought me back upstairs. I didn't get a good look around, but the place looked fully furnished with the usual household goods. I imagine his private space was on the second floor. I didn't get that far.''

''Do you think you made enough of an impression to see him again?'' Lucas wanted to know. He was watching her closely, assessing her state after her first encounter with the target.

She moved her hands over her face and through her hair. ''I think so. Maybe. It's difficult to tell. He's so guarded.'' She looked directly at Lucas then, or at least at his image. ''There's something wrong with this guy, Lucas. Something really wrong.''

''Anything you picked up on could be helpful. I've got a profiler standing by.''

She nodded. ''It's more than just the fact that he kills for a living, obviously.'' She tried to think how to label it…but nothing that came to mind felt accurate. ''He's deeply troubled. I got the distinct impression that he's not afraid of anything, death included.'' She shrugged. ''It's weird. It was nearly impossible to get any kind of reaction out of him. It's like he blocks all emotion. Doesn't feel a thing. And the scars.'' She shook her head as she thought of the marks on his body. ''I've never seen so many. He's had it rough at some point. But the lack of emotion was the biggest thing I noticed. I could scarcely get a reaction out of him at all.''

Ramon lifted a skeptical brow and eyed her skimpy attire. ''Are you sure he isn't dead?''

A pained laugh burst from her. ''Oh, no. He's very much alive…just buried somehow.''

''What about prints?'' Maverick tossed into the conversation. ''We could ID this guy if he's in the system.''

Lucas nodded. ''Possibly, but we've run his picture through the system and didn't find anything. Still, there's always the possibility that he's had his appearance altered. Did he give you a name?''

''Seth.'' Tasha tugged off first one boot, then the other. She reached into her right boot for her cell phone, handling it carefully. ''He handled the boots and the phone.''

Maverick and Ramon took custody of the items.

''I don't think that's his real name, though. Not that I expected to get the real thing,'' Tasha said to Lucas. ''But I studied Egyptian mythology as an elective in college. Seth was a sort of dark god, a slayer. The irony of it is too coincidental I think.''

Lucas nodded his agreement. ''We'll see what we can find on the name Seth. It may be an alias he's used before.''

''What now?'' she asked Lucas, then glanced at the two men who served as her backup.

''Now we wait,'' Lucas announced.

That felt like such a waste of time. Tasha spread her hands in a gesture of uncertainty. ''Maybe I should have tried to plant some sort of tracking device on him. He could be meeting with the guy who hired him right now and you can't allow a tail to get close enough to find out." She didn't want Lucas disappointed in her performance and he certainly hadn't given her any real reason to think he was pleased at this point.

Maverick spoke up first. "No way, little lady. This guy's a pro. He'd have found it, known you were the one who planted it, and that would have been the end of that, if you get my drift."

She nodded. The end of her, no doubt. "You're right. It just feels like I should have done more. He has my number, but who knows if he'll call."

"You got a lot farther than we expected for a first encounter," Lucas said pointedly. "And you're alive to tell about it. He'll call."

She supposed that was close enough to a pat on the back. And she sure as hell hoped he was right.

There was only one thing she could do now.

Wait.

CHAPTER FIFTEEN

TASHA MOANED SOFTLY as the steam rose around her. It felt so good to just soak for a while. She'd taken a shower after her debrief this morning, then a power nap that lasted for three hours. But this...this was pure luxury. She needed this. Her muscles loosened...relaxed as the heat chased away the stress and soreness. It might just take hours to soothe all the kinks and stiffness.

She apparently had the time. *He hadn't called.*

Her eyes opened and she lay there, her gaze searching for anything in the foggy room to focus on. She didn't want to think about him...not yet. Draping her arms along the sides of the tub, she forced his image away.

But not quickly enough. An entirely different kind of heat coiled inside her. She cursed herself for allowing it. He was a killer...the enemy. And yet, somehow he'd gotten to her on a level over which she had no control. It was totally unbelievable. She tried hard to pinpoint the precise root of the feeling. It wasn't sympathy. There was a definite physical attraction, despite his lack of personality. But that wasn't such a big deal. As Ramon would say, she wasn't dead. Any woman breathing would be attracted to Seth on a physical level. But she could handle that. He was an assassin...a very dangerous man...a bad guy...the enemy. Taking him down wouldn't be a problem.

That last thought echoed hollowly. "Shit," she muttered. This couldn't happen. She'd just met the guy. Taking him down was her mission...but something felt wrong.

How could she even think about screwing up this badly? She shook her head slowly from side to side. This was the opportunity of a lifetime. Lucas Camp had come to her! She couldn't let anything get in the way. Why the hell had she chosen psychology for her major, anyway? If she hadn't, maybe then she wouldn't have bothered looking beneath the surface.

She scrubbed a hand over her face and cursed herself again. This wasn't about what made the guy tick. This was about stopping a killer—a hired assassin—before he accomplished his mission. Her primary goal, outside seeing that he didn't accomplish his, was making the connection between him and the man who hired him. Nothing else mattered. All those scars… The overwhelming feeling that he was as much a victim as those he hunted was of no consequence.

He would be stopped, one way or another. And so would the man who'd hired him. Lucas's intentions were crystal clear. He wanted this guy dead. Tasha felt it all the way to her bones. It was personal somehow.

A knock at the front door jerked her from her troubling thoughts. Water sloshed as she pushed upright. Her heart kicked into a faster rhythm.

She shifted to her feet, the steam rising off her skin, and stepped out of the tub onto the fluffy bath mat. Shouldering into the robe without bothering to towel dry, she reached for her weapon next.

As she padded down the short hall, her bare feet leaving a trail of water, she chambered a round in the weapon Maverick had given her. Another knock rattled the hinges as she crossed the living room. She peered through the peephole, her heart pounding, and saw Maverick.

Heaving a relieved sigh, she shook off the tension and opened the door. "What's up?"

Maverick stepped inside, and she closed the door behind

him. "Just wanted you to know that we lifted his prints from your cell phone but they were useless." He passed the phone back to her.

A frown nagged at her forehead. "He wasn't in the system?" The guy was clearly a high-end professional, getting caught wouldn't be in keeping with his skill level. And unless he'd been caught and charged with some crime, he wouldn't be in any system.

He shook his head and handed her the boots she'd worn last night. "Can't tell. There's too much alteration, not enough legible lines to go for a match."

"He doesn't intend to be ID'd." This just kept getting better and better. Seth was really on top of his game. He'd had his fingerprints altered.

"It's professional work, too, not a homemade job."

That's why she hadn't felt any particular roughness when he'd touched her. This wasn't a hack job to alter any prints he'd leave behind, this was one of those cutting-edge "escape clinic" laser jobs. Very expensive, very cleverly done. Either Seth or the man he worked for knew how to remain anonymous.

"If he calls," she offered, "I can try and get a look around his place. See what I can find."

Maverick nodded. "Just be careful." He looked at her a moment before he continued. "Lucas would like you to try and get a DNA sample. We don't know how much good it'll do, but it's another avenue of identification."

The various ways a sample could be obtained flashed quickly through her mind. "All right."

Maverick looked away briefly before adding, "You know a shed hair won't get us what we need. If you could lift his toothbrush or razor, assuming it's not the electric type, that would be better."

She nodded. "Got it."

"Just be careful, North." Maverick shook his head, his

expression cluttered with more concern than she would have expected from a man of his background. "You're right when you said there's something off about this guy. He worries me more than most I've run across in my time. Lucas said the same thing."

At least she wasn't the only one picking up those vibes. "Don't worry, I've got it under control."

That was a flat-out lie, but he didn't need to know it. In the event that he was fishing for Lucas, she wasn't about to give him any information that could discredit her in any way.

"I'll be right downstairs." He glanced at her robe. "Don't forget to put another patch in place."

"Will do."

When he'd gone, she retraced her damp path to the bathroom, drained the tub and cleaned up the mess she'd made. She set her weapon aside, reached into the medicine cabinet and got the box that contained the patches. To anyone else they looked like a simple birth control prescription. Lucas's people covered every base. If her target decided to check her out, he'd find nothing that would suggest she wasn't who she said she was. They'd even furnished the second bedroom of the apartment, complete with young, female wardrobe, to give the illusion of a roommate.

Tasha pressed the patch into place and checked out her reflection. The bruise on her cheek was pretty much gone now, and her lip was way better. A dab of makeup and she'd be good to go. Her side was still a little tender, but not so bad.

The firm knock on her front door made her jump. Damn, she was edgy. Forgetting her appearance for the moment she strode back into the living room. What did Maverick want now?

She opened the door without bothering to check the peephole.

Her target filled the doorway, those piercing blue eyes covered by dark shades.

For one second she was sure she had to be imagining things, but she blinked and he was still there.

He removed the concealing eyewear and focused that fierce gaze on her. "Ask me in."

A shiver raced across her skin as much from the sound of his deep voice as from those eyes. She summoned a semblance of control and stepped back, opening the door wide. "Come on in."

He reached down and picked up a bag she hadn't noticed since she was too busy staring at those unsettling eyes. Idiot, she railed silently. Details. She wasn't supposed to miss any.

Once he'd stepped inside, he closed and locked the door behind him. That move should have set her on edge but didn't. Maverick and Ramon would be watching. Her apartment was rigged for surveillance. Seth looked at her, surveyed her lack of proper attire and then settled his gaze on hers. "I have a job for you."

For just a second it kind of annoyed her that she found not a glimmer of approval in his eyes. She was standing there naked but for the robe, and he didn't even notice. God knew that she'd absorbed every damned detail about him. Black T-shirt beneath a pale blue cotton button-up shirt. The telltale bulge of the weapon he wore, well-fitting jeans and those made-for-traction ankle boots. If she hadn't enjoyed the perusal so much she could have chalked it up to merely being part of her job. But the heat funneling beneath her belly button made a liar out of her. She pushed the disturbing sensation away.

"What kind of job?"

"You need money, right?" He said this as he surveyed what he could see of her apartment. It was a nice enough place and wasn't the reason he asked the question. She remembered telling him that she didn't have a job yet and was pretty much broke from coughing up her share of the rent.

"Yeah, I need money," she said bluntly. "But not badly enough to do anything illegal." She looked him up and down, pausing briefly at his crotch. She looked away just as quickly. Either the guy stayed aroused all the time or he was extremely well endowed. Why she would notice and why it would have such an effect was beyond her. What the hell was wrong with her?

"There's nothing to worry about." He offered her the shopping bag he carried. "Put this on."

Still trying to read his expression, which was impossible, she accepted the bag that turned out to be a good deal heavier than it looked. Inside was a brown uniform. "What's this?" Her senses moved to a higher state of alert. Even folded up as it was she recognized the delivery-service getup.

"I'd like you to make a delivery for me. It's very simple."

"What kind of delivery?"

When he looked at her this time, there was no way to miss his impatience. That he allowed her to see the emotion surprised her and served as a warning at the same time.

"Don't ask so many questions."

She shrugged and headed to the bedroom with the bag in hand. For a second or two she allowed the elation of his return to bolster the nagging worry over where this might be headed. For the moment he was back, and that was all that mattered.

Moving quickly, she dragged on a pair of panties and a bra. Surprisingly the uniform was a good fit. Maybe he'd noticed more than he'd let on. The weight in the bag was the shoes. He'd thought of everything.

She brushed her hair and pulled it up with a claw clip,

grabbed her purse and sunglasses and readied for whatever the hell he had in mind.

He waited right where she'd left him. Maverick and Ramon would know whether he'd looked around. She would find out later.

Seth scrutinized her from head to toe. "Perfect."

"Why not just have the package delivered in the usual manner?" she asked as they exited her apartment.

"I have my reasons."

She locked her door and followed him to the stairs. Fourteen floors, either the guy had a phobia where elevators were concerned or he didn't want to get trapped in one in case he had to make a run for it.

He didn't speak again even after they were in his SUV and headed into city traffic, which was no big surprise. He only spoke when he had something to say or she forced a response out of him. She occupied herself with attempting to determine their destination.

A few minutes later he parked in the lot of a large office building right off the Magnificent Mile, Chicago's main street of shops, restaurants and ritzy office buildings.

He reached into the back seat and picked up a package. Eight-by-ten, she estimated. Wrapped in a plain brown paper. Addressed to... She leaned toward him slightly to read the name and address.

The name slammed into her with all the force of a runaway train.

Victoria Colby.

She was his mark.

"You know..." Calm, stay calm. She forced her heart rate back to a normal pace and focused on slowing her respiration. She couldn't let him see that she recognized the name. "Maybe this isn't such a good idea."

He nodded toward the building. "Fourth floor. The elevator opens right into the Colby Agency lobby," he went on as if she'd said nothing. "Ask for Victoria Colby. Don't let anyone else sign for the package except her. Do you understand?"

She moistened her suddenly dry lips. Somewhere in the back of her mind, she realized that he'd just said more to her at one time than any other time since they'd met. "What's in the package? You're sure—"

"Go." He pushed the package and an electronic clipboard toward her and pressed her with a gaze that warned her not to argue. "Now."

She took the package and the clipboard and climbed out of the SUV. She walked slowly across the parking lot, praying that Maverick had her location. She forced her mind to consider what could be in the package. It felt a little light for any kind of elaborate explosive. A detonator would be required. But then again there were all kinds of lightweight devices. She considered the possibility of some sort of poison. Something absorbed through the skin or inhaled like anthrax.

Resisting the impulse to scan the lot for Maverick's vehicle, she opened the main door and stepped inside. She strode straight up to the lobby desk.

"I have a package for Victoria Colby," she said in as professional a tone as she could manage. He could be listening, watching even. Who knew what sort of gadgets he could have added to the innocuous-looking uniform. There'd been no time to check it out thoroughly.

"Fourth floor," the watchman said without even asking for ID.

It was the uniform. It was too much a part of everyday life for anyone to give it a second thought.

Tasha went to the bank of elevators and pressed the call button. She let her respiration and heart rate increase faster and faster as a signal to Maverick that something was wrong. By the time she reached the fourth floor, her skin felt flushed and she'd all but hyperventilated. Even if Seth had some way of monitoring her now, he would expect her to be nervous going in.

The receptionist greeted her with a smile and a pleasant, "May I help you?"

"I have a delivery for Victoria Colby."

The receptionist reached for the package. "I'll take it for you."

Tasha knew a moment's panic. "I'm sorry," she said, grabbing back control. "Ms. Colby has to personally sign for the package."

"Oh." The woman's expression turned to one of confusion, or maybe irritation. She pointed to the corridor on Tasha's right. "Her secretary's office is the first one on the left."

Tasha forced a smile. "Thank you."

She passed a couple of people in the corridor, both male and wearing suits. Colby Agency investigators, Tasha presumed. Each one surveyed her thoroughly before moving on. She wanted to scream, "Doesn't anyone suspect anything is wrong here?" But she only smiled stiffly.

"Good afternoon. You have a delivery?" This from a pleasant-looking middle-aged lady whose name plate read, Mildred Parker.

"Yes, for Victoria Colby."

"Well, generally the receptionist would sign for any packages," she offered kindly.

Tasha glanced at the clipboard. "The sender requested that Ms. Colby sign for the package personally."

"Very well."

The secretary stood and moved toward the door on the other side of the room. Tasha followed. The older woman knocked once and pushed it open.

"Victoria, there's a special delivery for you. This young lady needs you to sign for it."

Mildred opened the door wider and stepped to one side for Tasha to enter.

Her pulse racing, Tasha met the dark gaze focused on her from the other side of the massive mahogany desk. So this was Victoria Colby. She looked every bit as dignified and sophisticated as Tasha had expected.

What she hadn't expected was the incredible complacency where security was concerned. Wasn't Lucas supposed to have men watching her? Forcing her feet into action, Tasha moved across the room.

Victoria Colby reached for the clipboard Tasha offered. "Good afternoon," she said with a smile.

Tasha forced an answering smile and nodded.

Victoria signed the clipboard and passed it back to her, her open hand waiting for the package.

As she slowly extended the package toward the woman, Tasha tried to warn her with her eyes...tried to make her see that something was wrong.

If Victoria noticed, she didn't show it.

"Thank you," she said as she settled the package on her desk.

Tasha managed a stiff "Have a nice day" and left. She punched the down button at the elevator and fought the need to tell someone that this was all wrong. A part of her braced for the sound of an explosion or for a scream of agony.

When the elevator doors finally slid open, what felt like a lifetime later, Tasha drew up short when a tall, dark-haired man moved to exit the arriving car. He paused and looked directly into her eyes for two beats. She prayed he would see the warning there. When he at last moved past her he allowed his hand to brush hers.

The rush of relief was so profound that she scarcely stepped forward quickly enough to catch the elevator before the doors closed.

Whoever the guy was he had to be one of Lucas's men. The look he'd given her was one of assurance, the physical contact a sign that he understood something was wrong. Maverick had gotten word to Lucas.

She stabbed the button for the lobby and sagged against the closest wall. Taking long, deep breaths she calmed her racing heart and slowed her frantic respiration.

When she reached the SUV, Seth didn't ask any questions, just drove away once she'd climbed inside.

The silence that hung in the air ignited a fury in her belly. By the time he pulled up to the curb in front of her apartment building her temper had raged out of control.

"I want to know what was in that package." She turned on him, glared at him with all the anger she felt inside.

He didn't even bother taking off his sunglasses or looking her way, he simply offered her a wad of cash.

She almost told him where he could shove the money, but that would be out of character for the role she played. Instead, she snatched it from him, startled to note that it was five one-hundred-dollar bills.

"You can dispose of the uniform."

She grabbed her purse, shoved the money into it before slinging it over her shoulder. She started to get out, but hesitated, then shook her head. No way was he getting off this easy.

"I don't like being used," she told him. "If that package was dangerous and that lady—"

"There was nothing in the package that could physically harm anyone. It was merely a message…a reminder."

She closed her eyes for one second as another blast of relief hit her.

"Get out."

Renewed fury obliterated all other emotion. "You're unbelievable. You come to me for a favor, then you treat me like a piece of trash you can toss away."

He remained silent, motionless, seemingly oblivious of her heated emotions.

In a lightning-flash move, she snatched off his sunglasses and glared at him. "You really are—"

Before she could finish the statement, he'd jerked her across the console and trapped her between his chest and the steering wheel. The look in his eyes was murderous, his expression hard, his breathing shallow and harsh.

"Don't ever do that again."

Ignoring the fury seething in every part of him, she lifted her chin defiantly and demanded, "And just what will you do about it if I do."

He kissed her.

Savagely.

Then he drew back and looked into her eyes. "Get out."

She didn't hesitate this time. She scrambled out of the vehicle and strode to her building without looking back. Not until she was inside her own apartment, with the door closed and locked behind her, did she allow herself to breathe easy.

She thought of all she'd learned about him from their brief encounters. The way he'd locked her in that basement. The bizarre tattoo…the way he tried to hurt her even when he kissed her.

Whatever else she felt or imagined she felt, one thing was a certainty…this guy was dangerous.

Extremely dangerous.

To her.

CHAPTER SIXTEEN

"WHERE'S LUCAS?"

"He's on his way, ma'am," Logan told Victoria. "I've checked the package thoroughly. It appears to be safe, but I'd rather you wait for Lucas's arrival before we open it."

Victoria looked to Ian and then to Simon. Both men looked as uncertain about this as she felt.

She hadn't needed John Logan to rush in and snatch the package from her hands to know something was wrong. The young woman who'd delivered it had given her the undeniable impression that she should be afraid.

Victoria closed her eyes and tried to steady the spinning in her head. She wasn't sure she possessed the fortitude to get through this. It was bad enough that an assassin was stalking her, but the ice cream...now this.

Leberman, the son of a bitch, why didn't he just confront her face-to-face? Why all the subterfuge? All the games?

Because the sick bastard gets off on the pain he inflicts. She knew the answer. Understood perfectly why he was doing this to her. Still, she couldn't fully come to terms with it.

Victoria opened her eyes and stared at the package. Her only regret was that she couldn't kill the bastard here and now.

From his hotel only minutes away, where he'd set up a mini command post, Lucas arrived just then, his gaze going first to her, then settling on the package lying in the middle of her desk.

"That's it?" He looked to Logan and then to Ian.

Both men nodded. Logan told him, "I can't find any indication of explosives or poisonous substances. Scans indicate a nonmetal object."

"Clear the room," Lucas commanded. "I don't want anyone in here when I open it."

"Absolutely not," Victoria argued. "The package is addressed to me, I'll open it."

"I'll open it." Simon stepped toward her desk.

Simon had a new wife. Ian had a wife and two children. And Logan had a wife, as well. Victoria looked to each of the trusted men and ordered, "Leave my office. I want to do this alone."

Ian shook his head. "Not going to happen, Victoria. Either allow one of us to open the package, or we'll stand here and debate the point all evening."

She surveyed the determined male faces around the room. All were prepared to die to protect her. Every damned one of them was as stubborn as she was.

"All right." She stepped back. "Open it."

Simon quickly stepped in front of Ian. Simon had done time with the FBI and was fearless when it came to doing his duty. He was just one of many fine investigators Victoria employed. She prayed the evil that had followed her life for nearly two decades would not touch him now.

Using the gloves and utility cutter Logan had brought into the office, Simon carefully slit the packaging. He pulled back the outer wrapping and cut the tape sealing the lid on the small box. He dragged the package a little closer and cautiously lifted the lid.

He studied the contents for a moment before allowing his gaze to meet Victoria's. She saw the uncertainty there a split second before he turned the box around where she could see what it held.

A small blue sneaker was the only item in the box.

She didn't have to touch it or inspect it in any way. She recognized it immediately. She knew everyone in the room was waiting for her to say something...but she couldn't speak. She could only stand there, as the tears spilled down her cheeks, and stare at the small shoe her son had been wearing the day he disappeared.

CHAPTER SEVENTEEN

HE DROVE BACK to the house in Oak Park well after dark. He'd waited until Victoria Colby had left her office, her protector, Lucas Camp, and his two men close by, and then he'd followed her home.

It hadn't been necessary for him to see her face as she opened the package. He saw all he needed to in her pained, stoic profile while she pretended to go about her daily routine as she left the office. He was satisfied.

They knew he was watching, but they did nothing. He'd wondered at that in the beginning but he understood now. They had what they considered an ace in the hole. And Victoria Colby would want to see how this game played out. She wanted the truth. She wanted Leberman.

As, he imagined, did Lucas Camp.

He laughed softly as he considered what lay before them. Victoria Colby couldn't possibly imagine the horrors in store for her before the blessed relief of death would come. He almost hated to allow it to end that way.

He backed into the driveway that flanked the house he used for the time being. He hated coming back here, but it was a necessary part of the strategy. Though he enjoyed the buildup, the crescendo of death would be lessened immensely, in his opinion, by this grandstanding.

But it was not his decision to make.

As he did each time he returned, he searched the grounds, considered the windows and doors for any subtle change in the way he'd left them.

He knew immediately that he had a visitor.

A careful one.

Like smoke, soundless and camouflaged by the darkness, he stole into the house. His visitor waited in the darkness of the inner hall, like a cancer lying dormant before it struck its unsuspecting victim. Being in this house again with him gnawed at Seth's gut like the sharp hunger pains he'd once known in that dark place he'd called home.

"What do you want?" he demanded.

He didn't want him here. Had no desire to speak with him or to see him.

Leberman flipped on the overhead light switch, leveling the playing field since he could not see so well in the dark. He blinked to adjust his vision.

"You made the delivery?" he demanded without preamble.

"Yes." Seth squashed the sensation of fear that, even now...after all these years, tried to surface. He reminded himself that he was not afraid of anything—most especially this son of a bitch.

Leberman nodded. "Good. And the rest is on schedule?"

"I don't want you here." He clenched his jaw hard to hold back the emotion he refused to allow. Control was essential.

Leberman met his gaze, those beady eyes showing no fear. The tables had turned in recent years. He was a fool not to fear him. "I know you don't want me here. You despise me now." He circled him slowly, inspecting him as he had hundreds of times before. Seth resisted the instinct to stiffen. "I know exactly how you feel about me," Leberman continued. He moved back in front of him. "But that changes nothing. You owe me this. You will see it through."

Seth didn't respond. Leberman knew he would not fail.

As he said, he owed this to him. And then they would be even...finished.

Leberman leaned closer and sniffed. "You've been with a woman. I smell her perfume."

He didn't bother to respond to that comment, either, though a tendril of uneasiness slid through him. He banished it with the same indifference he displayed for his unwanted guest now. Theirs was not a relationship based on friendship or fondness of any sort. They had only one thing in common. Sheer hatred for the Colby name.

"Did you fuck her?" Leberman inclined his head thoughtfully. "I think not. Perhaps that's the reason for your foul mood." He smiled grotesquely. "She must have seen you for what you are. Pure evil...a beast. Did you let her live in spite of her rebuff?" He sniffed again. "You're not getting soft are you?"

Seth locked down all emotion and moved a step closer to the bastard, his fingers fisting tightly to resist the urge to wrap around that scrawny throat. Only with him did he still struggle with the human weakness of baser emotions. "Unless you came here to provide additional instructions, we have nothing to discuss."

Leberman peered up at him, studied his face, seemingly oblivious to the hatred radiating in his direction. "I trained you so well. You don't show the first hint of emotion. Anger now and again, perhaps, but nothing more."

This was a waste of time. "Say what you came to say and *go.*"

"Pain, death, none of it touches you, does it?" Leberman persisted. He smiled. "You are magnificent." He shook his head slowly from side to side. "You have no idea how proud I am. Every moment I've waited will have been well worth it." He sighed mightily. "You're prepared for tomorrow?"

The question was unnecessary. "Of course."

"Good. I'm looking forward to this step more than you can know."

Seth said nothing.

A beat of silence passed. When Leberman would have gone, Seth reluctantly issued a warning of a different sort, "They're watching me closely now. I don't think I was followed, but it's a possibility." Though he didn't really care if Leberman was caught or not, it would ruin his own plans at this stage.

Leberman cocked his head. "Really? I'm surprised you let them that close." His eyes narrowed. "That's not like you. It's *her,* isn't it?"

"I'll create a diversion so you can go undetected," he offered and walked away, leaving the bastard to think what he would and not bothering to answer his question. He didn't give a damn what surprised him.

If Lucas's men were out there, as he suspected, all he had to do was set a course for Victoria Colby's private residence, and they would follow.

He glanced back at Leberman once more and warned, "Don't come back."

"Just so you know, I will be watching tomorrow," Leberman told him, an underlying threat in his tone. "I'll be very careful to stay out of sight, but I will be watching."

Seth just wanted him out of his sight. If he chose to watch tomorrow it was of no consequence to him as long as he stayed out of the way and away from him. The death of Lucas Camp only served one purpose as far as Seth was concerned.

To torture Victoria Colby.

CHAPTER EIGHTEEN

TASHA LAY IN BED at midnight with no sign of sleep in sight. She couldn't stop thinking about what Lucas had told her. The package had contained a small boy's shoe. One of the shoes Victoria Colby's child had been wearing eighteen years ago when he'd gone missing.

Victoria had been devastated then and today.

Tasha thought of the woman she'd met briefly when she delivered the package. Strong, steady, still very attractive at fifty or so. But that woman had been brought to her knees by a horrible reminder of the past.

Why would Seth do that? Tasha felt certain that he was following Leberman's orders. Lucas had told her that they suspected this man named Leberman of having taken the child. Once he'd disposed of the body he'd obviously kept souvenirs for later.

Leberman wanted to make Victoria suffer before he ended her life. Lucas was sure he had more dirty tricks up his sleeve. Tasha also fully understood Lucas's personal ties now. Victoria Colby.

Tasha's thoughts turned to Seth then. Was it about the money? She'd turned the uniform and the bills he'd given her over to Maverick for fingerprinting in hopes of finding Leberman's or anyone else's who might be connected. She wondered how much a man like Leberman would pay to hire a man as skilled and ruthless as Seth to carry out this well-planned drama that was supposed to end in death.

She wondered at the brutalities Seth must have suffered

to make him the kind of man he was. She flopped over onto her other side. Why the hell did she care? He was a killer. It didn't matter what made him that way. Her only job was to stop him once they'd located Leberman.

Tasha pushed up from the bed and shuffled into the kitchen for a drink. Sleep wasn't coming. She might as well give up and do something useful. Maybe some yoga. She could definitely handle some relaxation exercises.

The telephone rang, startling her.

She blew out a breath. Damn, she was going to have to get a grip here. She strode over to the table next to the sofa and picked up the receiver. It wouldn't be Maverick, he'd knock on her door.

"Hello," she said softly as if she'd been awakened, though she really didn't expect to hear from Seth again this soon.

"There's a cab waiting outside."

Seth.

Anticipation seared through her. "A cab? Where am I going?" She glanced at the clock, 12:35 a.m.

"I think you know."

An audible click told her he'd hung up.

She lowered the receiver and dropped it back into its cradle.

For a while Tasha simply stood there trying to decide if she could take this step or not.

She knew what he wanted.

Had felt the primal urgency in his kiss that afternoon. Had also felt his resistance. He didn't want to want her.

She closed her eyes and ordered her heart rate to slow. Sleeping with him was supposed to be a last resort. But nothing was as it should be with him. She needed that closer connection with him. She needed him to need her. Seduction was her only option.

Rather than stand there rationalizing further, she did what she had to do.

She dressed for the occasion.

Short black skirt, matching thong, even shorter gold top, no bra, no hose. She slid her feet into strappy black sandals and looked herself over. The hesitation she saw in her own eyes was unlike her...she shouldn't hesitate. This wasn't personal. It was business—essential to the mission. She'd known going in that it might come to this. She shook her head and looked away from the lie in her eyes. Somehow, stupidly, she had waited for this moment. She hoped like hell her motivation was grounded in the mission. But she had a very bad feeling that it wasn't.

Tossing her toothbrush and other essentials into a bag, she glanced at the gun she'd left lying on the toilet tank. But she couldn't risk him finding it. She had mace. That would have to be sufficient. He was a lot bigger than her, but she could fight as well as any man. On second thought she removed the patch and tossed it into the trash. Maverick knew his location. She wasn't going to risk having to explain the patch to Seth. Or worse, have him detect its signal if he chose to do a body sweep.

As he'd said, a cab waited at the curb. She climbed in, and the driver pulled out onto the street without asking for directions. Maverick would be furious, but it wasn't like they didn't know where Seth lived now. Her apartment was monitored, they would know she'd left.

She relaxed into the seat and cleared her mind. She wasn't going to argue with herself anymore. Whatever happened happened. End of subject.

She knew what she had to do.

A few minutes later she leaned forward and surveyed the street signs.

"Why aren't we headed for Oak Park?"

"That's not the address I was given," the cabbie offered with a shrug. He smiled then. "Maybe it's a surprise."

Uneasiness slid through Tasha. An all-too-familiar sensation these days. There were surprises and there were *surprises*. This was definitely one she hadn't anticipated. Failure to anticipate her target's moves was a dangerous weakness. He looked more and more as if *he* was a serious weakness.

THIRTY MINUTES LATER, after traveling through several exclusive neighborhoods, the cab braked to a stop in front of a massive ornamental gate. She squinted to make out the house that lay beyond but couldn't.

After a moment the gate opened and the cab rolled through and toward the house at the end of the drive. As they neared the structure she could make out the soaring, contemporary lines and angles. A high wall enclosed the property for as far as she could see, and if her sense of direction was on track they were near the lake. That would explain the elegant homes they'd passed.

"Here you are." The cabbie glanced back at her and smiled with masculine approval. "The fare has already been taken care of."

"Thanks." Tasha stepped out of the cab and looked around for a bit before moving toward the house. The cab left through the gate, and she heard it close behind him. The house looked dark except for foundation lights that up lit from the well-landscaped shrubbery. But Seth liked the dark.

She moved toward the front entry, wondering where his SUV was parked. A side entry garage perhaps.

As she moved up the steps, the front door opened and he stood there waiting for her. He didn't speak, just waited. Her pulse reacted and she chastised herself for the lack of control.

If Maverick had tried to follow her, he was nowhere to be seen. But then, that was her fault for removing the one link between her and her backup.

It was just *him* and her.

She was on her own.

When she'd stepped inside, he closed the door behind her and turned on the lights, the setting far dimmer than she would have preferred.

"Looks like you've moved up in the world," she said to him when he remained silent. Even in the low light she could see that the house was elegantly decorated and expensively furnished.

"This way."

She followed him up the grand staircase. Surely this wasn't his home. Maybe Leberman's? That didn't make sense, either. Lucas and Victoria would certainly know if he were this close. This place didn't exactly have a lived-in feel, but it didn't have that closed-up smell or feel about it, either.

When he stopped again and turned on a light, they were in a generously sized bedroom with French doors that likely led out onto a balcony. She imagined there was a view of the lake. The furnishings were just as exquisite as the ones downstairs, including the massive king-size bed.

He took her purse, then leveled that piercing gaze on her. "Take off your clothes."

She walked over to him and reached for the buttons of his shirt. "How about we take off yours first?"

Strong fingers encircled her wrists and pulled her hands away from his shirt. "Take them off."

She backed up a step and considered her limited options. She could refuse and blow this now—maybe have to fight her way out of here—or...

He unzipped her purse then removed a thick fold of bills from his pocket and dropped them inside. When he'd tossed the bag aside he issued his order again. "Now, take off your clothes."

Unbridled fury scorched through her. "You think I'm some kind of hooker?" She glanced at her bag for emphasis.

When he didn't answer she huffed in disbelief. "Oh, man." She stormed out, didn't even bother with her purse. She wanted to make the right connection with the guy. Earn his trust. This kind of connection would get her nowhere fast.

By the time she reached the landing he was right behind her. She ignored him and kept moving. She was down the stairs and halfway across the entry hall when he stopped her. He whirled her around to face him, his hold on her arms brutal.

"No one walks away from me."

"Let me go," she warned.

Something changed in his expression. "I thought you needed a job," he countered, his eyes narrowing suspiciously.

She tried without success to jerk free of his savage hold. "I need a job not a john. Now let me go!"

He released her as suddenly as he'd grabbed her. He took a step back physically and emotionally. "Get your bag. I'll take you back."

Tasha couldn't move for a moment, unable to look away from that fierce gaze just yet. When she could break free of the spell, she turned and hurried up the stairs. She cursed herself every step of the way for being the fool she was. She should be glad that he hadn't out-and-out raped her. Instead, he'd turned off the desire she knew he had felt as easily as he turned off a light switch.

And, unbelievably, she was disappointed.

CHAPTER NINETEEN

HE PERFORMED his usual check of the perimeter of the Oak Park property before entering. Thankfully no one waited for him this time. A quick sweep for alien electronics and he relaxed.

If Leberman showed his face once more he might just kill him now and put them both out of their misery. Dread, or something on that order, hardened in his gut. He tamped it down. Hated those old sensations Leberman so easily engendered in him. When Victoria Colby was dead they would be even, anyway. What difference would a few days make? Once his score with Leberman was settled he intended to kill the bastard if he ever came near him again. Just looking at him made Seth remember the past, and he didn't want to remember.

He climbed the stairs to his room without bothering with light. He was as much at home in the dark as he was in the light, maybe more. The dark had always been his friend. No one could see him in the dark.

Before he could stop the mutinous memory, Leberman's words echoed in his head. He knew what he was all right. He was pure evil…a monster. Hadn't he been marked long ago? That was just one more reason he couldn't trust Tasha. She pretended to see what wasn't there…pretended not to care what he was.

But he knew differently.

He knew a great deal more than she suspected. He knew exactly what she was doing. Leberman had his sources.

He untied his shoes and toed them off, then shouldered out of his shirt and dropped it to the floor. The weapon and holster he shrugged off and lay on the bed. A gun had been his only sleeping partner for more than a decade. He was never without it. Never intended to be, as long as he was still breathing.

As he peeled his T-shirt up and off, he caught a glimpse of himself in the mirror. He moved closer to inspect the numerous scars that marred his otherwise well-maintained body. Ugly, brutal marks that told the story of his past. A past he wanted to forget. He studied his face and the slash on his jaw that had been the last one inflicted by the bastard who'd trained him.

He banked the fury that ignited instantly whenever he allowed himself to dwell on the past. His lips flattened into a grim line. The bouts of anger he'd been dealing with lately were nothing but an indicator of his one weakness— the past. When he had paid his final debt he would never think of the past again.

The image of Tasha flashed through his mind, sending a new kind of fire straight to his groin. She was proving a weakness, as well. He'd allowed his curiosity to get the better of him…. That had been a mistake.

It wouldn't happen again.

He had no reason at this point to kill her, but he would if she got in his way.

The curiosity she'd sparked in him was the only reason she wasn't dead already.

But she was toying with him…there could be no other explanation.

He knew what he was, and no woman would want that.

Unless she was paid to want it.

He shook his head in self-disgust when even the mere thought of her got him hard. Not once since becoming a man had he allowed any woman to hold that kind of power over him.

Sex, he decided, was only about his body's need for physical release, nothing more. He stepped back into his shoes and tied them. Then reached for his shirt and weapon. Well, physical release would be easy enough to obtain.

There were plenty of women out there who knew how to use their mouths for something more than talk.

He didn't need Tasha.

Any woman would do.

They were all alike—manipulative, clingy, untrustworthy. Though admittedly they had their uses, he had never met one he needed.

He didn't need anyone or anything.

CHAPTER TWENTY

TASHA SAT IN THE DARKNESS of the compact car Lucas had provided. She peered at the house where Seth had held her prisoner just forty-eight hours ago. Though the place was dark, she knew he was in there, his SUV was in the drive.

Tonight—this morning, actually, since it was well past midnight—when he'd dropped her back at her apartment, she'd been too furious to think before she reacted. He hadn't uttered one word to her the entire trip. He'd simply driven her back as he said he would and stopped only long enough for her to get out.

Even now renewed fury burned away all reason. She'd entered her apartment building, given him thirty seconds and then exited again. She'd jumped in her car and driven straight back to the lake house with no rational thought as to the consequences. She'd sat there for a few minutes watching the eerily dark house, but that extra instinct of hers had nagged her into going back to the Oak Park residence. She'd sensed that he wasn't at the lake house.

Somehow, incredibly, they'd connected on a level that she couldn't begin to understand. The only thing she did know with a certainty was that she'd lost a good deal of her objectivity way too fast. She felt angry at him for drawing her close, only to turn her away when she refused to do things his way. The idea that he could so easily turn off any need or desire made her want to scream with frustration.

Bottom line, she'd wanted him to want her. Which meant

one thing, she'd crossed the line. Hell, she hadn't simply crossed the line, she'd pole-vaulted over it.

This wasn't supposed to be personal, even if sex were involved. It was business—the mission. Somehow she'd allowed the amateur psychoanalyst side of her to get sucked into his world. She was so busy trying to figure him out that she was losing all perspective on reality.

He was a killer.

An assassin.

He tortured and murdered people for money.

Her career would be over if the Agency or Lucas Camp discovered that she'd crossed that line. Worst of all, she feared her lack of objectivity was even more deeply personal than her overwhelming need to know what made him tick.

Maybe her career should be over if she couldn't maintain proper perspective any better than this.

The headlights of his SUV suddenly glared through the darkness.

She tensed…forgot all else and moved to a higher state of alert. Where the hell would he be going now? To Victoria Colby's house? That didn't feel right. He was surely aware that she would be tucked in for the night with maximum security. He was on to Lucas now, probably had been from the start.

The SUV he'd backed into the driveway rolled forward onto the street, in the direction of Chicago proper and away from her position.

Slowing her respiration and pulling her focus on track, Tasha eased into a nearby driveway, turned around and followed him. Maintaining a visual would likely be impossible since she couldn't risk getting too close. At this hour the very idea of tailing a target was ludicrous. There were no other vehicles on the quiet residential streets with which to blend.

But she'd give it her best shot.

Even if he didn't spot her, she was in deep trouble. Maverick would have her hide whenever she showed up back at her apartment. She was supposed to wear the monitoring device at all times. When Seth had called about the taxi she'd foolishly assumed the destination. Now she had nothing to blame but plain old stupidity. She'd been so angry she followed him without taking the proper precautions. She'd acted on the moment...on instinct. What the hell good was backup if she left them in the dark? She imagined Maverick would report her carelessness to Lucas.

Somehow she had to make tonight worth the risks she'd taken. Going back empty-handed wasn't an option. She needed something.

Something only *he* could give her.

And that was the bottom line. As much as his actions had rubbed her the wrong way, pushed some button he shouldn't even have access to, she'd walked away with nothing and no guarantee that she would see him again. Unacceptable. She was better than this. She would get to him...she would give Lucas Camp what he wanted: Leberman.

As they neared downtown, traffic appeared, which facilitated her ability to duplicate Seth's turns without the risk of detection. Since she'd never visited Chicago before this assignment, she didn't know the name of the area he selected for his middle-of-the-night cruise. But it didn't take her long to recognize he was headed toward the seedier side of town.

Block after block of adult-entertainment joints, hole-in-the-wall newsstands, pawnshops, dive bars and the occasional sleazy-looking motel. The heavy flow of pedestrian traffic made it look like a Saturday night on Bourbon Street in New Orleans rather than a plain old weeknight in the low-rent section of Chicago.

He pulled over to the curb, and Tasha did the same. From her vantage point a block behind him and parked between two other vehicles, she watched a hooker approach the passenger side of his SUV. Since he'd passed at least a dozen in the past three blocks, she could only assume that he'd decided this one suited his taste.

Try as she might to watch the scene evolving before her with cold, clinical objectivity, a mixture of rage and something she wasn't prepared to label seethed inside her. He wanted someone he could control, someone who would play the game his way.

Seth eased away from the curb, drove to the end of the block and turned into a small parking area. Seconds later he approached the woman waiting outside an adult entertainment club. He followed her inside.

Tasha, wishing like hell she had her weapon, fished for her cell phone. She had to let Maverick know where she was. She might not be thinking as clearly as she should, but she wasn't completely stupid. According to the display, she'd missed three calls. Oh, yeah, Maverick would be pissed. With the phone set on vibrate there had been no ring. "Dammit." Even worse, she had no signal now. *No signal.* How could she be in a city this large and not get a signal?

"Hell with it." She tossed the phone to the passenger seat and emerged from her car. Her senses on full alert she started in the direction of the club. She ignored the comments tossed her way by the men, as well as the women, she passed along the way. At least she was dressed to fit in.

The club Seth had entered was a narrow two-story building sandwiched between a pawnshop and a sleazy restaurant that was closed for the night. No bouncers waited at the entrance to check for weapons or to stamp her hand.

Management apparently had a lax door policy. No surprise there.

Inside, music blared and multicolored lights flashed and throbbed in sync with the rhythm. Tasha surveyed the crowded room, careful to stay in the shadow of the tight clutch of weirdos hanging near the entrance. Seth and his hooker were nowhere in the throng. Tasha peered beyond the masses enjoying lap dances and watching porn videos on the array of wall-mounted screens, her gaze locked onto a dimly lit corridor and set of stairs on the opposite side of the club. She moved in that direction.

"You got an appointment?"

The male voice halted her in her tracks, and she glanced over to the man standing at the end of the battle-scarred bar. The numerous body piercings and tattoos did little to enhance his thin, haggard frame.

She smiled flirtatiously and leaned on the counter to look up at him. "Do I need one?"

He jerked his head in the direction of the corridor marked Employees Only. "You do if you're going in there." He looked her up and down when she stood back and adopted a put-upon expression.

She reached into her purse and withdrew the wad of cash Seth had dropped in there earlier. "I only want to watch."

The bottom feeder behind the counter grinned grotesquely. "Baby, this'll buy you just about anything we have to offer." He flexed his bare, tattooed arms as he braced against the counter and leaned forward. "Including me."

How could she resist? she thought loathingly. "As tempting as that sounds," she lied, "there's something else I need to do first. A big guy, blond hair, dark glasses came in here a couple minutes ago with a redhead."

He nodded to the corridor again. "Last door on the left upstairs."

She gave him a million-dollar smile that suggested a promise she definitely didn't intend to keep. "Thanks."

Tasha pushed through the crowd and made her way up to the second floor. Nine doors lined the dark corridor, most were partially open, offering glimpses of sexual depravity involving whips and chains and parties of three. The music still thumped loudly, adding a sick score to the nefarious acts taking place.

She slowed as she came nearer to the final door. Like the others it stood slightly ajar. A warning blaring in her skull, she eased into the entryway, allowing the door to shield her to an extent. She peeked into the room, telling herself that she just needed to know what he was up to. But that was a lie. This had nothing to do with her mission…this was personal. She knew it, but the realization didn't stop her. She had to know. Had to see.

Swaying provocatively the woman undressed in front of him. Tasha watched his unchanging profile as the hooker gave it all she had without eliciting the first visible reaction from the man. Completely naked, her body pressing close to his, she reached for him, but he pushed her hands away. Yet something passed between them. He hadn't spoken, Tasha was sure of that. The hooker must have seen some indication in his eyes of what he wanted.

She knelt in front of him, her red hair swishing around her shoulders as she moved her upper body brazenly, showing off her large breasts. Taking her time, to draw out the tension, she unfastened his jeans. First the single button at his waist, then slowly, ever so slowly, she lowered the zipper of his fly.

Tasha watched in morbid fascination, unable to move or think…she could only watch as some heretofore unknown genetic defect allowed her body to respond as if it were her touching him. Her breath stalled in her lungs. Heat slid through her, and she was helpless to stop it.

With his fly gaping wide, even from across the room,
Tasha could see that he was naked beneath the worn-soft
denim. Her mouth parched unbearably as the hooker took
him. The breath hissed out through Tasha's parted lips as
his fingers plunged into the woman's hair. His reaction startled Tasha...damaged her somehow. He hadn't reacted to
her touch...hadn't allowed her to reach him.

Stunned by her own fierce reaction, she forced her gaze
upward to look at his face...to measure his response...

But he was looking at her.

She jerked with the impact.

He held her in a firm grasp with nothing but an Arctic
glare. The sheer force of it cut all the way across the room.
She stumbled back a step.

"See something you like?" another male voice uttered
harshly in her ear.

She froze. The fine hairs on the back of her neck stood
on end.

"He's beautiful, isn't he?"

Behind her, to the left. Hidden from Seth's view as well
as hers.

She cautiously reached for the mace in her purse.

"Don't move," he threatened as he pressed a cold, steel
muzzle to the back of her head. "Keep your hands where
I can see them, and I'll let you watch. Make the slightest
move and you'll die on the floor of this den of iniquity."

Tasha tried frantically to place the voice. Refined, no
accent whatsoever...evil.

The music rose and fell, punctuating the wanton cries
and demands echoing from the other rooms.

Seth never took his eyes off her. He still couldn't see the
other man, the one with the gun to her head. Tasha wanted
to tell him somehow but between the cold barrel poking
into her flesh and the woman drawing her mouth back and
forth along his hardened length, she could only stare help-

lessly, wishing that she could taste him, that it was her hair that his fingers were plunged into. She licked her lips...need sharp and demanding unexpectedly paramount to all else. It was crazy...but she couldn't stop it.

Seth abruptly shoved the hooker away.

Tasha blinked. The strange spell suddenly broken.

He fastened his jeans and was across the room before his intent fully assimilated in her brain. He drew his weapon and plowed through the doorway, knocking her out of the way in the process.

By the time she regained her balance he and the man who'd jabbed her with his weapon were facing off in the corridor. The hooker cowered in the room, belatedly holding her blouse to her chest.

"I warned you not to let anyone too close," the other man said.

Tasha scanned the details of his face, recognition slammed into her instantly.

Leberman.

"I told you," Seth growled, his tone chilling, deadly, "to stay away from me."

"She followed you here. *This* is a mistake."

Tasha's fingers itched to grab the mace and do what she could to take control of the situation but that would only get her killed. If Leberman didn't get a round off, Seth would. He wouldn't hesitate to kill her. She knew it. It made her obsession with him all the more insane.

"I'm out of here," she announced, determined to take some sort of action. If she could only get to a phone while they continued their standoff...if she'd only worn that damned tracking monitor.

Seth manacled her arm and jerked her back when she would have walked away.

"Don't move."

Tasha held perfectly still and used the time to study Leberman. He wasn't very tall, five-ten or -eleven maybe. Hundred fifty pounds, she guessed. Gray hair...but those eyes were dark and menacing. He glowered at Seth with a mixture of awe and irritation. The situation was too weird to explain, but one thing was crystal clear. Seth hated Leberman. He might be working for him but he damned sure didn't like him.

"Come near me again and I will kill you," Seth warned him. There was more than anger in his voice this time...fear or desperation maybe.

Leberman stiffened ever so slightly, but Tasha picked up on it. He didn't like being ordered around by his hired help. Seth's reaction was a little harder to assess. What power did this man hold over him? How could this weasel instill any sort of fear in a man like Seth?

"Your mission is too important to let anything—" he glanced at Tasha "—get in your way."

Seth tightened his grip on his weapon. Leberman flinched. "Nothing—" every muscle in Seth's body looked taut, ready to snap "—will get in my way, including you."

Leberman lowered his weapon. "This is not the time to allow mistakes."

Seth kept his weapon aimed directly at the other man's frontal lobe. "I never make mistakes."

"See that you don't." Leberman turned his back on them both and walked way.

Startled, Tasha looked from one man to the other. Not until Leberman had descended the stairs did Seth lower his weapon. He turned on Tasha then.

When that icy gaze collided with hers there was something new there...something she couldn't quite define. Whatever it was, she shivered at the intensity of it.

"If I see you again, you're dead."

He walked back into the room where the hooker still

cowered like a frightened animal and slammed the door behind him.

For five trauma-filled seconds Tasha didn't move, just stared at the closed door. Then she blasted into action, running for the stairs.

Leberman couldn't have gotten far. Weapon or no weapon she had to do something. She had to find him. Had to get word to Lucas.

Leberman was here...in Chicago.

CHAPTER TWENTY-ONE

THE MINUTES TICKED PAST like hours.

Victoria roamed her den like a prisoner anticipating his final walk down death row. She'd slept less than an hour...hadn't been able to turn off the images inside her head long enough for more than that.

She remembered so well dressing him for school that morning. The jeans...Cubs T-shirt...and those blue sneakers. His favorite pair.

After school she'd picked him up and they'd gone home, just as always. She never stayed at the office when she could be with Jimmy. The sun had been shining...spring had arrived after a long, arduous winter. She'd loved the spring.

He'd gone out into the yard to play.

She'd been distracted for only one moment.

And then he was gone.

Her life had plunged into an abyss of pure hell. James had done everything he could to find their son. Lucas had helped, as well. But none of it had mattered...he was gone.

She stopped in the middle of the room and closed her eyes in an attempt to regain her equilibrium.

Why had he waited all this time?

She had assumed that since he hadn't tortured them with the idea that he had possession of their son, that he wasn't the one. Leberman wanted to hurt them...used every means at his disposal. But this—this just didn't make sense.

It had been eighteen years.

Did this particular time of year hold some significance for him? It had been October when James had interviewed Leberman's wife, nearly twenty years ago. Nineteen to be exact. James had long since left his work with military intelligence, choosing instead to start the Colby Agency where he would never have to worry about being separated from his family. But an old friend had needed him to help with an investigation involving one of James's former men, Leberman. Errol Leberman had served under James's command. Had been an excellent intelligence officer.

But Leberman had committed treason, had sold military secrets to the enemy, and James had uncovered the evidence, had driven the final nail in Leberman's coffin.

When Leberman went into hiding to escape prosecution, James questioned his family as to his whereabouts. But his wife had claimed no knowledge of her husband's whereabouts or his troubles. She had feigned shock at the news that he was wanted for treason. James had pushed...that much was true. If only he had known how unstable the woman was...maybe he could have prevented what happened next.

Mrs. Leberman had taken her life that same night, but only after taking the lives of her two children first. She'd left a note stating that they simply could not live with the weight of her husband's shame.

That had been the beginning of the end.

Leberman had successfully evaded capture and made it his life's work to get even with James Colby for, in his twisted way of thinking, killing his wife and children.

Victoria exhaled a heavy breath. Dear God how he had gotten even.

He'd killed their son. She closed her eyes and fought the tears that welled. All this time she had hoped...for a miracle. Had hoped that her son was alive and well somewhere with people who loved him. But he wasn't. He was dead.

Leberman wouldn't have allowed him to live. It hurt too much to even imagine what the bastard had put her child through before taking his life. Then, when she and her husband had suffered through endless nights of praying and hoping and endless days of searching—three long years' worth—Leberman had killed James. Though there was no rock-solid proof it had been his evil work, she had known.

Just as she knew he was behind this assassin…this heartless reminder of the child she had lost. Her fingers tightened into fists of rage. He'd let her hope all these years only to dash that hope. Just when she'd been ready to resume a real life. It was if he knew. As if he'd waited for this moment to start sending back the pieces. He had done the unthinkable. She knew it.

Lucas knew, as well.

Leberman wanted to destroy them both. He wouldn't stop until he did. If Victoria went into hiding as Lucas urged her to do, it would change nothing. He would just keep coming back until he destroyed everything connected to the Colby name. She felt certain he was the one responsible for various troubles the agency had run into over the years. She had to face this monster once and for all. Or she would never be free…and neither would Lucas, for he was guilty by association.

Victoria had lost enough.

This time Leberman was going to be the one to die.

Her doorbell rang, and she glanced at the mantel clock above her hearth—7:00 a.m. It would be Lucas. He'd decided not to go back to his work in Washington until the Leberman situation was resolved or until he could talk her into disappearing, whichever came first. He wasn't going to like her decision.

As much as she hated to admit the weakness, his concern warmed her. She needed him right now. But she also needed him to understand her position.

She checked the peephole in the front door for safety's sake, disarmed the security system and opened the door for him.

"Good morning," he said as he stepped inside, his gaze scrutinizing her immediately.

He would see that she'd had no sleep and would guess that she'd lacked any appetite as well. He would fuss. She sighed wistfully. And she would be thankful for him…for his constancy in her life. She inhaled deeply, enjoying the subtle, clean scent that was the same one he'd worn for as long as she'd known him. An enticing combination of sandalwood and plain clean skin. She resisted a shiver. Only Lucas could make her feel so alive under present circumstances. And she was so very tired of reliving the haunting past. She couldn't bear it any longer.

"Good morning, Lucas." She decided to do something she rarely did, go to the office late. "Would you like to have coffee with me this morning?"

That charming smile he had perfected to a science—the one that warmed her insides—spread across his handsome face. "I can always handle a second cup of coffee." He locked the door behind him and followed her to the kitchen.

It had been a long time since she'd prepared morning coffee for someone besides herself, but it felt good. Once she'd slid the carafe into place and pressed the start button, she turned to Lucas.

She might as well get this part out of the way while they were in her territory. "I've decided to stick by my schedule for the next few days. Mildred reminded me last night when I'd pulled myself together a bit that I have that Woman of the Year luncheon this evening." She held up a hand to hush his protests and continued, "You know I don't care about the honor. It isn't about that at all. It's about not allowing that bastard to put my life on hold again. He's not taking anything else from me."

"Victoria." Lucas propped his cane against the closest cabinet and took her hands in his. "You wouldn't let me comfort you last night." He searched her eyes for answers. She knew what he wanted to hear...but could she give him what he longed for after all that had happened?

It would feel too much like running.

They'd both waited so long. But she was so very tired of living with the threat of Leberman hanging over her head. He represented all of her past pain...she wanted to banish him forever. Wanted to make him pay for what he'd done to her son.

The worry in Lucas's eyes very nearly undid her. "You refuse to go away with me. You have to give me something to work with here. Please." He squeezed her hands. "Please, let me keep you safe."

She had known Lucas Camp for more than half her life, and this was the first time in all those years that she had sensed his emotions so near to the surface. Certainly it was the first time she'd heard him skate so close to outright begging.

She looked into those loving gray eyes and she tried with all her might to ensure that the depth of her feelings for him shone in her own. "Lucas, I know you want to keep me safe, but I can't run from this. If I do, it will never end. We have to stop this bastard. Face this enemy. Now."

"I have a strategy in place," he countered. "One that doesn't require you to take these kinds of risks. Whatever precautions we take at this evening's affair, there is still a strong possibility that he'll get close enough to hurt you. Let me bring him down my way. You have my word that I'm working on that as we speak. I *will* make it happen."

He wasn't making this easy. She looked away, gathered her scattering courage before allowing her eyes to meet his once more. "Lucas, I'm certain that you're doing all you can. But it might not be enough." Pain tightened her chest as she saw the new lines of worry forming on his beloved face. "Yesterday when I looked into that box and saw that shoe I almost slipped over a precipice that I'm not completely sure I could have returned from. It's been that way for a while now. It's like I'm performing a balancing act on an emotional high wire."

She shrugged, hoped her words were making sense. "I can't do this anymore. *He* won't let me put the past behind me and move on as I'd hoped to do. You and I will never be free to live our lives as long as that bastard is breathing."

Lucas nodded, his eyes suspiciously bright. "You're right. I know that, but knowing the facts won't prevent me from going crazy with worry for you."

Tears brimmed behind her lashes and she took a breath, moistened her lips and tried her damnedest to hold them back. "And that's just one of the many things I love about you."

He searched her eyes again, his own clearly startled by her admission. Though they had each recognized for some time how the other felt, they'd refrained from verbalizing that emotional commitment. Not out of fear or uncertainty, out of respect for the man they'd both loved in different ways. But James Colby wasn't coming back.

"Victoria, you must know," Lucas began, his voice filled with the same emotion she saw in his eyes, "that I am deeply, profoundly in love with you."

She smiled. God, how she did love this man. "Of course you are. I've known it all along."

For several boundless moments they simply stood there, holding hands and staring into each other's eyes while the scent of fresh-brewed coffee filled the air around them. She moved first, leaned forward just far enough to lift her mouth to meet his.

And then he kissed her.

His lips were as firm as she'd known they would be, his taste pleasant, sugared coffee flavored with just a hint of French vanilla—the kind they sold at the coffeehouse near his hotel. When he reached up to gently cup her face in those strong hands she moaned softly. How long had she waited for that simple touch? Desire sung vibrantly through her veins, sending a long-forgotten heat to the very core of her being…to the part of her that made her woman.

And then she forgot to think at all.

CHAPTER TWENTY-TWO

AT SEVEN-FIFTEEN on Tuesday morning Tasha walked into her apartment building on North Dearborn. The strappy sandals she'd donned the night before hung precariously from her right hand.

The long walk had cleared her mind of the confusing emotions she'd experienced in that club. She'd gone from outraged and obsessed to furious with herself to numb. Total exhaustion had left her defenseless and completely disillusioned about who she'd thought she was.

Some jerk had stolen her car while she acted like a jealous lover. Her useless cell phone had been in there for all the good it would have done her. And, on that sleazy side of town, there hadn't been a cab to be seen in the wee hours of the morning.

She walked. Oh, she'd turned down a couple of offers for rides, but she had known, judging by the sleazebags tossing out the invitations, that she would have ended up walking, anyway—after she'd had to beat the crap out of one of them.

But worst of all, she'd looked Leberman straight in the eyes and hadn't been able to do anything about it.

That screw-up alone was enough to get her tossed back to Langley. She jabbed the call button for the elevator, too damned tired to even consider the stairs.

Not that she could blame Lucas for sending her back. She'd failed. Gotten personally involved practically overnight. She shook her head in self-disgust. All this time she'd thought she was all set to become a hotshot under-cover operative. She could do anything. Kick ass all day long and never miss a beat. Boy, had she been wrong.

She slunk onto the elevator when the doors opened and selected floor thirteen. No doubt it would stop there, any-way. Might as well save Maverick and Ramon the trouble.

The elevator surged into motion making her stomach turn over with renewed dread. She hadn't wanted it to end like this…she hadn't meant to…

The gentle bounce that signaled she'd reached her des-tination dragged her attention from her self-pity session. This was it. The doors slid open and Ramon waited in the corridor, one elbow braced on the arm folded over his mid-dle so he could tap his chin like an impatient teacher.

He did a quick but thorough appraisal. "You look like hell, honey."

"Where's Maverick?" Why beat around the bush? She was done. *Finito.*

Ramon hitched his head in the direction of the apartment directly beneath hers. "He was too pissed off to greet you in the corridor." His expression turned sympathetic. "You might want to brace yourself."

She nodded, appreciative of his concern, but wholly un-deserving.

Ramon led the way. She followed, not bothering to brace herself. Whatever she got, she deserved. She could be ready to head back to the east coast in less than an hour. Martin might not even want her back after this fiasco. She gritted her teeth and blocked the image of Seth that tried to haunt her. If she never saw him again it would be too soon.

Yeah, right.

He was the whole reason she'd screwed up so badly… he'd messed with her head. Another image, this one in-volving him and the hooker, flashed before she could stop it. Seriously messed with her head.

"Just one thing," Ramon said, hesitating outside the door, "the car thing was his idea. Not mine."

Bewildered but too depressed to care, Tasha followed him into the apartment to face the wrath of Maverick.

He stood in the middle of the living room, his arms crossed over his wide chest. Every feature of his formidable frame vibrating with tension. "Sit," he ordered with a distinct nod toward the chair directly in front of him.

She dropped her sandals onto the floor, flinched at the loud *thwack,* and took the seat he'd indicated.

"Do you know how stupid what you did this morning was?"

She looked straight into those furious eyes. "Yes."

"Did you also know that I have never lost an operative? Never. And you're hell-bent on smudging that perfect record."

"I just—"

"Don't speak," he warned, his tone lethal. "It was a rhetorical question."

His high-handedness kind of ticked her off, but she knew he was right so she squashed the retort that had risen immediately at his scathing remark.

"You went into that club—*without backup*—after a known assassin. He could have killed you and there would have been nothing we could do about it."

"But I—" His words echoed inside her head, derailing the thought before she could voice the rest of it. Club? How the hell had he known about the club?

She looked up at him. Her confusion no doubt obvious. "How did you—" And then it hit her. These guys were specialists—the best of the best. They would have all bases covered well in advance.

"I'm an old hand at this business, North. You're nothing but a green recruit." Before she could argue the point, he went on, "Did you really think I'd give you enough rope to hang yourself?'' He shook his head. ''No way. I knew you'd screw up.''

Before the mental order to stay seated issued by the more reasonable side of her brain could synapse she was on her feet. ''Okay, you're right, but I got through it. And…and I came face-to-face with Leberman. You should—''

''We know.'' His expression went from furious to grim in less than a heartbeat.

She blinked. ''You know?''

''We had a tracking device in your car. A new one we're trying out. It's supposed to be undetectable, but we're not prepared to take unnecessary risks with it yet. Still, we figured bugging your vehicle would be safe enough since you usually rode with our target anyway.''

''Why didn't you do something?'' she demanded before she could catch herself. ''I mean,'' she said in a more controlled tone, ''what did you do?''

''When one of our men spotted Leberman he tailed him in hopes of getting a clean shot. Halloween's this weekend, some prick in the local adult entertainment industry decided that every night this week they'd party like the world was coming to an end over in that crime-ridden zone where we located you. The cops probably won't even bother trying to stop them as long as no one gets murdered. But the whole scene made for crowds, and my man lost Leberman before he could take a clean shot. But we have confirmation that he's here.''

She nodded. ''Yeah, he's definitely here.'' The standoff between Seth and Leberman tugged at her thoughts for a few seconds before Ramon's insistence that the car wasn't his idea jarred her gray matter from its distraction. ''You took my car,'' she accused as her gaze connected with Maverick's once more, then narrowed with suspicion as the concept solidified.

"Damn straight I did. Once I knew you'd live through your stupidity, I figured you needed a lesson in humility."

So Maverick was the jerk who'd stolen her car.

She shook her head in defeat. Might as well admit now that she wasn't good enough for this mission. It wasn't as if she hadn't given them a clear picture of her inadequacies. Lucas was looking for sharp people like Maverick…not impulsive hotheads like her. "So, I guess it's over then. I failed. I'm out, right?"

Maverick laughed, which really pissed her off. "Lucas said you'd feel that way."

Her humiliation was complete now. "You've talked to Lucas already?" She felt every bit as hollow as her voice sounded.

"Honey, I talked to Lucas the moment you sashayed outta here in that taxi right after midnight."

This was it. She'd get her walking orders now.

"Look, North, you screwed up," Maverick offered, his tone gentled now. "You survived it. But that doesn't mean you're not cut out for this gig."

How could he know exactly what she was feeling?

"This is the real thing, not training. You're inexperienced in the field. No way can you expect to perform in that setting the way you did in training. Not in the beginning. It's a whole different world. We understand that and so should you. Lucas picked you for this mission because he knew you were good." He gave her a knowing look. "He also knew that you possessed a key element that would get you closer to our assassin than anyone else on our team. You're a virgin."

"Like hell," she blurted, then cringed. There were some things she was experienced in, but she hadn't meant to say it out loud.

Maverick chuckled. "Not that kind of virgin."

Tasha just wanted the floor to crack open and swallow

her up. Could this get any worse? Her face flamed so hot, she cringed.

"Our guy obviously picked up on your innocence in a professional sense or you'd be dead now."

Admittedly, a part of her had known that. He hadn't been threatened by her. Annoyed maybe, but definitely not threatened or intimidated in any way. She'd almost convinced herself that he trusted her just a little. But that wasn't the case. He just didn't see her as a threat.

"You not only got close to him," Maverick continued, his tone openly approving now, "you got to him on some level or he would have killed you last night."

Damn, the man was a mind reader. "Leberman told him not to let me too close...said I'd get in his way. But he let me walk despite that warning."

"You got to him," Maverick reiterated. "He doesn't want to hurt you."

Her brow furrowed into a frown as she recalled Seth's final words to her. "Well, he did say that if he saw me again he'd kill me."

"That's bullshit, baby," Ramon piped up.

Tasha turned toward him.

Ramon smiled at her, his apparent approval shoring up her resolve. "You did good, girl. If our boy had wanted you dead, he wouldn't have wasted time talking, and you wouldn't have been walking."

The guy missed his calling, she mused. He should have been a poet. "I guess that's true." A big part of her sure hoped like hell it was.

"We know Leberman is close," Maverick said, drawing her attention back to him. "That means whatever is going down will be happening soon. We have to be ready. We could still use an ID on that assassin. Anything we can learn would be helpful."

Tasha shrugged and dropped back into the chair. Damn

she was tired. "I can try going to his place. Making contact again."

Maverick shook his head. "You have to play by his rules. He has to make the next move. You don't want to push his generosity. He doesn't want to see you again, but if you got to him the way we think you did, he'll be back."

If only she could be that lucky. "So we wait." She looked from Maverick to Ramon and back. "Again."

"We wait," Maverick confirmed, then gave her a quick once-over. "You look like you could use some rest, anyway."

She nodded and pushed to her feet. The memory of that house by the lake zoomed to the forefront of her thoughts. "He took me to a house by the lake. Could it belong to Leberman?" That seemed the most likely scenario. If they'd been tracking her movements, they would know which house she meant.

Maverick and Ramon exchanged a look. "No," Maverick told her. "That house belongs to Victoria Colby."

CHAPTER TWENTY-THREE

LUCAS SURVEYED the palatial lobby of Chicago's Cultural Center as Victoria chatted with well-wishers. Soaring arches created a kind of echo chamber and allowed the classical music to gently resonate throughout and then upward. It was 6:45 and they had just started to move toward the grand staircase. He didn't like the crowd pressing in around them. Liked even less the endless possibilities the Greek and Romanesque architecture offered in the way of hiding places.

His men had scoured the five-story building and had set up the tightest security net possible, considering that hundreds of guests were expected for tonight's gala. Every single person who entered the lobby had been screened, as was the current protocol for all major public events. Not one of the tuxedoed or sequined attendees looked villainous. Every security guard and police officer on site had been briefed as to the descriptions of Leberman and the assassin. All imaginable precautions had been taken. And yet, he somehow knew that it would never be enough.

His team had not been able to pick up either Leberman's or the assassin's trail since four o'clock this morning when things went to hell in that sex club.

But there was nothing else Lucas could do. Victoria insisted on going through with this. His gaze moved to her and his heart surged into his throat. She looked incredible. More beautiful than he had ever seen her. The exquisitely simple white gown didn't need any glittering embellishments. The woman wearing it was jewel enough. His mouth parched as he remembered the kiss they had shared. He'd waited so long for that moment. The kiss had held many promises, and even now made his body harden with desire.

He couldn't help wondering if tonight would be the night. That, too, would be Victoria's decision. He would not rush the issue. As much as he wanted to make love to her, he would wait until she made the first move. Just as he had with the kiss. He took a deep breath, every fiber of his being anticipating more of those wonderful kisses.

Moving farther up the staircase, he studied the walls of white marble. Shimmering mosaics winked in the light of the bronze sconces and the chandeliers draped from the three-story, vaulted ceiling. This was the kind of place where Victoria belonged, amid luxury and beauty, the grandest of which could not rival her own. She deserved all that life had to offer, and he would go to his death trying to give her whatever her heart desired, including this moment.

Every instinct warned him that this was a dangerous risk, but his heart would not allow him to deny her.

When they reached the landing, the staircase spilled into Preston Bradley Hall and more of the palatial savoir faire. Spectacular stained-glass domes, lush ornamentation and intricate coffered ceilings. Lavishly decorated tables filled the enormous hall. A stage and podium had been erected beyond a towering archway adorned with mosaic scrolls and rosettes. Opulence abounded. The perfect setting for this prestigious honor. His gaze settled on Victoria once more. And it was all for her.

Lucas smiled in spite of the tension vibrating inside him. No one knew better than he what an amazing woman Victoria Colby really was.

STANDING BEFORE the full-length mirror, Seth adjusted the lapels of the tuxedo, then checked the bow tie. Perfect.

He picked up the elegantly embossed invitation from the dresser and walked out of the master suite belonging to the man whose name was inscribed beneath the words *requests the presence of...* He would be among the last to arrive at the gala event, but no one would notice since he had taken meticulous steps to alter his appearance.

The eyeglasses, brown-tinted contacts and the temporary rinse he'd used to darken his hair provided a slight resemblance to the man who had been conveniently called away on business. Leberman had seen to every necessary detail. But the most important aspect of Seth's camouflage tonight was the layers of skin-colored latex that added fullness to his face and neck and simultaneously covered his one readily visible distinguishing mark, the scar on his jaw. The carefully applied makeup that allowed for the other man's lighter coloring, face, throat and hands, and finally, the padding that piled on the extra forty pounds that completed the image.

All in all he felt confident that no one, not even Lucas himself, would recognize him.

Twenty minutes later, after allowing the valet to take his borrowed Mercedes, Seth put his skills at disguise to the test. As he expected, he was waved through by local security without a second glance.

Now all he had to do was move into position.

Five days ago he had come to the Cultural Center in response to their frantic call for maintenance on the heating and cooling system. With an electronic monitor on the land line he had easily intercepted the telephone call. The problem was simple, especially since he was the one who'd rigged the fault. He'd taken his time, explored the ventilation and return ductwork until he found what he wanted. Access to Preston Bradley Hall. The necessary returns placed about the enormous room provided several different angles in the event the stage was not positioned as he expected.

Escaping once he'd accomplished his goal would not be such an easy task, since he would still need to get out of the building and would have already shed his disguise. So he had arranged a couple of diversions. With a crowd this size it wasn't a difficult task. A fire alarm and then, ten seconds later, a small explosion near the first-level rear entrance. The hysteria that followed would provide all the distraction he needed.

Once he'd reached the access area, he shucked the tux and peeled off the disguise, contacts included, and shoved them out of sight. He donned the coveralls and assembled the weapon he would use for the job, all of which he'd stashed five days ago.

After attaching the silencer, he eased into the long galvanized-steel tunnel that wound around and eventually took him to Preston Bradley Hall.

He slipped into position and peered through the louvers he'd pried apart just enough to facilitate the tip of his weapon. He'd disposed of the filter, which left nothing but the thin louvered metal door between him and the crowd settling at their respective tables.

Now he would wait.

Because of the large crowd anticipated, the thermostat had been set to a lower temperature to ensure comfort during the exclusive event. Despite that step, sweat had already beaded on his forehead.

Leberman was here already. It wasn't necessary to spot him in the crowd or to recognize the disguise he used. Seth sensed his presence just as one sensed a coming storm in the air. The very atmosphere changed. Every nerve ending cracked as an anxiety he'd thought behind him inched up his spine. He gritted his teeth and forced away the memories that threatened. He would not be distracted.

Forty-one long minutes passed with one politician after the other raving about their beloved city of Chicago and the glorious Victoria Colby and all her worthwhile accomplishments as an entrepreneur and businesswoman.

His gut clenching with anger as every accolade echoed in the enormous hall, he tuned out the meaningless words. Politicians were fools, anyway. He wondered how lofty Victoria Colby would feel a few moments from now. A smile stretched across his face. Now, there was something to look forward to.

Finally the mayor stepped up to the podium to make the presentation they had all waited for.

A standing ovation accompanied her as Victoria Colby rose like a regal queen and advanced to the podium. When she began to speak, the crowd stopped clapping and resumed their seats. She made what she must have considered a moving speech that garnered her yet another round of enthusiastic applause.

As she concluded, Lucas Camp made his way to the stage, dressed in his black tux, his silver-handled black cane making him look all the more distinguished. He extended his hand to Victoria as she descended the first of three steps leading down from the stage. The delicate crystal Woman of the Year award clutched against her chest with one hand, she reached out to her beloved protector with the other.

Seth squinted into the scope, snugged his finger around the trigger as he steadied his aim, then took the shot.

Lucas Camp fell forward.

The Woman of the Year award shattered on the marble floor.

Victoria caught Lucas in her arms, his weight pulling her downward, the blood from his head wound turning her lovely white gown a sinister crimson.

CHAPTER TWENTY-FOUR

HE STOOD IN THE DARKNESS, his eyes closed as he absorbed the sounds. Allowed the tension to drain from him. His respiration slowed as he gradually became one with the night. Years of surviving in the darkness had given him power over the night.

He was not afraid...not afraid of anything or anyone.

Not anymore.

The stillness crept closer...the night sounds like a familiar lullaby. He'd learned to embrace the darkness and to let go of all else. That had been his only means of existence.

It was true that he was alone, but that had never mattered. He needed no one...nothing.

Her image slipped into his meditation, etching a frown across his brow. She'd followed him last night, not that he was really surprised. He had wondered at her seeming innocence. She was not like any of the other women he had known. Certainly not what he had expected considering her chosen occupation. He almost laughed at that. There had never been a time when he'd bothered to know anyone. He wouldn't miss or need what he didn't know.

He didn't need her.

Perhaps it wasn't about need.

He simply wanted her.

His eyes opened and he stared beyond the dark, beyond the cloak of trees that sheltered his position, to the lake that glistened like glass beneath the moon's pale glow. She was out there. Not so far away. He could have her. He was certain of it. Her eyes had given her away…the way she'd licked her lips as she'd watched another woman take him. Even now his body reacted to the yearning that had clearly surprised her. Though, like him, she'd sensed the connection from the beginning.

She'd wanted to touch him that way. To feel the weight of him in her hands, the thrust of him inside her hot, lush mouth. He'd wanted the same thing. It was the thought of her that had sent his fingers plunging into the other woman's hair. Not once had he touched a woman that way—with tenderness or intimacy on any level other than the requisite physical contact necessary for release.

But he longed to touch Tasha that way. He couldn't shake the fiercely primal craving. Couldn't completely block thoughts of her.

His frown deepened. Mere curiosity kept his thoughts going back to her. It couldn't be anything else. Desire alone would not be enough. He'd conquered that emotion long ago.

The intensity of her own desire had shaken her, and still she hadn't been able to look away from the carnal act taking place before her.

But *he* had interfered.

Seth clenched his teeth at the thought of Leberman. He should have killed the son of a bitch then and there. But he'd sworn to repay this one final debt. He might let the bastard live to see that debt fulfilled and then he would finish him if their paths crossed again. Never again would the bastard control him…punish him. *Never.*

His lips tipped into a smile when he thought of how outraged Leberman would be that the day had not ended as he had decreed. He'd laid out the plan he wanted carried out step by step. Every move calculated so carefully.

Too bad. Seth had developed his own plan. The end result would be much the same, but it would be carried out his way whether *he* liked it or not.

He cut his eyes to the right, his senses moving instantly to an elevated status of alert. He inclined his head, listening for any sound that would confirm his instinct. A leaf crunched under the weight of a silent footstep. Ten meters away.

He was certain no one had followed him here tonight or any other night. No one had any idea he came to this place. Tasha had been to the house once…but he'd warned her to stay away. There was only one who knew of his draw to this particular spot. That singular, deep-rooted urgency to occupy this place and know control over his own destiny.

The brush of foliage against fabric…closer.

Seth stepped back, shielding himself behind a towering oak tree. His skin prickled with a familiar warning.

"I knew you'd be here."

Seth moved toward him with the stealth he'd learned long ago to avoid punishment.

The tip of his 9mm pressed against the man's skull before he suspected Seth had approached him. "Are you ready to die?" he asked from between clenched teeth. He'd warned him twice already.

Leberman turned, faced him and the weapon with its chambered round as if the risk of death were of no consequence to him.

"You disobeyed my orders."

The statement was spoken far too casually. Seth tensed. Tightened his grip on his weapon. This was not like his hated mentor. He resisted the apprehension nagging at his gut.

"This day was very important," Leberman rambled on, as if discussing the latest political uprising in some third-world country. "It was the perfect occasion. I had waited for this moment so very, very long. Yet you blatantly disregarded my wishes.''

"The result was the same," Seth ground out, quickly growing sick of the bastard's presence despite his uneasiness. "You saw the look on her face the same as I did. The horror...the surrender. She would gladly have traded her life for his in that split second.''

"That's all quite true but not the issue at hand." He eased closer, allowing the business end of the weapon to bore into his chest, then slapped Seth hard. Seth refused to flinch...clenched his jaw. His grip on his weapon tightened so that his arm trembled, but he would not back off. Wouldn't give the bastard the satisfaction.

When Leberman spoke again, his tone was accusing...threatening. "You expressly disobeyed my order. I will know the reason for such insubordination.''

For one instant panic trickled through Seth, but he brutally squashed it. He would not feel that fear again. "The job will be finished on schedule," he said between gritted teeth. "But I have decided that the manner and timing of events will be at my discretion." He lowered his weapon. "End of subject.''

"Your discretion?" Leberman echoed haughtily.

Seth turned his back on the man he despised almost as much as he did the final target of this mission and walked away. The past was over. Only the future could bring him the peace he sought.

"This is how you thank me for saving your life.''

Seth stilled. The words rang out like a death knell from the church tower in a medieval village, dragging him back in time regardless of his determination not to go, twisting his gut with remembered agony. The pain...the confusion and endless punishments. He didn't want to go back there. Wouldn't go back there.

Taking his time, he faced his ruthless, self-proclaimed

savior. "Yes," he said harshly, his breath growing more shallow and rapid with each passing second. "You saved me from certain death, and I will repay that debt."

Leberman released a melodramatic sigh and waved his arms in orchestration as if the words he intended to utter were a garish symphony regaling his selflessness. "I taught you everything you know...made you all that you are. Without me you wouldn't have survived. I am your maker...the man who created you. You owe me *everything.*"

Claimed by renewed fury and hatred, Seth took two long strides toward Leberman before realizing he'd moved. He beat back the emotions that would undermine his control, but it proved more difficult than usual. "You made me all that I am, rightly enough. I have the scars to prove it." Before he could stop himself he was toe-to-toe with Leberman once more. "I suffered your endless beatings... days on end without food...and the training." He laughed, the sound as evil as that of the very savior who had schooled him so well. "Do you have any idea what they did to me?"

Long-exiled memories came flooding back...threatened his already strained hold on control.

"They did only what I instructed," Leberman said bluntly. "Everything happens for a reason. The torture made you untouchable...made you stronger."

"Go to hell, you bastard," Seth snarled. "I'll do what I came here to do because I want it." He pounded on his disfigured chest. "I want to watch Victoria Colby die just as much as you do, maybe more." He took a moment to slow his ragged breathing, to steady his shaking hands. "Final warning. Don't come near me again. Or the teacher will become the student, and I don't think you'll like your first lesson."

He walked away without looking back.

For the last time.

CHAPTER TWENTY-FIVE

AT 4:00 A.M. Victoria took a deep breath and made the journey to the private waiting room where Ian and Simon, as well as two of Lucas's men, waited. She produced a faint smile for the police officers, Chicago's finest dressed in their stiffly starched dark blues, gathered in the corridor outside the doors marked "No Visitors Beyond This Point" that she had just exited.

Chicago PD had gone above and beyond the call of duty. The shooting as well as the fire alarm and minor explosion had sent the crowd into a panic-stricken mass exodus. Only with the quick and levelheaded thinking of the boys in blue had the evacuation occurred without additional injuries or worse. That was the only level of involvement by the local authorities that Lucas had allowed thus far.

At the waiting-room door she drew together the lapels of Ian's jacket. He'd cloaked her shoulders with it hours ago, more to cover the gruesome bloodstains on her dress, she imagined, than to shield her from the brisk October night. One last deep breath and she prepared to deliver the news.

She entered the room and all talk ceased.

Vincent Ferrelli and Ramon Vega, two of Lucas's Specialists, Ian and Simon all turned their attention to her and waited expectantly. Each still wore his tailored tux—except Ian's jacket was missing—and all looked very much like the remainder of the old regime still standing after a conquering military invasion.

"You'll all be able to see him soon," she announced, knowing the words would banish a good deal of the tension thickening the air in the room.

A collective sigh of relief sounded.

"But first," Victoria said, pushing all emotion away, "I'd like to clarify my position on this latest turn of events."

Dead silence settled over the room once more.

Victoria looked from Ian to Simon, her most trusted men, and then to those Lucas trusted just as much. "Leberman was there last night, just as the assassin was. You can be assured that he's close now, waiting to hear if the assassination attempt was successful. Lucas wants him to believe that it was." She allowed the one emotion that would get her through this. Absolute fury flamed as hot as Hades inside her. "I don't give a damn what he believes. I want him dead. Do you understand what I'm saying?" She surveyed the grim faces. "I want him dead...*today*."

Ian moved toward her. "Victoria—"

She stopped him with one upraised hand. "No one is going to change my mind. I want both of those bastards dead. I don't care what it takes."

Ferrelli shrugged nonchalantly, like any good Italian who had a score to settle. "Sounds like a plan to me."

Ramon shot him a quelling look. "Mrs. Colby," he offered, "we should wait to see what Lucas has to say about this."

"Listen to him," Simon put in, "he's right. Besides, Leberman isn't coming out anytime soon. You know that. He'll stay in hiding, savoring his coup for at least a couple of days or until he finds out the attempt failed."

Victoria shot Simon a scathing look. "I think I know Errol Leberman better than anyone in this room and I know what he wants." She turned to Ian then. "You put the word out on the street that I want a face-to-face meeting with him. Anyplace, anytime as long as it's soon.''

Ian gave his head a slow, deliberate shake. "I won't let you do that. That's what he wants.''

Victoria lifted her chin in challenge. "That's what I want as well. I don't care if I have to put out a personal plea on the local radio stations. Whatever it takes. I want a face-to-face with Leberman *today*.''

"Over my dead body.''

The sound of Lucas's voice propelled her into an about-face. "What're you doing up?'' she demanded.

John Logan and a tall young man in a surgical scrub suit trailed behind him. Victoria recognized the young man as the surgeon who'd taken care of Lucas. "He won't listen to a word I say,'' the doctor lamented.

Victoria doubted anyone in the room was surprised.

A bandage covered Lucas's forehead. He looked pale, weary, and her heart lurched as the whole scene played out in her mind's eye once more. He'd fallen into her arms, blood pouring from his head wound. For three endless beats she'd been certain he was dead. And then he'd taken her down to the floor with him, telling her to stay down as blood covered his face completely.

"He wouldn't even let me put him under to do the repairs,'' the doctor who'd patched him up told her. "Had to do it with local anesthetic.''

Lucas flitted a glance at him. "I didn't live this long without enduring a little pain. I'll be fine.''

The doctor's eyebrows shot up. "I removed a sizable section of skin from your back to repair the damage on your forehead. You might be tough, Mr. Camp, but don't be foolish. Infection is still a serious risk.''

Victoria felt the bottom drop from her stomach and she had to work to keep her legs from wobbling. The bullet had more or less grazed his forehead, tearing away a portion of tissue. Though the wound wasn't deep, like all head wounds, it had bled profusely. All the blood. She shuddered. That had been the most frightening part. Not knowing exactly how badly he was hurt had almost sent her over the edge.

"Thanks, Doc. I'll be in good hands." Lucas looked from the doctor to the men in the room. "We have work to do."

With a defeated sigh the doctor added, "I'll write up your release order." He turned to go without further argument. He, apparently, knew a brick wall when he hit one.

Victoria also knew, without doubt, that it wouldn't have mattered what the doctor said, as long as Lucas was breathing and able to stand, he would go on with his work. He was that much like her. Or maybe she was like him. She couldn't help smiling at the thought.

"We're going to go with the assumption that Leberman thinks I'm dead," Lucas said when the door had closed behind the doctor. He rubbed his jaw a moment then. "I do find it difficult to believe that our assassin missed. I had him pegged as a lot more worthy than that." He snorted a laugh. "God knows I'm glad his game was a little off. Still, it doesn't feel right. For now we'll—"

"Excuse me." A nurse eased into the room, her hesitation evident in her expression and in the way she loitered in the doorway. She held a large floral arrangement in her hands. "Mr. Camp?" She looked to Lucas since he was the one wearing the bandage.

"Yes?" He looked annoyed but tempered it with a stab at a smile.

"These were delivered down at the E.R. a little while ago." She blinked a couple of times as if befuddled. "We usually don't get deliveries at this hour. But, anyway, they're for you."

Lucas's less-than-stellar smile drooped. "Thank you."

When he would have reached for the flowers, Logan stepped in. "I'll take those."

The nurse nodded jerkily and rushed away.

Victoria couldn't help wondering if they looked that intimidating. She surveyed the classically dressed, well-trained agents in the room, and then hers as well as Lucas's bloodied attire and shivered. Oh yes. They definitely looked lethal.

Logan settled the vase onto a nearby table and fished out the accompanying card.

The smell of freshly cut white carnations drifted across the room and only then did Victoria really look at the arrangement. A frown furrowed her brow. Something about the flowers disturbed her somehow.

Logan passed the card to Lucas. "It's him."

Those two simple words tightened like a steel band around Victoria's chest, drawing her attention away from the flowers.

"Next time," Lucas read aloud, "will be for real." He looked up, his gaze settling on hers. "He signed it 'Fate.'"

"You were right," Simon commented dryly, "he wasn't off his game. The miss was intentional."

Lucas nodded. "It would seem so."

Victoria started to shake. Couldn't control it. She hugged her arms around her middle. "We have to do something. We can't let him get away again." The scent of the flowers drew her gaze back there once more. Carnations made her think of death...funerals...graves.

Lucas came to her, pulled her close. "I won't let him get away this time," he murmured for her ears only. Then he turned to the men awaiting instructions. "Ferrelli, you and Simon go to the house in Oak Park our assassin calls home. Tear it apart." His jaw clenched, he added, "If there's anything there I want it found."

"Won't we need a warrant for that?" Simon suggested, ever the rule player.

Lucas smiled, but the grim expression held no humor. "Not for this." He leveled his most intimidating stare on Simon. "You only need paper if you fear repercussions, which I don't, or when you plan to prosecute. This man isn't going to live to go to trial."

Just then a memory struck Victoria. Carnations. She'd ordered carnations for James...for the funeral. She'd placed a single carnation in his hand...before they closed the lid. That one had been for the son they'd lost.

The little boy they hadn't even been able to bury.

The lights dimmed.

She could hear Lucas calling her name.

Arms grabbing for her.

Then the darkness took her.

CHAPTER TWENTY-SIX

LUCAS SAT on Victoria's bedside and held her hand. His head throbbed viciously, and the spot on his back they'd robbed of skin burned like hell, but he couldn't worry about that right now and any sort of pain reliever that might actually help was out of the question.

He had to stay sharp. Couldn't let down his guard.

"I should be at the office," Victoria said, her voice thin with exhaustion and the devastation of the night's events.

"You won't be going to the office today," he insisted as gently as he could while remaining firm. "Ian has everything under control. He said he'd call you this afternoon for a general briefing."

She nodded resignedly and lapsed into silence.

There was so much Lucas wanted to say. He wanted to reaffirm his love for her with more than just words. But now wasn't the time. She was far too fragile. He could practically see her breaking apart right before his eyes.

And he was helpless to stop the momentum.

"I want you to rest now. I'll be right here."

She nodded again, not bothering to look him in the eye.

But she didn't have to say anything for him to know what she was thinking. She wanted this over...she wanted Leberman dead. She was more than ready to face death herself to end this nightmare. Lucas would not allow that to happen.

He left her resting and moved quietly to her den. He scrounged up the remote for the television set and the VCR

and·switched them on. After locating the surveillance videotape in his briefcase he slid it into the machine and fast-
forwarded to the part that kept nagging at him.

On the videotape, Tasha North opened the door and allowed *him* inside her apartment. Lucas studied the way he
moved, the sound of his voice. There was something
vaguely familiar about the bastard who had taken a chunk
out of his profile, but he couldn't place it.

He was smart. Damned smart and well versed in all the
right tactical maneuvers. As soon as the Cultural Center
had been cleared, Logan and Ferrelli had determined exactly how the shooter had pulled off his hit. He'd posed as
a repairman the week prior, plotted his access to the hall
where the Woman of the Year banquet would be held, then
stored his necessary equipment. Since the equipment was
stored within the cooling system's metal frame, their scans
for weapons hadn't picked it up. He'd used C-4 for his
explosive, not enough to do any real damage, just a little
fear factor tossed into the mix to create mayhem. The
smoke bomb had been a stroke of genius, as well. It had
set off the fire alarms and assured mass hysteria.

He'd thought through the whole scenario very thoroughly. Hadn't missed a trick. He'd known that escaping
would be impossible without a diversion, so he'd planned
ahead.

Lucas would bet his life that Leberman had been there,
too. Ramon was reviewing the Cultural Center's surveillance tapes right now, but Lucas doubted he would be able
to ID the scumbag. His disguise would, like the assassin's,
be elaborate. The man the assassin had impersonated had
called the police this morning to report that his home had
been burglarized while he was away. It was yet to be determined how Leberman had managed an invitation and
under what name. But Lucas would find all the answers
in time.

He rewound the tape a third time and watched it once more, concentrating hard in an attempt to capture that fleeting sense of recognition. What was it about this guy?

"What's that?"

Lucas looked up to find Victoria standing behind him. He switched off the tape. She didn't need any more stress today. When Simon and Ferrelli reported in with their finds from the Oak Park house, he would have to see that Victoria was distracted. He intended to suggest that the timing of Ian's briefing would coincide.

"Just another surveillance tape I wanted to take a second look at," he said, as he pushed to his feet. "Join me and I'll call out for some lunch." Neither of them had eaten today. Nourishment of some sort would be good right now.

Victoria didn't bother to sit down. "I've been thinking for the past few minutes."

Lucas tensed. He didn't want her coming up with any plans that included her personal involvement in baiting Leberman.

She moved toward him, her eyes glittering with unshed tears. He blinked, kicked himself for not noticing her emotional state sooner. "Don't let him get to you any more than he already has," he urged. "He wants to hurt you. Don't give him the pleasure."

He reached for her and she came to him without hesitation. She walked into his arms, pressed against his body and it felt right. So right. Lucas closed his eyes and reveled in the feel of her...the warmth...the softness.

"It's not me I'm worried about," she murmured, then drew back to look at him. "I can't bear to lose anyone else. Especially not you." She shook her head as one tear, then another slipped past her lashes. "I've been selfish. Only thinking of my own need for revenge." She peered deeply into Lucas's eyes. "He almost killed you last night. Every time I play it over in my mind I lose my breath. I can't allow that to happen again."

"Victoria, I swear to you that I will stop him."

She moved her head side to side. "No more. I want us to leave. To go far away. Someplace where he'll never find us. I want this over even if it means I have to walk away from everything."

Dear God, could she know how much he wanted to believe that? He would love to take her away and keep her safe forever, but she would never be happy. He knew that for a certainty. The Colby Agency meant too much to her. Running wasn't her style.

He pulled her to him again. Inhaled the delicate scent of rose oil. So sweet and elegant, just like the woman. "We will go away." He drew his head back far enough to meet those worried eyes. "But we're not running. We're only taking precautions. I'm going to get him before this is over. That's a promise."

"Kiss me, Lucas," she urged. "Kiss me and make me forget for just a little while."

He'd waited a lifetime for this moment. She wanted him to take her to bed. She didn't have to say the precise words. He understood what she wanted…needed. He wanted and needed the same. As much as he feared her request might be based on the stress of the past few hours, he couldn't resist or deny her anything.

He pressed his lips to hers. For one long moment he simply savored the taste of her…the gentle heat that made him crazy with desire. How he loved this woman, wanted to make her happy above all else. She melted into his arms, the tender contours of her feminine body making his harden in an instant.

Her kiss was greedy, desperate, and her arms tightened around him as if she feared she might lose him. He held her tighter to reassure her. She was his, and no one was going to harm her. Heat flooded his body, and he surrendered to the kiss…putting all else aside.

This was their time.

A knock on the front door jerked him from the heady embrace of desire. He stilled, praying it was a mistake and whoever was at the door would go away. But the banging came again, more insistent this time.

He drew his mouth from hers, his whole body crying out at the loss of contact. "I should get that."

She smiled, all signs of tears gone now. "You should. We'll continue this as soon as you've gotten rid of whoever it is."

A grin tugged at the corners of his mouth. "You'd be surprised how fast an old man like me can work."

She stepped aside and he reached for the cane he'd abandoned on the sofa. "Don't move," he told her. "I'll be right back."

"I'll be waiting," she tempted as he made his way toward the entry hall.

It felt good to hear her tease him. Going away now was not only necessary but it would be beneficial to both of them. They needed time to themselves, where work and the past couldn't touch them.

When they had consummated and solidified their fledgling relationship, then they could return to face the past.

Logan waited on the other side of the door, Lucas noted with a quick glance through the peephole. A part of him wanted to threaten that this interruption had better be important, but Lucas knew it would be. His men were too well trained for him to expect anything less.

"The postman just delivered this package for Mrs. Colby."

Lucas glanced at the package, then back at Logan. The grim expression on his face told Lucas he'd already checked it out and it wasn't good.

"It's from him?"

Logan nodded.

Lucas reached for the package, but Logan stopped him with a warning, "You'd better close the door. I don't think you're going to want Mrs. Colby to see this."

Lucas moved forward a step and pulled the door closed behind him. He propped his cane against his hip and reached for the package once more.

When he raised the lid, tissue paper concealed whatever was inside. A note read: "A memento from the past."

Lucas shoved the note aside and drew back the layers of delicate white tissue paper.

His breath evacuated his lungs. Ice slid through his veins as his heart pumped one last time before shuddering to a near stop.

A small T-shirt bearing the Cubs logo, the best he could make out, lay neatly folded in the box.

The entire shirtfront was soaked in dried blood, an ugly brown with age.

Lucas didn't need Victoria to identify the shirt for him. He knew whose it was.

This was the shirt her child had been wearing the last time she saw him.

CHAPTER TWENTY-SEVEN

TASHA PACED the length of her living room once more. She knew Maverick could see her. He had to know she was going crazy down here, and still she heard nothing.

Seth had taken a shot at Lucas. Thankfully he was okay, but it had been a close one. According to the last word she'd gotten he hadn't intended to kill him.

This time.

Failure stung sharply.

Dammit. Why hadn't she been able to get close enough to the guy? She was better than this.

She kept playing that scene in the sex club over and over in her mind until she was going crazy with it.

He'd watched her watching him. Had known how bewildered and, at the same time, fascinated she'd been by the intimate act playing out before her.

How sick was that?

She'd gotten turned on watching another woman go down on him! She'd been so damned caught up in the twisted moment that she hadn't even sensed Leberman coming up behind her.

She *always* sensed danger.

Her advanced precog receptors had never failed her.

But this time had been different.

This time she'd let herself get infatuated with the target. Obsessed with the mystery of him. What made him kill? How had he gotten all those scars?

She'd been so focused on playing the voyeur that she hadn't even felt the enemy coming.

Maverick told her not to beat herself up, but he hadn't been there, and she wasn't about to tell him exactly what had distracted her.

She'd lost it. Hell, maybe she'd never even had it.

She spun on her heel and stormed across the room again.

The waiting was driving her mad. It was worse than sitting behind that damned desk at Langley, reading those monotonous reports.

She had to get out of here.

It had been almost a week since she'd run or worked out at all. Her physical as well as sexual frustration capacity had maxed out.

She couldn't stand it any longer.

Turning thought into action, she strode determinedly toward the door, flipped the lock and yanked it open. At least a walk out in the open air would be better than this. Maybe she'd run into some safe-looking guy on the street, screw his brains out and get this crazy obsession out of her mind.

Maverick towered in her doorway.

"Lucas wants to talk to you."

She blew out a breath and waved the big guy in. "It's about time." Her body literally vibrated with tension.

The suspicious way Maverick looked at her as he entered the room had her hoping he couldn't read minds. While the big cowboy turned on the monitor and Webcam for the briefing, Tasha made herself comfortable on the sofa. She rolled her shoulders, took a couple of deep breaths and banished the thoughts that had haunted her for the past forty-eight or so hours.

When Lucas's image filled the screen, she produced a smile. "Good morning." She made a conscious effort not to scrutinize the bandage on his forehead. Seth had gotten too damned close. And where the hell was the hatred she should be feeling for the bastard right now?

"Morning."

Lucas's tone told her immediately that whatever he had to report wasn't good.

"Yesterday afternoon Victoria received another package."

The memory of the package she had delivered on Monday and its contents sent dread pooling in Tasha's stomach. "What was it this time?" Her voice sounded stilted, but it was the best she could do. She couldn't even begin to imagine what a mother who'd lost a child went through—even eighteen years later.

Lucas hesitated and in that moment she saw the anguish in his eyes. But it vanished in a flash as he composed himself once more. "It contained the T-shirt Victoria's son was wearing the day he disappeared. We're waiting for DNA analysis."

DNA analysis. She swallowed hard. That most likely meant blood. The shirt had probably been bloody. She closed her eyes for a fraction of a second and sucked in a steadying breath. Leberman was ruthless.

"There's still no sign of Leberman or the assassin."

She'd noticed that Lucas refused to call him Seth. They still didn't have a last name. She wondered if using first names made it too personal. Lucas always called her North. With a shudder she imagined that it would be easier to kill a man you'd never called by his first name.

"Did you find anything at the house?" Ramon had told her that they were going through the Oak Park house where Seth had held her hostage, but she hadn't heard any results.

Lucas nodded, his expression going even more somber if that were possible. "We have reason to believe that Leberman and/or our assassin have used that house on and off for some time. We found a few usable prints. Some old magazines on guns, mercenaries and porn. But not much else. There's indication that the basement where he held you has been used for that sort of thing before but that's about all we know for now. We've got a couple of forensics techs going over the place from top to bottom to see if they can find anything else.''

Tasha nodded. The gruesomeness of it weighed heavily on her chest. How could she have feelings for such a monster? She thought about the number...666. Who had marked him that way? Branded him a beast? "Tell me what I can do, Lucas.'' She looked straight into the Webcam and turned up the intensity in her eyes. She had to do something. She couldn't just keep sitting here, waiting. It was Thursday, she hadn't heard from Seth since just before dawn on Tuesday when he warned her to stay away.

''I know it's difficult, but I really need you to sit tight for a little longer. Considering this latest turn of events Victoria has agreed to disappear. That means Leberman will get desperate.''

She lunged to her feet and braced her hands on her hips. ''How the hell is that going to help me get close to Seth again?'' She had to do something. Get out there and find him. Take her chances.

''Sit down, North,'' Lucas ordered.

With a disgusted sigh, she dropped back onto the sofa. ''Dammit, Lucas, I just need to do something.'' Her eyes widened the moment the words were out of her mouth. What was wrong with her? She'd just addressed him as if he were her buddy not her superior.

''I didn't want it to come to this,'' he said quietly.

Oh, God, here it was. She'd screwed up one time too many. He'd ship her back to Langley—if they'd have her.

Lucas heaved a breath. ''But we're out of options.''

Okay, so maybe he wasn't sending her back. She dispensed with the self-pity session and listened up. ''Just tell me what you need me to do. Whatever it is, I'm ready for it."

Lucas looked at her from wherever the hell he was, but those gray eyes peered into hers as if he were right there in the room. "When Victoria and I disappear, we need our man to lead us to Leberman."

Tasha nodded. "Right. That's been the plan all along."

"Yes, we discussed that strategy in the beginning. But our guy hasn't responded to you the way we'd hoped. He's chosen to keep you out of the game."

It was her fault. She'd failed. She hadn't possessed the skills to reach a man as far gone emotionally as him. "If you'll let me get back in the game I can find him. I'm sure of it."

"We're going to have to take extreme measures," Lucas suggested, either in conjunction to her offer or oblivious to it.

"I agree," she said quickly, maybe a little too quickly. Uneasiness slid through her and goose bumps rose on her skin. "What's our first move?" She resisted the urge to flinch at the intensity emanating from that screen.

"I'm going to give you up, Tasha. It's the only way. He'll try to get to us through you. Are you prepared for that?"

It was the first time he'd called her by anything other than North. That alone gave her pause. She moistened her lips and held the fear screaming in the back of her mind at bay. "You're going to put the word out that I'm part of your team."

It really wasn't a question.

She knew the answer.

And it made perfect sense.

Lucas nodded. "Only if you're prepared to take that risk. I'll tell you now that if I were in your shoes, I might choose to stand down. I won't hold it against you if you do," he hastened to add. ''My original offer still stands. You've got a job with me for as long as you want it. Your decision now won't change anything.''

Well, she appreciated his leniency. But then, if she got the job that way she wouldn't really be earning it. And Victoria Colby would never be free. She wouldn't even allow Seth to enter the equation. If she was successful— major *if* considering her recent job performance—she might just have to kill him herself. Protecting Victoria Colby was top priority. His attempts to complete his mission had to be stopped at all costs.

The real question here wasn't whether or not she was prepared to take the risk, because she was.

What escaped her completely was whether or not she could kill Seth if it became necessary.

CHAPTER TWENTY-EIGHT

"YOU PLANT THIS somewhere in his SUV." Maverick handed her the tiny electronic bug. "It'll be useless, since he has a jammer, but he doesn't know that we know that. He'll find this thing in a hurry, so don't hang around after you've put it in place."

She nodded. "Then I wait some more." That was the part she hated the most.

"Not for long. As soon as he's found the bug he'll know you're working with us, or at least that will cross his mind. Then when he realizes Victoria and Lucas have skipped out on him, he'll come looking for you."

She understood that part perfectly.

"Now, this," Ramon said, drawing her attention to him, "is an entirely different matter." He showed her a small object about four inches long, similar in design to an ink pen. "Don't try writing any checks with this baby."

She picked it up and looked it over. "What is it?"

"It's a high-pressure puncture device, kind of like the ones diabetics use to deliver a blast of insulin, only this one delivers a drug that debilitates the human body within seconds." He took the pen-shaped device from her to demonstrate. "Just stick him with it, ensuring that you push with your thumb against the button as if you were clicking the pen into place to write."

"It takes a tough enough punch that you're not likely to do it accidentally just by rummaging around in your purse," Maverick added.

That was a good thing. She looked to Ramon for confirmation. "This will render him unconscious?"

He nodded. "For about an hour. It's powerful stuff. You could put down a bull elephant with that stuff. And since you'd never get in the club with a gun in your purse, this is the only protection you'll have."

Tasha gingerly dropped the pen into her purse, then tucked the tracking device into the bag's small, zippered compartment.

She glanced at the clock. Half past nine. Things would be jamming at the club by now. "I should get going."

Maverick and Ramon exchanged a glance. "Just be careful," Maverick warned. "Don't take any unnecessary chances. And remember, press against the implant if you need us. We won't be far away as long as we don't lose the signal."

The latest technology in tracking-warning devices had been inserted subcutaneously on the underside of her right forearm. It was a passive transmitter which emitted its signal only once per hour. If Seth swept her for tracking devices he'd find nothing. However, all she had to do if faced with trouble she couldn't handle was press hard against the device and an altered signal would be generated immediately, indicating distress. This one had a longer range and a better warning system than the patch. It also fluctuated the pitch of its signal to help override jam frequency. But it was brand-new and could present unforeseen glitches. Still, they had decided that it offered the technology they most needed at this point.

"I'm ready." She took a breath. "I'll see you guys when I see you."

They all three stood there for a moment, just looking at each other, not saying anything. There was really nothing to say. Seth had warned her to stay away, but she was going after him. If she survived the encounter, the likelihood of surviving his fury when he discovered who she really was amounted to something less than zero.

That was the deal.

TASHA DROVE PAST the lake house. The one she now knew belonged to Victoria Colby. There was no sign of Seth. Maverick had given her the entry code for the gate and front door, but going in that way would give her away too quickly if he did happen to be in there.

Instead she hung around outside for a while, watching and waiting. When she felt reasonably sure enough time had passed for him to have approached her if he were there, she headed back to town. It was only Thursday night but there was always the possibility that he would be at the Metro Link. En route she had driven down the street past the Oak Park house. Though she felt fairly confident he wouldn't go back there after Lucas's order to take the place apart.

Before she headed over to the Metro Link, she decided to cruise down *porn* avenue and see if she saw him there. Maybe he liked the redhead enough to go back for a repeat performance.

The street was almost too crowded to maneuver. The Halloween festivities were in full swing tonight, masks and elaborate disguises included. Though Halloween wasn't actually until Saturday, that didn't appear to bother any of this party-hearty group. No sign of his SUV. Of course, he could be driving something else now. She couldn't be sure. Shooting a guy like Lucas definitely upped the stakes. Seth might feel it necessary to change a lot of things, including the places he usually frequented.

The possibility that she might not find him at all nagged at her but she refused to think that way. She had to find him. Lucas had said that the club where she'd first met him was his favorite hangout. Maybe she'd find him there.

She had to find him…she needed this second shot at proving she was as good as Lucas Camp had thought her to be when he'd brought her on board for this mission.

Maybe he didn't consider her performance so far a failure, but she did.

And that was unacceptable.

The music thumped loudly, its rhythm inviting, as she strolled up the walk to the Metro Link's main entrance. The place was almost as crowded as it had been on Saturday night. Thankfully she didn't find any Halloween masks here. The same bouncer was waving his metal detecting wand. He smiled when he caught sight of her, then gave her a slow perusal.

She'd opted for a skirt. Very short, very tight. Very red. A red spaghetti-strap top that showed off her flat midriff and four-inch leather stilettos that accentuated her legs. She might not be supermodel material but she knew how to use what she had. Returning the flirtatious bouncer's smile, she opened her matching red bag for him to survey the contents. She'd made sure a package containing a neon-purple condom would be right on top.

He lifted it between two fingers and waved it in front of her. "Got big plans tonight?"

"You bet, sugar." She leaned a little closer. "I've always got *big* plans."

He dropped the condom back inside and glanced briefly at the cell phone and pen, lip gloss and few bills, then waved her through. His no-personality partner stamped her hand a little more gently this time.

"Great shoes," he commented, eyeing her legs lasciviously.

She moistened her lips and gave him a sexy smile. "Why, thank you."

The only thing she could think as she entered the

crowded club was that the guy must have gotten laid this week. His mood had certainly improved.

She cruised the place for a while, weaving through the crowd, watching, smiling, keeping a constant eye out for Seth. Just when her hopes started to plummet she saw him near the bouncers at the entrance. Her gaze narrowed as she watched him slip something to the guy with the wand who then waved him through without hesitation.

So that's how he got inside with a weapon. He'd either given the guy money or drugs. Making her move before he spotted her, Tasha latched on to the closest available guy.

"You wanna dance?" the guy asked, his words slurred.

"Absolutely." Her arms went up around his neck, and he pulled her close.

"I haven't seen you before," he muttered close to her ear. The music made hearing almost impossible this close to the band.

She kept the shouted conversation going as she slowly but surely lured him farther from the band and closer to the bar…to Seth. He'd claimed an empty stool and was surveying the crowd the way he had before.

She sensed the instant he saw her, felt his eyes on her. Snuggling up to her dance partner, she widened her smile and from time to time as if he had her undivided attention. He seemed to be thrilled with her attention, though she wasn't sure how he stayed vertical considering the degree of his inebriation.

"I need a drink," she finally told him.

He walked her to the bar, keeping one arm around her shoulders. Plopping unsteadily against the counter, he ordered himself a beer and then looked down at her.

"The same for me," she said sweetly, keeping her adoring gaze focused on him, though she could feel Seth's cutting right through her.

When the bartender set the beers in front of them, she

leaned closer to the guy. "What was your name again?" she asked, though they hadn't exchanged names, but she doubted he would remember.

"Kevin," he said after downing a gulp of his beer.

"I'll be right back, Kevin," she assured him. "Gotta find the ladies' room." She gave him a quick peck on the cheek. "Save my spot."

Kevin smiled down at her, his eyes blurry. "Count on it."

Tasha looked for the signs marked Rest Rooms and headed in that direction. She passed right by Seth without sparing him a glance. She rounded the end of the bar and followed the narrow, dimly lit corridor to the bathrooms. There was an emergency exit at the end of the hall. This one exited to the opposite side of the building from the main parking area, probably into another alley. She shivered instantly as she thought of the one Seth had dragged her to the first time they met.

As she reached for the ladies' room door, her skin instantly pebbled with goose bumps.

Strong fingers manacled her arm. "What're you doing here?" that deep masculine voice growled, sending shivers up her spine.

She whipped around and faced him. Before she could utter the scathing comeback she'd planned her gaze moved over his body, taking in every last detail. Well-fitted jeans, faded chambray, button-up shirt. And those eyes. She could never get her fill of looking into those eerily clear blue eyes…so ice-cold and yet so intense.

"I'm having a good time," she told him with an indignant little sway of her shoulders. "Now, if you'll excuse me—" she tried to tug free of his hold "—Kevin is waiting."

Fury blazed in those eyes, turning them a glistening

aquamarine blue. Her pulse reacted. "I know what you're doing. I warned you to stay away from me."

She laughed ruefully. "Don't flatter yourself. I have better things to do. Besides—" she moved in close and peered up at him, allowing her breath to feather across his lips and simultaneously hoping he wouldn't see the way his proximity affected her "—I don't think I'm your type."

For three seconds he didn't move…she held her breath.

"Guess there's only one way to find out." He yanked her toward the emergency exit and once again no alarm sounded as they barreled through the door, allowing it to slam hard behind them.

"What the hell do you think you're doing?" she demanded, tugging uselessly against his barbaric grip. A thread of panic needled its way through her.

He didn't stop until he'd reached his SUV and jerked the passenger-side door open. "Get in."

She drew back as far as his brutal hold would allow. "No way. I'm not going anywhere with you." It was a lie, of course. But she couldn't make this too easy.

He trapped her between the SUV and his muscular body. "I don't like games."

Her breath caught at the renewed intensity in his eyes. "I'm not playing games with you."

"Don't lie to me. I know what you're doing and I know what you want. Now you're gonna get it."

She swallowed, moistened her lips and reached for the calm that had promptly deserted her. "Maybe I changed my mind about what I want."

"Get in."

Exhaling shakily, she looked away from that intimidating gaze and climbed into the passenger seat. He shut the door and moved around the front of the vehicle, his gaze never deviating from her.

Focus, she ordered her whirling mind. This was good.

This was the first step.

She had to get close to him and find his vulnerable spot…had to do this right.

He got behind the wheel and drove straight to a hotel a mere five blocks away. She recognized the chain and felt some amount of gratitude that it wasn't a complete dump.

''Don't move.'' He cut her a look that would form icicles in the desert.

Steeling her nerves, she watched as he entered the lobby and paid for a room, a mixture of anxiety and anticipation welling up inside her. There would be no talking her way out this time.

The point of no return, Tasha, she told herself.

Prepare to go through with it or get out and run like hell.

The decision had to be made *now*.

She watched the clerk accept the cash he offered.

Tasha reached for the door handle.

If she ran, this one last chance would be over and there wouldn't be another.

Seth took the key card.

But if she stayed…

She reached into her purse and retrieved the small tracking device. She tucked it into a niche in the console then dropped her hand back into her lap as he exited the lobby.

This was the only way.

He slid behind the wheel and drove to the far side of the parking lot.

A test, she told herself. A simple test to see if she had the right stuff to do this job.

As determined as she was resigned, she followed him to the room, first floor, facing the parking lot. Quick access to his vehicle if he needed to make a run for it.

The room was small but neat. She purposely looked away from the bed as he locked the door behind them and tossed the keys to his vehicle onto a table.

She dropped her bag on a chair and went into the bathroom and closed the door. On second thought she locked it. She braced her hands on the sink and stared at her reflection in the mirror. She could do this. Operatives often sacrificed a great deal more.

Summoning her resolve, she pushed off the sink and turned back to the door. If she gave herself too much time to think about this, she'd lose her nerve. That couldn't happen.

She opened the door and took a deep breath. She was attracted to him…she could do this.

The room was dark, the dim glow from the bathroom providing the only illumination. But then, he was most at home in the dark. She blinked rapidly to adjust her vision, and located him sitting in the chair near the door where she'd left her purse. He'd tossed the red handbag onto the table next to his keys, the contents scattered across the laminate top. He'd gone through her bag.

"Take off your clothes," he ordered, a raw edge to his tone.

She knew what he thought. He thought she would run away again. Well, this time she intended to see it through. He would be the one wishing he'd run. If she had this guy pegged even half to rights, he wasn't accustomed to a woman like her. Tasha had never believed in doing things halfway.

Seth the slayer was about to learn a very important lesson.

Slowly, taking her time, she released one button after the other, until her tight little top fell open, revealing her unrestrained breasts. He watched. The pale, frosty blue of his eyes cut right through the semidarkness, like those of some unearthly nocturnal being.

She shouldered out of the blouse, allowing it to fall to the floor. Without hesitation she reached behind her and lowered the zipper to her skirt. She slid it over her hips and down her thighs until it, too, puddled on the floor like a circle of blood.

Stepping out of the ring of shed garments, she stood before him naked but for her thong and stilettos. "Now your turn," she said tautly, the anticipation of seeing his nude body already making her want to squirm. She reached for his hand and pulled him to his feet, which would have been impossible had he not wanted to do her bidding.

"Turn out the rest of the lights," he ordered in that ominous growl she'd come to associate with the man.

She shook her head. "I want to see you." Her nipples pebbled at the thought.

He stood perfectly still as she reached for him. When she released the first button of his shirt, she expected him to bolt, but he didn't. She released button after button until she'd reached the waist of his jeans, then she tugged his shirt free of that confinement. His only reaction was a slight increase in the rate of his respiration, but he remained very much in control. She had to fix that.

She pushed the shirt off his shoulders, ensuring that her hands molded to his bare skin and that her breasts grazed his chest as she leaned close. Heat sizzled deep inside her. When she reached for the shoulder holster he captured her hand and shook his head firmly side to side.

She moved on to the closure to his jeans but all those scars captured her attention once more, startled her all over again. They were so brutal...and there was so very many. Trying her level best to keep the shock from her expression, she touched each one, committed it to memory. Had he been some sort of prisoner?

Slowly, not wanting to set off any internal alarms, she moved around behind him. Her breath caught in her throat, the resulting tremor quaked all the way to her hands. He tensed beneath her trembling touch. If she'd thought the scars—the hideous indications of torture—on his chest were unsettling, the ones on his back were indescribable.

Grappling for composure, she did the only thing she could, she slowly kissed first one and then the next. Soothing each injury with a gentle touch. She could feel the tension rising in him with every graze of her lips. His fingers tightened into fists. Before she could finish he turned to face her, his expression hard, angry.

"I don't need your pity," he snarled. "I am what I am."

She looked deeply into the fiery depths of those eyes and said what she knew in her heart with complete certainty, "I know."

Before he could demand to know what she meant by that remark, she dropped to her knees and released his jeans, her heart pumping fiercely, foolishly as she considered that she had longed to do this since watching him with the other woman. She didn't slow down to think how insane it was. She only wanted to touch him…to taste him. She lowered the worn soft denim over his hips, freeing his engorged sex. Her pulse leaped as she inhaled the earthy smell of him. She pressed a kiss to his hip, allowing his long, hard cock to nuzzle against her neck. He was so hot.

His move came lightning fast and with all the brutality she knew him to be capable of. He jerked her up and pinned her against the door, his body pressing hard against hers.

She started to ask why he'd stopped her, but before she could his mouth came down savagely on hers. He ripped her panties from her body and crushed his pelvis against hers, the full size of his rigid sex grinding into her bare mound.

She braced her hands against his chest, knowing she should stop him…at least slow him down. The condom… it was right behind him on the table. But she couldn't slow the momentum, every part of her begged for his touch… yearned for his possession. She couldn't have stopped him…he was just as far over the edge as she was. Her thoughts fragmented, forced all reason from her mind as her hands learned him, molded to the muscular contours of rock-hard flesh.

Her fingers went into his short, thick hair and her mouth opened wider, inviting his invasion. She couldn't stop herself. She wanted this…wanted him. He thrust his tongue inside, then retreated, over and over again as if he couldn't get enough of tasting her, delving inside her. He lifted her legs up and she obediently wrapped them around his waist.

Long, blunt-tipped fingers parted her expertly. She writhed anxiously, needing to feel him inside her. The insistent nudge of his cock sent a spasm racking through her entire body a split second before he rammed into her, stretching her opening and dragging along her feminine walls until she cried out at the sweet unbearableness of it.

He hesitated only for a second, his lips mere centimeters from hers, his breath ragged, then he drew back and thrust hard again, jamming that generous length deep inside her, his mouth plundering hers once more. His hands latched on to her breasts, squeezing savagely, his fingers still damp from delving between her slick folds.

He pumped long and mercilessly, every stroke pushing her closer to the edge, slamming her against the solid wooden door at her back. Her flesh was on fire, her insides quivered with the urge to ignite…to erupt with the tension mounting. He hitched her legs higher, increased the depth of his penetration. She cried out with the pleasure-pain of it, the sound a primal signal that set him off. He pounded harder, flexed those powerful hips back and forth, allowing the full length of him to slide in and out…over and over again—base to tip.

The release that had felt faraway, deep, deep inside her abruptly crashed down around her, as if he'd dredged it from the farthest recesses of her soul. She screamed with the force of it.... Her body bucked in his powerful arms.

And then he came. Hard. Long. The heat and fury of it setting her on fire all over again.

He thrust one last time, a guttural sound escaping from between his clenched teeth. The agonized sound caused her eyes to flutter open. Her brow creased in confusion as she watched the dance of unreadable emotions across his face. He pushed her legs off his hips and withdrew, his cock gleaming with their commingled fluids, leaving her sagging against the door, her limbs quivering.

While she stood there trembling, her entire body limp and tingling, her mind swathed in bewilderment, he hoisted up his jeans and fastened them. He reached for his shirt and then looked straight at her, "Get dressed."

She took an unsteady breath and pushed away from the door, her legs so weak she very nearly staggered in the high heels. As quickly as she could she went into the bathroom and cleaned herself up, then put on her clothes, sans her destroyed silk thong.

When she came back into the room he still stood there silently waiting, the keys to his SUV in his hand.

Unable to bear the silence any longer, she looked directly at him, not bothering to shield her utter confusion, and asked, "What's with you?"

"You were right. You're not my type."

CHAPTER TWENTY-NINE

IT WASN'T EVEN MIDNIGHT when he pulled up alongside her sedan in the parking lot of the Metro Link. The club was still packed, the music still blasting. How could she have failed yet again in less than two hours' time?

He was her target...and she'd fallen for him.

Fallen hard. Let things get personal.

Her mission was to stop him...terminate him if necessary. After all, he was a cold-blooded killer, a man who tortured innocent people for money. And yet, more than anything else, she wanted to save him.

She was seriously messed up.

"I could stay the night at your place," she offered, her voice sounding too fragile. God, this was totally pathetic. But she had to try. It was her job—the whole mission depended on her being able to get to Leberman. She had to do this. Had to find a way to stay close to him.

He didn't respond, just sat there waiting for her to get out. Even in the dim glow cast by the dash's display, his profile looked stony, every line and angle rigid with some conclusion only he understood. Dammit, she was certain he'd felt something.

She'd watched the unreadable emotions play across his face...had felt his body's response to hers. It went beyond the physical, she couldn't shake the connections. But he didn't want it that way...he didn't want any strings. For some reason her response to him disturbed him. It damn sure disturbed her.

Was it the scars? Had someone made him feel ugly? Deformed? Or did he simply choose to be this way to facilitate his profession? From the beginning she'd felt something wasn't right here…something intrinsic to his very being.

But it went too deep to be recent or merely about sex. This was way bigger than that.

Then again, maybe she was reading too much between the lines in an effort to let herself off the hook for indisputable failure.

He looked directly at her, giving her a start with the abrupt move. "Do yourself a favor and walk away."

She shifted in the seat to face him more fully. Anger, mostly at herself, frustration and hope, dammit, *hope*, funneled inside her, making her desperate to reach him…to salvage this operation.

"I don't want to walk away. I want to know you." She blinked, only then realizing that moisture had gathered in her eyes. What was wrong with her? This shouldn't be happening. And then she knew…if she couldn't get to Leberman—if she were factored out of the scenario for good—Lucas and his men would have no choice. Seth would die. Because he wouldn't stop…they would stop him. She'd totally screwed up this mission. Broken the first rule of ops: never get personally involved.

That penetrating gaze focused fully on her, the ferocity of it making her tremble in spite of her determination not to react outwardly. "There's nothing to know." Two endless beats passed before he shifted his focus forward. "Now, get out."

Tasha didn't argue this time. She couldn't risk letting him see more of the emotions that hovered far too close to the surface. The moment she'd scrambled out of his SUV and closed the door he drove away.

Just like that.

Her heart rammed against her chest as she tried with all her might to focus on getting the keys into the ignition of her car. She had to get out of here before she lost it completely. She needed a bath. A long, hot soak to wash away his scent…the very feel of him lingering on her skin.

She sucked in a jagged breath and put the car in gear. No way could she consider the consequences of her futile act right now. They hadn't used a condom, and the sacrifice she'd made had been for nothing. She'd still failed to keep his attention. She didn't have it in her to go there…to analyze it. The next time she saw Seth—if she saw him at all—it would be on a whole other playing field. He would be seeking her and it wouldn't have anything to do with sex.

SHE LEANED AGAINST the wall in the elevator as it moved upward, eventually stopping on the thirteenth floor. Vaguely she wondered if they'd chosen that floor in defiance of the significance of the unlucky number. Or maybe it was the only one with every room vacant. After all, who wanted to live on the thirteenth floor?

Her mind was rambling…her emotions a wreck.

She couldn't think…couldn't reason.

It was over.

What was there to think about? Other than keeping herself alive when he turned those killing instincts on her. Well, if her performance continued on its present course she was dead already.

Fury ignited inside her. She was a complete idiot. She'd let this guy get to her. Let him draw her into some kind of spell, and she'd lost all illusion of being in control.

Not once in all the scenarios they'd thrust her into during training had she failed so miserably.

It was the human element, she knew. They'd warned her that when it was for real she might not feel so damned cocky. But she'd convinced herself that she was better than that. Didn't need any warning. She could handle anything. Well, she'd handled it all right. She'd handled herself out of the game.

The elevator doors slid open, and Maverick waited in the corridor for her. She didn't know and didn't ask how they'd gotten back to the building before her, but the flicker of concern in his eyes was impossible to miss.

They'd been tracking her every move…they knew just how far south this op had gone.

"Did you plant the bug?" he asked as they strode side by side to the apartment that served as a sort of command center.

She nodded. "He'll find it next time he sweeps the SUV."

"Good." Maverick opened the door leading to the apartment and waited for her to go in first.

Ramon turned toward her when she stepped inside. "You okay?" he asked, surveying her disheveled appearance.

She shrugged. "I'm okay."

"Our boy opted not to take you back to wherever the hell he's staying now," Maverick stated the obvious. "We'd hoped he would keep you close long enough to pinpoint that location."

Tasha moved to the couch and sat down. "Thanks for reminding me." Like she needed the cowboy to rub it in. She'd failed. "He told me to get lost, as usual."

"Did you have to approach him or did he approach you in the club?" Maverick wanted to know, the analytical wheels turning in his head.

"He approached me," she said wearily, though for the life of her she couldn't see what difference it made at this point. She was out. Another wave of anger washed over her, and she racked her brain for possibilities of what she could have done differently. There had to be a way to reach this guy on a level he couldn't resist.

"That means he's hooked," Ramon suggested, jerking her from her troubling thoughts. "He'll be back in touch."

She looked up at the two men, regret pricking her. She hated to burst their collective bubble of hope, but that wasn't going to happen. "He's not the kind who can be hooked," she said, setting Ramon straight. "He doesn't want any connections. If he comes back it'll only be because of the bug and his assumption that I'm connected to Lucas."

"There's nothing we can do but wait and see," Maverick said pointedly, either to get her to lighten up on herself or in an effort to thwart her self-pity session. She'd seemed to be doing a hell of a lot of that lately.

"There is the other…" he began, looking directly at her.

"I got it," she said before he could ask. That was the one thing she'd done right in all this. Her means might lack originality, but success was the bottom line. She looked directly into his expectant gaze and said, "I got the DNA sample Lucas wanted."

"That'll be helpful." Maverick's expression didn't show his relief but she heard it in his voice. "I'll notify Lucas right away. He'll want analysis started immediately."

She moistened her lips and said the rest, the reality that they hadn't used a condom reverberating in her head again. "There's just one thing. We're going to need a rape kit to retrieve it."

CHAPTER THIRTY

AT DAWN Seth took up a position with Victoria Colby's private residence within his sights. Lucas Camp had taken her there from the hospital two days ago and she hadn't left since. But Seth knew she couldn't stay holed up in there forever. Eventually she would come out. Quite possibly this very day if his calculations were correct.

Lucas's men had the gated community staked out quite thoroughly, but that didn't present a problem for Seth. He didn't need to be that close. All that he required was a position within striking distance. He was a top marksman, had learned the skill from the best snipers in the mercenary business. He'd risen above even the masters. A weapon felt as much a natural extension of his body as his right arm.

His focus shifted back to the small but grand house Victoria Colby called home now. He wished he had been there to see her open the package containing the T-shirt. He couldn't fault Leberman's uncanny foresight. All those years he'd kept the evidence of his crime. Anyone else would have wasted no time in destroying any and all evidence. But not Leberman. The bastard had known the power it held. The soul-deep anguish it would awaken. He had planned this final game for nearly twenty years. Now the end was near. There would be one last moment of shocking discovery and then death would swoop down upon Victoria Colby and her protector before they could hope to escape.

Seth was the instrument of that certain death. He existed

for that sole purpose. It would fulfill his obligation. Would sever the connection between him and Leberman. Once and for all. A twinge of something that felt too damned much like regret twisted inside him. He almost laughed out loud at the sensation. Was he supposed to grieve the loss of his *creator?* The only caretaker he'd ever known? He thought of the endless persecution and decided the answer was no. He hated Leberman. Despised him.

It was that very hatred that made him good at his work—he had no fear and no hope for anything beyond the moment. Death was no threat to him. Nothing could stop him.

She slipped into his mind…made his body tighten with remembered visions of them together. He clenched his jaw and pushed thoughts of her away. He'd given her what she wanted…what she needed to accomplish her part in the grand finale. He wouldn't see her again. Like he'd told her, she wasn't his type.

Another laugh rumbled in his throat. He didn't have a type. And he knew without reservation that there was a reason for her physical reaction to him as there was for everything. Leberman had taught him that unforgettable lesson well. However innocent on certain levels Tasha appeared, he was not fooled. Nor was he a fool. He knew that no woman would want him…would look at him with anything other than disgust in her eyes. Even the hookers he hired to relieve his sexual tension didn't want to look at him except for the money. And if at any time he started to forget just what he was, Leberman always reminded him. He was nothing, could depend on no one…trust no one. But he could deliver death without fail…without flinching. And when his own death came, that ability would define who he had been. Nothing…no one—a ruthless killer.

They thought they had him figured out, thought they knew what he was about. But they had no idea.

The bug she'd left in his SUV hadn't been necessary. He

had known she was the enemy from the moment they met. The only reason he hadn't killed her that first night was because she had tripped some internal trigger he hadn't known existed…made him curious. Made him feel a strange kinship with her. He usually didn't allow distractions of any sort, but he hadn't been able to deny himself this one indulgence. It could prove a mistake, but he wasn't concerned at this point. She knew what he wanted her to know, nothing more. She had not hindered his task. To the contrary, she had facilitated his effort, unknowingly of course.

Tasha North would be the messenger who carried the final blow to the mighty Victoria Colby.

Leberman didn't like that part. He'd wanted her out of the way from the start, but Seth had refused. Considered his inspiration to make her a participant as ingenious as any of Leberman's schemes. The more he'd thought about it the better he liked it.

She would provide the pivotal key without even realizing it until it was too late.

She wasn't part of the Colby Agency or any member of Lucas Camp's organization. Lucas had selected her from someplace else. She had some training, he knew, but she lacked real experience. Just another unknown factor that nagged at his curiosity.

Though he knew it was her job to get close to him, to learn what she could for Lucas Camp, her sincerity gave him pause. He'd felt her body's reaction to him. That kind of response couldn't be faked. Irrationally, his own body reacted instantly at even the thought of thrusting deep inside her. Admittedly, he had been shaken somewhat by the overwhelming physical connection. Had experienced unfamiliar sensations deep in his gut. But there had been much more on her part. She was either very, very good at pretending, which he doubted, or she'd let herself get emotionally involved.

The last didn't make sense, since Lucas Camp would never select someone so lacking. Yet, Seth was anything but convinced of her ability to pull off such a genuine performance. His instincts had screamed a warning at the depth of her vulnerability when he'd pushed her away afterward. That was the part that didn't make sense to him.

He needed to know more.

He lowered his binoculars and considered more closely his motivation for such a step. What did it matter who she really was or where she had come from? Or even what made her react as she had? She was simply a useful tool, one he would, without hesitation, dispose of if she got in the way.

His teacher had ensured that he possessed no emotions, other than rage. Determination, if one considered that an emotion. His ability to block such distractions was necessary to his existence…to his mission. Nothing else mattered.

Still, he needed to know about her. Some aspect of her background might prove useful at a critical moment.

Not that it would change the outcome.

Nothing could change the events to come.

CHICAGO'S CIA FIELD OFFICE, like all offices even remotely related to national security, worked more man-hours now than in the past two decades. The Domestic Resources Division and its once-secret collection-and-analysis work within the boundaries of the United States were no longer a closely guarded secret. Constant analysis and briefings were expected from every available source. The pressure was on.

But one CIA officer, Walter McCone, now understood just how scary things could get in his otherwise sedate job.

Three seconds after Seth pressed the muzzle of his 9mm to the man's temple, he had provided the necessary retinal and thumb print scan to allow access to the Central Intelligence Agency's vast database. The moment he'd entered his personal identification code and the screen confirmed its acceptance, Seth had landed a swift blow to just the right spot, rendering him unconscious. Killing him hadn't been necessary. Seth wanted him to report the security breach. It was time Lucas Camp realized just how much Seth knew.

He shoved the man's limp body aside and settled into the chair behind his desk. He typed in the name Tasha North and waited for the search results.

Half an hour later, despite the dead ends he'd encountered, his persistence paid off.

Everything he wanted to know about Tasha North spilled across the screen in front of him.

The more he knew, he reminded himself, the more power he possessed.

CHAPTER THIRTY-ONE

"YOU KNOW," Victoria said thoughtfully, "Max has that cabin near Crystal Lake. We could go there." It certainly wouldn't be the first time the Colby Agency had used one of their own people's hideaways for a safe house.

She tried to read Lucas's face or his eyes as she waited for his response to the suggestion, but he'd guarded his emotions very closely for the past two days. The assassin must be closing in, she concluded, it was the only reason he would work so hard to keep her in the dark. He feared for her safety...worried that he wouldn't be able to do enough to spare her from harm. Lucas was not so young anymore, the worry was taking its toll on him.

Her jaw clenched tightly. She hated Leberman and his assassin for that. They still knew nothing about this killer—where he'd come from, his reputation. She wondered, fury and hatred seething inside her, if this man, this assassin, felt even a moment's remorse for what he'd been hired to do. She knew the answer. No. He felt nothing.

What kind of man could kill without thought or hesitation? Could induce the kind of pain she had endured having to look at her child's bloodied T-shirt? Tears welled instantly at the thought. She would not think about that. Leberman, the bastard, had kidnapped and killed her child. She didn't need the DNA analysis Lucas had put a rush on to confirm it. The shirt was his...the blood was his, as well. She could feel that truth in her very soul.

Though she had known that her son was most likely

dead, had accepted that fact on some level. The knowledge did little to lessen the devastation when she'd peered into that box and seen that small, bloodied garment. Agony squeezed her chest whenever she considered what her baby must have endured at that bastard's hand. She would kill him. Whether Lucas wanted her involved or not. She wanted to fire the weapon that ended his pathetic life. That was precisely why she had no intention of going too far from here.

As much as she feared for Lucas's life, and she did, dear God, she did, she had to end this. They would never be free of this horrible past until Leberman was dead. The delivery of the T-shirt had driven that point home. She wanted him dead soon.

And she hoped he burned in hell for all eternity.

"I had a more remote location in mind," Lucas said after lengthy consideration of her suggestion. He braced on his cane a little more heavily than usual and walked over to join her at the hearth. Just another indication of how hard the past week had been on him.

Though it wasn't that cool outside, she couldn't seem to get warm. She'd had Lucas light the gas-powered fireplace. The heat from the flame scarcely made a dent in the cold cloak of dread that had swathed her. The chill came from deep inside and she had a feeling that she wouldn't feel warm again until this was over.

She looked directly into Lucas's caring gray eyes and told him the truth. Being evasive wouldn't help matters. "I know you want to keep me safe, Lucas. There's nothing in this world I want more than to see that you're safe, as well." Tears burned in her eyes as the images from that night—when he'd fallen into her arms...blood streaming down his face—rushed one after the other through her weary mind. "We can't risk allowing Leberman or his assassin to get too close. But, by the same token, we can't run from this. We have to get him this time. There's no other option.''

Lucas nodded. ''I agree. I have a place in mind that isn't so far away. We'll be safe but close enough to react in a timely manner if the need arises. I just don't want to risk utilizing any known locations.''

There it was. Ian and Simon had warned her that Lucas considered even her trusted employees at the agency a possible threat. She could scarcely believe it then or now. Of course, her two most trusted men hadn't told her about their covert meetings with Lucas until after there was no way to hide the truth any longer. But that only proved their dedication to her welfare.

Still, it annoyed her that Lucas would even consider one of her people less than trustworthy.

''I know what you're getting at,'' she said flatly. ''You won't find a traitor at my agency. Can you say the same for your own?'' That was unfair. She didn't have to see the surprise in his eyes to know that she'd tossed out that scathing remark without grounds. Lucas's Specialists were above reproach just as her Colby agents were. ''I'm sorry. That was uncalled for.''

Lucas splayed his hands in uncertainty. ''Perhaps it isn't. I can't be positive.'' He leveled that knowing gaze on hers. ''Just as you can't. There are too many variables in this world to be that certain.''

''True,'' she admitted, though with great reluctance. ''That's why you chose someone outside yours or my sphere of professional affiliation to make contact.''

''Exactly. The woman we have undercover is someone I selected personally for this mission. Someone outside this circle.''

Victoria had wondered about that. She remembered her from the day she'd delivered the package. This young woman was risking a great deal. She hoped that the personal wager was not more than she realized. "Does she know the full risk involved?"

Lucas nodded. "I believe so, though I'm certain her youth colors her perspective a bit."

Victoria's instincts went on point. She read the regret in Lucas's eyes in a heartbeat. "You're that worried about her?"

He exhaled mightily. "I am." He turned away then, looking at something beyond her…or maybe nothing at all. "I chose her because she was untried in the field, lacked the hard edge of experience. I wanted her vulnerability to show. I didn't want him seeing through her cover. But I may have overestimated her emotional limitations to some degree."

Victoria definitely knew how that felt. She'd done the same once. But only once. She'd chosen a young woman right out of the Colby Agency's research department—unaware that the woman had a congenital heart condition—for those very reasons and sent her out to bring in the kind of man, though a good guy, not unlike this ruthless assassin. Fortunately that mission had succeeded…this one might have an altogether different outcome.

"Are you going to pull her out?"

Lucas regarded her for a moment before he answered. Something more bothered him but he wouldn't tell her until he was ready. "Yes, I am."

Victoria's heart skipped a beat. As hard ass as Lucas Camp would have the world believe him to be, he would not risk a life unnecessarily. His honor wouldn't let him. Just more proof of the many reasons that she cherished him so dearly.

She put her arm through his and drew closer. "Tell me about this place you plan to take me." Warmth spread through her and she allowed it, let it wash away the cold worry and fear. She loved this man, wanted to spend the rest of her life with him if it amounted to nothing more than a few hours. She wanted those precious moments to be with him.

He laid his hand over hers. "It's definitely off the beaten path."

Victoria smiled. "That sounds perfect." She very much needed a place just like that right now. A place where she could forget the past and concentrate on whatever time she and Lucas would have in the present.

If destroying Leberman took her life, she wanted to spend the time they had left wisely. She'd wasted far too much already.

LUCAS READIED for his conference with Tasha.

He considered again the intel he'd only just received, and his decision solidified. He had to pull her out now. Whatever happened from this point forward, he could no longer in good conscience ignore the risk to her life.

When her image appeared on the monitor, he produced a smile for her benefit. "Good work, North," he told her. Maverick had already informed him that she'd taken the assassin's rebuff far too personally. "The DNA evidence you provided is being analyzed as we speak. If this guy is anywhere in the system, we'll find him."

She nodded firmly, but her eyes gave her away. She knew she'd failed to accomplish the ultimate goal, and the guilt weighed heavily upon her. "Thank you, sir."

"I received intel a few minutes ago," Lucas told her, paving the way for the blow to come, "that indicates our assassin has accessed CIA's database. He now knows who you are. I had hoped that change in our strategy might facilitate our efforts to locate Leberman, but now I'm not so sure. Considering the risk involved, I've decided to sequester you in a safe house until we eliminate the threat."

Something changed in her eyes. All signs of uncertainty vanished. "No."

Lucas leaned forward a bit, wanted her to see the irritation in his expression. "That wasn't a suggestion, North, that was a direct order. You've done all you can. Certain additional developments have greatly reduced your value as an asset in this mission. Now, you *will* go into protective custody until we neutralize this situation."

"With all due respect, sir," she said with just as much annoyance as he'd shown, "I'm not finished yet."

Lucas tightened his hold on his cane. A part of him wanted to give her a lesson in following orders, but another part of him wanted to cheer her undying determination. "I'll be taking Victoria to a safe house as planned. When we've disappeared he will come after you in hopes of discovering our location—"

"That's what you wanted, right?" she countered. The determined tilt of her chin as well as the rigid set of her shoulders warned him that she wouldn't give in easily.

"That's what I wanted before," he allowed, "I have reason to believe your objectivity has been compromised." Personal involvement on that level spelled disaster. He knew it, and so did she. That was the first rule of deep cover. Though he didn't relish the necessity to dash it in her face.

"That's why you picked me in the first place, isn't it?" she accused, hitting the proverbial nail right on the head. "I lacked any field experience which would prove to my advantage in fooling our target. The fact that I lost perspective only lends more credibility to my act."

Well, she certainly had him there.

"The bottom line is I won't let this go any further," he said pointedly.

"Pulling me out will blow your best chance at getting Leberman," she retorted, knowing he couldn't deny her words. "I think you're smarter than that, sir. I'm a more valuable asset than ever at this point. I'm willing to take the risk. You'd be a fool not to take advantage of the opportunity."

A flare of fury ignited inside him. She might be right about many things, but she was wrong about him. He wasn't going to knowingly get her killed. She'd gotten too close to the guy. Every instinct warned him that she wasn't thinking like an agent…she was thinking like a woman.

"I may be a fool, but you have your orders. We'll bring down Leberman another way." He'd already considered his options. She wasn't the only bait he could offer. Once he and Victoria disappeared, he had a feeling that this guy would gladly follow any available avenue. He was too focused to let anything get in his way.

"In that case, I guess I'll head back to Langley," she said as she stood. "I have no desire to work for a fool."

She was angry. If there hadn't been some credibility in the words she'd flung at him he might have been angry himself. But she was more right than she knew. For that reason he let her insubordination go.

She walked out of the camera's visual range. He let go a heavy breath as he heard a brief, heated exchange between her and Maverick and then the slamming of a door.

"You want me to take her into custody?" Maverick asked as he moved in front of the camera.

Lucas nodded. A new kind of fury flamed inside him. Leberman always had a way of turning everything to shit. Even his own life. Leberman blamed James Colby, had tried to destroy all that was his because *he* had screwed up. "Don't let her get away or she'll be out there looking for him."

"Will do."

Maverick signed off to catch up with Tasha. She had a stubborn streak about her, Lucas had to give her that. But that determination he'd so admired was going to get her killed under the circumstances. He should have seen this coming. But he hadn't.

Maybe *he* was too personally involved to make reliable decisions. He shook his head and closed the laptop that had provided the face-to-face encounter without his leaving Victoria's home.

"Lucas."

He looked up to find Logan waiting in the doorway of Victoria's small home office.

"Yes." He stood and moved toward the door. "Did we get the results of the analysis?"

Logan nodded. "It's a match. The blood on the T-shirt definitely belonged to Victoria's son. And the age of the sample tested is consistent with the time frame of his disappearance."

There it was.

Leberman wasn't merely playing with Victoria's emotions, this was the real thing. Her son's actual shirt…his blood. The bastard had killed the child—violently probably.

Fury twisted inside Lucas. He would see that he died in a similar manner…screaming for mercy.

CHAPTER THIRTY-TWO

TASHA DIDN'T BOTHER slamming the door to her apartment since she knew Ramon was right on her heels. The door closed behind him but she didn't look back, just kept moving until she was in her bedroom, then she slammed the door as hard as she could. She wanted him to know how pissed-off she was, for all the good it would do. It was his job, she imagined, to keep an eye on her until Maverick finished up with Lucas, and then she'd be under house arrest so to speak.

Lucas wanted her out. Not that she could blame him. She'd crossed the line. It was true. But that didn't mean she was out. She could finish this if he'd only let her. She was very nearly positive that she'd gotten to Seth on some level. She'd felt it.

It wouldn't matter now because he was a dead man. Lucas's men would take him down. Every instinct told her that Leberman would get away. He was too smart to get caught by the usual means. Lucas knew that. That was another thing she was certain of. Yet, he refused to allow her to do what needed to be done.

He was protecting her.

Because she'd failed.

And, ultimately, it was his responsibility to know when an agent was no longer reliable.

A blast of fury obliterated the mixed emotions playing havoc with her ability to think.

Yes, she'd crossed the line. But she was still an asset.

And that left only one thing to do.

She went into the bathroom and lifted her arm, surveying the tiny healing cut where they'd inserted the tracking device two days ago. Tasha moistened her lips and braced herself for the discomfort.

Using a pair of tweezers she tore the tiny incision open and dug around under the skin. Her stomach roiled and a thin line of sweat broke out on her upper lip before she made contact. She grasped the tip and pulled out the matchstick-size device. Letting go a ragged breath, she wiped away the blood, careful not to leave any signs of her little surgical procedure, and shoved a small strip bandage into place. Another deep breath or two and the nausea had passed. She swaddled the device in a tissue and set it aside.

After pulling on her denim jacket, she tucked her handgun into the waistband of her jeans and groped around in her purse for that nifty little ink pen Ramon had given her. She tucked the pen into the right pocket of her jacket and shoved what cash she had and the tissue containing the tracking device into the other. Her sneakers would allow for stealth. She was good to go.

When she heard Maverick's voice in the living room of her apartment, she made her move. The hidden door inside her walk-in closet that concealed a laundry-chute-like egress route into the apartment directly below opened with ease. Five seconds later Tasha stood in the kitchen of the command center Ramon and Maverick called home.

She hurried to the front door, unlocked and opened it, praying that one of them wasn't one step ahead of her already.

The corridor was empty.

Releasing a tense breath she ran for the stairwell. She listened intently for someone else to enter the stairwell as she double-timed it down one flight after the other. Just as she reached the final dozen steps, she heard the echo of footsteps above her. She had to get out of there before she was caught. Whichever of the two wasn't bounding down the stairs would be coming down in the elevator. Time was not on her side.

She burst through the stairwell door into the first floor lobby and, without pausing, exited the building. Five-o'clock rush hour had turned frantic with drivers and pedestrians alike determined to get home to begin their weekends. She didn't hesitate. She pushed through the crowd on the sidewalk and shot into the street, dodging and weaving to avoid the cars. A horn blew and tires squealed, but she made it to the other side without ending up a hood ornament. When she would have darted into the alley between two upcoming buildings a taxi, sans fare, slowed to a stop practically right beside her.

It had to be fate.

She jerked his rear door open and rattled off an address. "How fast can you get me there?" she demanded, leaning forward, needing him to feel her urgency.

He shrugged. "In this traffic, I can't say."

"Just get me there as fast as you can. I'll make it worth your trouble."

No sooner than the words were out of her mouth than there was a break in traffic and the taxi eased left, then zoomed forward. At that precise moment she caught a glimpse of Maverick and Ramon on the sidewalk panning the street. She slumped down in the seat and didn't breathe easy again until the taxi had moved ahead several blocks.

When he reached the address she'd given him, she paid the fare plus a generous tip. "Do me a favor," she said, peeling off another hundred bucks, "drive around for a while. Maybe on the other side of town."

He took the money and smiled. "Sure, I got some errands I could take care of before I call it a day."

"Thanks." Tasha climbed out of the car, leaving the

. tracking device tucked safely in the back seat. She'd watched for a tail and hadn't noticed one. Maverick and Ramon were likely caught in the traffic. The chase the taxi would lead them on would buy her some time. But she couldn't afford to waste a second. Lucas would be notified and more of his men would pick up her trail. Unless he decided she wasn't worth the time and manpower.

When the taxi was gone and there was still no sign of Maverick or Ramon, she surveyed the Oak Park house. This was as good a place as any to start looking for Seth. Though she felt fairly confident he wouldn't come back here, there might be something inside that would give her an indication of where to start looking. Something the others had missed.

The fine hairs on the back of her neck suddenly stood on end.

The sound of a vehicle braking to a stop sounded right behind her. She swore, certain it would be Maverick.

"Get in."

She whipped around as recognition of the voice exploded in her brain cells. Seth's SUV sat at the curb, the passenger-side window down, his 9mm aimed directly at her. Was this her lucky day or what?

"Now," he commanded.

He hadn't needed the gun. She would have gone with him anyway. But he didn't know that. She climbed into the vehicle as ordered.

"Give me your weapon."

"What makes you think I'm armed?" she tossed back as he eased away from the curb.

Those piecing blue eyes cut in her direction. "The weapon," he reiterated, "give it to me."

She reached behind her and removed the gun from her waistband and placed it on the console between them. "This isn't necessary," she told him quietly. "I know you found the bug. But there are things you don't know."

He just drove, not even bothering to glance her way.

"We need to talk," she said bluntly, hoping like hell he would at least listen to what she had to say before he killed her.

He picked up her weapon and tucked it into his waistband. "Don't talk."

She should have expected that. He didn't mince words. She was the enemy. He would kill her.

Tasha faced forward and relaxed into the seat. She ignored the ache in her arm where she'd removed the tracking device. The idea that she'd probably made a mistake doing that flitted through her mind. No, she decided, that had been necessary. She had to do this on her own. Staring out the window, she couldn't be sure where he would take her to do the job, but between here and there, she needed to come up with a plan that would keep her alive and accomplish the mission at the same time. She resisted the urge to laugh. Piece of cake, right?

Yeah, right.

One glance at her captor's stony profile and she decided that staying alive might just be impossible. But impossible had never stopped her before.

The sun was setting, casting an orange glow over the treetops, by the time he reached his destination. She didn't recognize the house or the thinly populated neighborhood as he parked his SUV in the deserted drive. Woods bordered the back of the property. The house was dark, empty looking. A For Sale sign tucked into a front window told her the reason why.

"Get out."

His voice startled her after the long minutes of silence. She moved to obey, knowing that a play for her weapon would be futile, not to mention suicide.

As they crossed the yard, her heart rate accelerated. He

nudged her from time to time to keep her moving toward the wooded area.

"Where are we going?" Her voice sounded as shaky as she felt and she hated the weakness. He was taking her into the woods, to kill her no doubt. Panic trickled through her, but she pushed it aside. She wasn't dead yet. The pen in her pocket gave her some comfort. She hoped like hell it worked as fast and efficiently as Ramon had said, since it was the only thing standing between her and certain death.

"Just keep walking," he said in answer to the question she'd almost forgotten she asked.

After about fifteen minutes he finally said, "Stop here."

The broad canopy overhead blocked most of the sun's waning light, leaving them shrouded in gloom. She glanced around the area. There were trees on all sides but the smell was different here. She inhaled deeply, noting the deep woodsy smell and something else...something damp and earthy.

Water.

The lake.

She suddenly knew where they were.

Victoria Colby's lake house.

"Why are we here?" she asked, her skin prickling with a familiar warning. This place held some significance... that's why he kept coming back.

He leveled that chilling gaze on hers. Despite the near darkness, those eyes of his seemed to draw whatever light there was and reflect it as if he possessed some sort of supernatural power. She suppressed a shiver. Reminded herself that he was likely about to kill her. How had her instincts failed her so miserably where he was concerned?

"I told you to stay away from me," he growled.

She looked straight into those haunting eyes and told him the truth. "I couldn't do that."

That assessing gaze narrowed. "You want to die, is that it? Is your job worth dying for?"

She took a step closer to him, ignored the alarm bells going off inside her head. He was way bigger than her. And strong. The memory of those arms holding her firmly while he pumped in and out of her made her shiver in spite of her best intentions not to.

"I came back," she told him as she stared up into that unyielding face, "because I thought you were worth saving." Unfortunately for her, it was the truth. That's why she'd failed...because she felt something deeper...stronger. He was more than just a killer. Every instinct urged her in that direction.

He laughed, the sound a harsh bark bursting from his chest. "And just who do you think you have to save *me* from?"

"Lucas will eliminate you," she said flatly, a fierce combination of emotions warring inside her. Her loyalty to Lucas battled relentlessly with her yearning to save this man...this killer. "You could walk away now. All he wants is Leberman. Tell me where Leberman is and you can disappear."

Rage claimed his rock-hard expression. "You think you know what this is about? You don't know anything."

She held her ground beneath that intimidating glower. He hated talking about the past. She'd learned that very quickly. And this had everything to do with the past. "Then why don't you explain it to me."

"I have an obligation to fulfill, and nothing will stop me." His voice sounded calm and collected but she could sense the building tension, the hot fury beneath it. "Not Lucas Camp. Not you."

She shook her head. "This is about more than money. Whatever Leberman is paying you to do his dirty work, that's not what drives you." His guard went up instantly.

Checkmate. She gave herself a quick mental pat on the back. "There's a lot more involved. It's something in your past."

He tensed visibly. "Shut up." His fingers tightened on the weapon in his hand. "You don't know what you're talking about."

"Someone did this to you. Made you what you are. Your father, maybe?" she ventured, her pulse racing in anticipation of his answer. "A caretaker for certain. You don't trust anyone...you don't need anyone. You're a classic case of abused child turned raging adult. You don't even know why you do this...you just do it because it's the one thing you have control over. It's *all* you have."

"I said shut up!" He shoved the weapon against her temple. Every feature of that chiseled face turned to granite.

She ignored his threat and went on, "I knew when I saw those scars that someone had done terrible things to you. Someone you trusted to take care of you...someone you cared about."

"I've never cared about anyone," he said through clenched teeth.

"What did your father do to you, Seth?" She didn't let up. Laid her hand against his chest, knowing he hated to be touched. He flinched. "Tell me what he did to you." She threw down the gauntlet, knowing he wouldn't be able to resist the challenge. "Or are you too afraid to talk about it? I thought you weren't afraid of anything."

He laughed softly, the sound almost sinister. "You want to know what he did to me? You think all those stories you read in your psychology books have prepared you?" He tangled the fingers of his free hand in her hair, dragging her closer. "He punished me each time I didn't live up to his expectations. Kept me shackled in the dark in a basement like an animal...fed me when he decided it was convenient."

Her heart was pounding. She was getting closer. "What about school or training?" She winced as his fingers tightened a fraction more in her hair.

"I've only had one kind of training. The kind—" he leaned closer, until she could feel his breath on her face "—you can only get from men who are no longer men...they're animals who crave violence, who live for nothing else. The kind that teaches a fourteen-year-old how to be a ruthless killer."

"But you were just a kid," she protested, her heart aching at how horrible it must have been.

"That's right. And do you have any idea what they did to me? They beat me within an inch of my life for every misstep I made. They withheld food and water for days at a time if I failed in some way. Far more frequently and far worse than anything Leberman had ever done." A muscle jerked in his tense jaw. "When they couldn't break me that way, they made me their personal whore."

The brunt of his words made her shudder, brought the sting of tears to her eyes. Dear God...how...

Before her thought could mesh fully in her mind, he continued, "But I kept growing bigger and stronger until I wasn't a kid anymore." He made a guttural sound, a laugh maybe. "Then I had my revenge. I'd killed half the bastards who'd ever touched me before the others could stop me. They kept me locked up, afraid to come near me, until Leberman arrived to take me away." He tapped his head, right where that bizarre tattoo was. "That's when I got this. Leberman laughed and said that I wasn't human...that I was a beast."

Her whole body sagged beneath the weight of the words he's spoken. How could anyone hope to overcome that kind of violence. "How..." She cleared her throat and moistened her trembling lips. "How did you survive?"

He shook his head. "You don't get it, do you? *I didn't.*"

She saw the change in his eyes...knew what his next move would be. Her fingers wrapped around the pen in her jacket pocket. "I just want to help you," she urged.

"I don't need your help."

She jerked her arm upward and brought it down hard against his neck.

His body tensed.

For two beats she was certain she was dead.

The weapon bored more deeply into her flesh.

And then he dropped like a rock.

CHAPTER THIRTY-THREE

LOGAN ENTERED Victoria's home office, and Lucas looked up from his final preparations. "Any word on Agent North?"

Logan shook his head. "No luck with the CIA. Since she hasn't been upgraded to field work yet she didn't receive a tracking implant."

Lucas hissed a curse. He'd hoped they could locate her that way since she'd removed the one Maverick had implanted. He leveled his gaze on Logan's. "You keep me posted. Ramon and Maverick are on this?"

"I called in Blue and Noah to help them out. They're combing the city along with Maverick. Ramon's hanging out at the Metro Link in case our guy shows up there."

Blue Callahan and her husband Noah Drake were two of Mission Recovery's finest assets. Lucas should have thought to call them in. He sighed in self-disgust. "I appreciate the way you've stayed on top of things, Logan. I haven't..." His words trailed off as a wave of weariness washed over him. He'd tried to keep the exhaustion clawing at him at bay, but his efforts were quickly losing ground. "I haven't been at the top of my game this go-around."

"That's understandable, sir. Are we ready to go?"

They had waited for the cover of darkness. A switch-off would take place in the event that the still-unidentified assassin was watching. Ian Michael's wife, Nicole, disguised to look like Victoria, would leave with Lucas and two of his men in the SUV waiting outside. Nicole had arrived dressed as a man so anyone watching wouldn't suspect just such a setup. Thirty minutes after their departure, Victoria, disguised in the male clothing and wig Nicole had worn, and her two most trusted men, Ian and Simon, would leave in an SUV parked in a neighbor's driveway. Another of Lucas's men, along with two more of Victoria's, would be watching the small gated community for any sign of the assassin as Victoria departed. Vince Ferrelli would follow as backup. They'd covered every possible base.

Lucas didn't like the idea of being separated from Victoria, but it was the only way to ensure her safety at this point.

"Almost ready," he said in answer to Logan's question. "Victoria is briefing her people before leaving. Since we can't be sure how long she'll be away, she wants to ensure that both Ian and Simon feel comfortable in their positions as codirectors of the agency until her return."

"I'll be waiting outside," Logan said before he turned away.

"One more thing," Lucas said, waylaying him. "I've decided to change my orders on the assassin."

Logan looked surprised. Lucas rarely made last minute changes without overwhelming motivation. "In what way?" Logan inquired.

"Until now I've wanted him alive so he could lead us to Leberman. I think that might be a mistake. It's now clear to me that Leberman has grown impatient and will want this over just as swiftly as we do. I think he'll make a move with or without his hired help." Lucas looked directly at Logan then to ensure there was no misunderstanding. "If you get our assassin in your scope, take him down."

Logan nodded slowly. "Do you want him alive for any reason?"

"No." Lucas didn't hesitate. "I want him eliminated."

"Understood."

Lucas watched Logan go, then took a moment to ensure he'd taken care of everything in his makeshift command center. He considered the possibility of any loose ends and could think of none. Director Casey would continue to handle ongoing operations at Mission Recovery until Lucas's return. Assuming he returned.

Lucas closed his briefcase and exhaled another heavy sigh. His top priority right now was getting Victoria to safety. He touched his still-tender forehead and the fresh, much smaller bandage that had been secured there today. His back was still tender as well. There was no doubt in his mind that he would be dead right now had the assassin wanted him that way. More of Leberman's games, Lucas had decided. Well, he'd had enough games. It was his and Victoria's turn now. Whatever it took, Leberman was going to die.

He thought again of the video he'd watched when the assassin dropped by North's apartment. He couldn't shake the feeling of familiarity in the way the man moved. But he'd studied that video over and over and nothing had come to him. Familiar or not, he was a dead man, the same as the man who'd hired him.

"ARE THERE ANY other questions?" Victoria looked from Ian to Simon and back. The two men sat on the sofa, both watching her closely as she stood before them. She couldn't sit for more than ten seconds without squirming.

"None," Ian said.

Simon chimed in as well. "No questions."

Victoria nodded. "Very good." She propped her hip on the arm of a chair and pretended to relax, knowing she wouldn't be able to tolerate it for long. "If for any reason I don't return," she stated succinctly, "Zach has the proper instructions for continuing to conduct business." Victoria suddenly wished Zach were here. She missed his steady support. As the Colby Agency's top legal eagle, they worked closely together. But Zach was on leave back home in Indiana where his lovely wife was giving birth to their second child.

Victoria couldn't help a pang of jealousy. They had their whole lives ahead of them, just as Ian and Nicole, Simon and his Jolie did. Time was running out for her and Lucas, and here they were wasting it on a horrendous part of the past that wouldn't go away.

God, how she wanted Leberman dead. She wanted this over so she could move on. Eighteen years was long enough to grieve and keep fighting the same old battle. She couldn't change the past...couldn't bring her husband and son back. It was time to move forward.

She closed her eyes and thought of the way Lucas made her feel when he kissed her. So warm and contented. Happy in a way she had not known in a very long time. His kisses had been chaste the past couple of days, because of the mounting tension and all the horrible reminders of the past, she knew. But she was ready to move beyond that. She was sick to death of having her painful history dashed back in her face. Life was so fleeting. Why couldn't she have this time with Lucas?

"Victoria, are you all right?"

Nicole's voice dragged her back to the present, and Victoria's eyes fluttered open. She managed a smile for the young woman. She nodded then. "Yes. I guess I'm just tired." A frown worried her brow. "Nicole, are you absolutely certain you want to do this?"

Nicole Reed-Michaels smiled. "I'm positive. I can handle it. Don't worry about me." Nicole was former FBI. She knew how to take care of herself.

But that didn't keep Victoria from being concerned. A dark wig covered her blond hair, and she wore one of Victoria's suits. If the assassin or Leberman were watching, she was a target. Leberman was an evil bastard. His assassin had proven every bit as devious. Those kinds of men were capable of anything. Killing a lovely woman, wife and mother of two, would be nothing to them.

Victoria stood abruptly. "Excuse me a moment."

She rushed to the guest room to take care of a task she'd forgotten. A quick flip of the wall switch and light filled the space. Her gaze went immediately to the bed. A box, its contents scattered across the pale green comforter, drew her deeper into the room. Settling on the edge of the bed, she reached for a photograph of her young son. Tears gathered in her eyes as a bittersweet smile tugged at the corners of her mouth. If only she could have protected him.

She'd failed.

Laying the picture aside with trembling fingers, she surveyed the mementos of his short life. This was all she would ever have of him…it wasn't enough. She'd dragged out the box of painful memories earlier that afternoon, she had to look one last time.

He was gone.

She had to face the finality of that glaring fact.

With a heavy heart she pushed up from the bed and moved to the door without looking back. Freda would put things away…she didn't need to bother—to put herself through the pain. It was time to forget.

As hard as it was to do, Victoria turned out the light on that part of her past.

"It's time," Lucas said as she entered the den once more.

She nodded her understanding. "All right." She looked back at her trusted Colby agents and reminded herself to be strong.

Determined not to allow this moment to become an emotional farewell, she produced an appreciative smile for Ian and Nicole. "Thank you for everything." To Ian and Simon, she added, "I'll be in touch."

When the decoy party had moved to the entry hall, Lucas glanced back to Victoria. He wanted to take her in his arms, she could see the need shining in those caring gray eyes. But he wouldn't, not now.

"We'll rendezvous in one hour," he told her.

Somehow she managed to keep her smile tacked in place. "One hour," she repeated. "Be safe."

"Let's step back into the den, Mrs. Colby," Vince Ferrelli, one of Lucas's specialists, said.

Victoria's heart pounded so hard she feared she might be incapable of a response just then so she nodded and followed him from the entry hall. She wanted to say so much more to Lucas before he left. Wanted to tell him again how very much she loved him. She'd only told him that once.

Please, God, she prayed, don't let that be the last time.

"We'll wait here, Mrs. Colby," Ferrelli said. He gestured to the sofa. "Everything will be fine."

It had to be, she thought as she settled onto the sofa's edge. Fate couldn't be so cruel as to take Lucas from her. She'd already lost too much.

LUCAS'S CELLULAR PHONE vibrated in his jacket pocket. He frowned at the intrusion. He didn't need any distractions right now. But if it was one of his people it had to be important, otherwise they wouldn't risk talking over the air waves and interception by anyone who might be listening.

He hoped like hell it wasn't bad news involving North…or Victoria. He'd only left her minutes ago.

He fished the damned phone from his pocket and flipped it open. He didn't recognize the number of the caller. "Yeah," he said instead of identifying himself.

"Lucas?"

His frown deepened. "Ebb?" Dr. Ebb Deason was the genetics expert Lucas called upon whenever he needed the very best in DNA analysis. Not to mention he could count on his old friend dropping everything and working his team until he had results.

"I apologize for calling you like this," Ebb hastened to explain. "Maverick insisted it would be all right, considering the subject matter."

Maverick had given the doctor this number? It had to be important. "It's fine. Go ahead, Ebb."

"I finished that latest analysis you sent me."

The seminal fluid specimen North had provided. The memory pinged Lucas's conscience. "That's good to hear. What have you got for me?" Unless the doc had found a match in some database, a mere analysis wouldn't be much help.

"Well, I was a little bewildered at first. I knew immediately that I'd seen this DNA strand before."

Anticipation seared through Lucas. "You found a match in CODIS?" The FBI's Combined DNA Index System proved a useful tool for all government agencies. It contained DNA specs for violent criminal offenders. That would be the most likely source of a match considering the specimen donor's occupation.

"No…the match was with another specimen you provided."

Lucas stilled. Every sensory perception stood at attention.

"This specimen was a perfect match to the one from the Cubs T-shirt."

Lucas blinked, breaking the paralyzing spell the news had cast. "You're certain of that." Of course he was certain. He wouldn't have called otherwise.

"Yes. Quite certain," the doctor confirmed.

"Thanks, Ebb."

Lucas didn't remember terminating the call, but somehow his cell phone made it back into his pocket.

"Dear God," he muttered.

This was…impossible…

The assassin determined to kill Victoria was…*her son.*

CHAPTER THIRTY-FOUR

TASHA COLLAPSED on the floor in the massive entry hall. Her breath heaved from her chest as if she'd run a marathon.

It had taken her at least thirty minutes to drag Seth's unconscious body to the house. The woods, she discovered, bordered the side of Victoria Colby's lake house opposite the water. She'd used the code Maverick had given her to open the gate and then the front door. For once, since taking finals in college, she was thankful for her fantastic memory. She'd only seen the code once but it was forever imprinted across some brain cell that floated around in her gray matter just waiting for her to access it.

After getting Seth into the house, she'd tied him to one of the massive columns in the entry hall. She'd used the electric cords for the coffeemaker and the toaster to secure him. She glanced at the clock on the wall. She couldn't be sure what time she'd injected him, but she imagined he would be coming around anytime now.

She had both weapons and his cell phone.

Leaning back against the wall, she watched him and considered all that she'd bullied him into telling her. She would bet her life, which ultimately she'd just already done, that he'd never told anyone that horrifying story before.

She closed her eyes and fought the sting of tears when she thought about the child he'd been and how that bastard Leberman had brutalized him. Shackling him in the basement like an animal, restricting his food and water. No wonder he had such excellent night vision, he'd spent his formative years in the dark.

Then, worst of all, sending him to stay with those scumbags who'd done far worse things to him. At fourteen he must have believed that nothing could be worse than what he'd faced so far in his young life, and then he'd been left to discover that his nightmare had only just begun.

They'd tortured him…starved him…dear God, and they had raped him. Anguish roared through her. Leberman had made him a monster. He'd disfigured his body and then he'd killed his soul.

How…how did you survive? Even now tears burned in her eyes as that moment replayed in her mind. *You don't get it. I didn't…*

Seth was right. He hadn't survived. Whoever he had been back then had died. The man that he was now had been born of violence and despicable evil. A beast. Like Leberman said. Her fingers tightened around the weapon. She wanted to kill that bastard with her bare hands and now she had the bait.

She flipped open the cell phone and went through its menu. There were no numbers entered into the speed dial function. She checked the incoming call log and dialed the number from which he'd last received a call. Three rings passed before a very pissed off, male voice answered.

"Where the hell are you? They're on the move."

It was him. A shudder of dread quaked through her. It was *Leberman.*

"Seth's a little tied up right now," she said flatly, almost smiling at her own wit. "Why don't you come and help him out. I think you know where we are." She ended the call and tossed the phone aside. "Bastard," she hissed beneath her breath. She would kill him all right and never feel a moment's remorse.

"That was a mistake."

Seth's voice jerked her attention to him. His eyes burned like a high-octane blue flame. Fury didn't begin to describe what she saw there. She swallowed back the fear that threatened to clog her throat. "Maybe," she allowed, then cocked the weapon in her hand. "I'm of the opinion that he's got this coming to him."

Seth made that noise in his throat that was probably as close to a laugh as he got. "You think you have what it takes to stop him? Others have tried and they've all failed. Just ask your boss, Lucas Camp. He'll tell you."

That he'd tossed Lucas's name into the equation with such glibness made her want to shake the hell out of him. She eased out of her sitting position and moved toward him, settling again near his bound feet so she could read him better. She wanted to see even his subtlest reaction to what she was about to say.

"After all he's done to you, why would you care if I kill Leberman or not?"

He looked straight at her from beneath lids still heavy with the lingering effects of the drug. "Who says I do?"

She shrugged, deciding to go with her gut and not pretty this up in the least. "I don't know. Maybe it's because you haven't killed him yourself in all this time. After all, he did all those cruel things to you and still you let him live." She said the last with as much repugnance as she could muster, then pressed him with a fierce gaze of her own. "Maybe you liked it."

The change evolved instantaneously. The fury she'd noted before morphed into pure, unadulterated rage. But even that savage ferocity didn't hold a candle to the lethal intensity of his voice when he spoke. "Cut me loose now and I'll let you live. Drag this out and you'll end up dead."

She inclined her head and stared at him in amazement. With complete certainty she knew that what had happened between them in that hotel had affected him, maybe not to the extent it had her, but he'd felt something. And yet, he still appeared prepared to kill her. Or maybe the suggestion was his offhanded way of trying to save her.

"Still think I'm worth saving?" he taunted.

She looked him straight in the eye and said what she felt in her heart…in her gut. "Yes. I do. Despite the kind of man your father is—despite everything he did to you—I know there's something good inside you. It's just buried under so much pain and cynicism that I can barely see it."

He made another of those humorless sounds. "You don't know anything about my *father*. He was responsible for the death of an innocent family and caused all of this."

She'd tried hard to keep her emotions in check—to keep an objective prospective—that went out the window. "I know he did everything in his power to turn you into some sort of unfeeling monster. But it didn't work, did it?" She pushed to her feet, circled him slowly. He held very still, not even breathing. When she faced him again, she crouched down and peered into that feral gaze. "You felt something when we were together. I know you did. I felt it, too. So don't try and play dead with me, Seth. I know better."

He pushed forward as far as his bindings would allow and with heart-gripping sensuality and intimacy whispered, "Just because I fucked you and liked it doesn't mean I won't kill you and like it just as much."

The words were a direct hit to her more fragile emotions. Hurt hurdled through her, and she drew back slightly before she could stop the outward reaction. He smiled, the expression sinister.

"See, Tasha, that's the difference between us. We both have our causes, but I'm prepared to see mine through no matter what it takes. Can you say the same?"

For one long moment she stared into those eyes, knowing with complete certainty that he spoke the truth. He would kill her here and now if given the chance. Whatever it was about him that her instincts urged her to believe in, she damn sure couldn't see it at the moment. No matter the atrocities he'd faced as a child, as a man, he was still a killer.

And it was her job to see that he didn't fulfill his mission.

Long minutes passed in silence. There was more she wanted to say, but it wouldn't matter. The only thing she could do was wait.

He looked away abruptly...appeared to listen intently. The fine hairs on the back of her neck stood on end. Every fiber of her being went on alert as his gaze returned to hers.

"He's here. Cut me loose and I'll protect you."

She gave her head a little shake and rolled her eyes. "I think I'll take my chances on my own."

"Then you'll die."

Ignoring his comment, she stood, tucked his weapon in her jeans at the small of her back, and, at the same time, heard what he'd likely picked up on five seconds earlier. Leberman had come in through the back. The slightest shuffle of a single step touched her auditory senses. Moving away from the dim light of the entry hall and into the darkness of the dining room, she listened intently for more movement.

The kitchen.

A faint scuffling sound.

Moving in the direction, she frowned. What the hell was he doing? Trying to give himself away?

"Turn on the light, Agent North."

She flinched. The haughty sound of his voice grated across her nerve endings.

"Put your weapon down, Leberman," she ordered. Squinting, she could barely make out his silhouette in the darkness. Something was wrong...

"Turn on the light or she dies *now*," he snapped. "You

see,'' he went on in a much calmer voice, ''after your call I picked up a little insurance.''

She. Tasha's senses charged to a higher state of alert, she eased toward the wall nearest the door leading into the entry hall, where the light switch was most likely located. The fingers of her free hand located and activated the switch. She blinked quickly to adjust to the brightness and then her heart surged into her throat.

Leberman shielded his body with a young girl. Sixteen or seventeen, tops. Her eyes were wide with fear. Judging by the way she was dressed she was probably a prostitute. New at the profession, Tasha immediately determined. Her hair was too shiny, too full of body and life, her skin still looked clear and smooth. Dammit. Where the hell were her parents?

Leberman held a knife, probably from this very kitchen, close to her throat. She cried out as he pressed the sharp stainless steel even harder against her soft flesh. The swift bloom of bright red tears beneath the shiny blade jerked Tasha from the stunned spell.

''All right,'' she relented. ''Let her go and I'll put down my weapon.''

Leberman laughed with the same haughtiness that he'd spoken. ''You put down your weapon and I'll let her go. That's the way it works. You see, Agent North, I'm in charge of this game. Not you. And certainly not Lucas Camp.''

She now had the distinct feeling that both Leberman and Seth had known from the beginning who she was…it couldn't simply have been since she'd planted the tracking device in his car to give herself away. Leberman exuded the kind of confidence that went with knowledge held over time…not recent, surprising news. He wasn't the least bit surprised. He'd known. She was sure of it. She just didn't know how.

She didn't want to give up her weapon…but those bloody tears slid down the girl's long, slender neck.

"Put it down now!" Leberman commanded.

Slowly Tasha laid her weapon on the closest counter. The thought of dying left a bad taste in her mouth, but at least she'd managed to distract both Leberman and Seth while Victoria and Lucas escaped to safety. That was something.

Then again, she wasn't dead yet. She looked straight at Leberman. "Your turn. Let her go," she said pointedly.

He shook his head. "Not quite yet." He nodded to the counter. "Lay the weapon on the floor and kick it over here."

She had one split second to make the decision.

Tasha reached for her weapon. It was cocked already.

She bent at the knees as if she planned to do as he'd asked.

Instead she fired.

He jerked when the shot hit his right shoulder.

The knife clanged to the floor.

Shrieking, the girl scrambled away from him.

When Tasha would have taken a second shot, one aimed right between his beady eyes, the muzzle of his weapon stared right back at her.

He'd been holding a gun in his left hand. The girl's blouse where he'd held her anchored to him by her waist had covered his hand and the weapon.

Shit.

Tasha straightened to her full height, kept the weapon leveled carefully between his eyes. "I guess we have the proverbial Mexican standoff."

Leberman smiled sardonically. "Well, I do have a bit of leverage, Agent North."

"Really?" She lifted a brow in question. "And what would that be, scumbag?"

"The man standing behind you."

She held perfectly still, allowing the rush of goose bumps over her skin to tell her that Seth was, in fact, right behind her. She'd tied him securely, but somehow he'd managed to free himself. He tugged his weapon from her waistband and she cursed herself.

Curled in the fetal position, the young girl sobbed quietly in the corner. That was the worst atrocity of all, Tasha told herself in the next moment. She was a trained agent. She'd known going into this thing that death was a possibility. But the girl—she was innocent on that score. Tasha's call had dragged her into this. For that she suddenly felt a truck-load of remorse.

"You know," Tasha said, deciding she might as well get her dig in while she could, "I just can't figure out why Seth would do your bidding after all you've done to him."

Leberman laughed again, that ugly, evil noise that erupted straight from hell. "Didn't he tell you? I rescued him...saved his life. He owes me everything. Without me...he wouldn't exist at all."

None of what he said made sense. "Saved him from what?" she demanded, unconvinced and allowing him to clearly see her doubt and disgust.

"Why from his negligent parents, of course. They didn't care what happened to him...left him all alone and lost. But payback is always a bitch, isn't it, Seth?" Leberman said the words to Seth but never took his eyes off Tasha. "You see, Agent North, we've both waited for this for a very long time. Final vengeance is close at hand, and you're not going to stop it. Neither is Lucas."

What was he saying? If he wasn't Seth's father, then who was? "I'm afraid you've lost me," she tossed back at him. "Call me dense, but I just don't get it."

Fury streaked across the slight man's face. A ferret, she decided. If not for the gray hair, he'd look just like a weasel-faced ferret. She shook off the thought no doubt spawned by hysteria and focused. She had his attention. He would want her to fully understand before she died. One didn't have to be a psych major to know his type. She had his number already. He only enjoyed the kill if the proper emotional impact was achieved.

"I told his father all those years ago before I killed him what I planned to do." Leberman laughed, his gaze suddenly distant. "You see, I knew watching *her* suffer from the loss of her husband would never be enough. So I waited all these years for her to finally put the past behind her and fall in love again before I staged the grand finale. But I told her beloved husband every detail fifteen years ago. He died with those horrible images in his head. God, it felt so good. It was almost enough…but not quite."

James Colby. He had to be talking about James Colby. Lucas had said that they suspected Leberman had killed Colby fifteen years ago. But what did that have to do with Seth?

"My God," she murmured as the realization rammed into her brain like a bull charging toward a taunting matador. Seth was…James Colby Jr. He was Victoria's son. Her gaze focused back on Leberman and a new kind of rage went through her. "You son of a bitch, you stole him away from his parents and then you did…" All those despicable things to him.

"I didn't have to steal him," Leberman lashed out, his control slipping marginally. "They left him all alone in those woods. He would have died from exposure or drowned in the lake if I hadn't rescued him. *I saved him.*"

That's why he'd taken her to the woods…that's why he kept coming back to this place. It had once been his home. A dozen sensations whirled inside Tasha all at once. She so wanted to face Seth and make him believe the truth that she knew. But she couldn't risk turning her back on Leberman.

"You're a liar, Leberman," she said flatly. "Maybe you've got Seth fooled, but I know the truth. You stole him from the people who loved him. Victoria still grieves for the son she lost...the one you *stole*."

"No! She left him, just like his father did. And now, the son she threw away will have his vengeance, as well as mine. He owes me that. I kept him alive...made him what he is. He will finish this. Kill her now!" he shouted at the man behind her.

She might be headed to hell but she was taking Leberman with her. Her finger tightened around the trigger.

The gun blast echoed in the room.

CHAPTER THIRTY-FIVE

LUCAS STARED OUT over the dark water as it rushed toward the shore. The moon and blanket of stars overhead cast down an ethereal glow which only made the water look more menacing. The isolation suddenly pressed down on him…made him feel small and completely inadequate in the scheme of things.

He had chosen this location precisely because of its isolation. Well north of Chicago, the small waterfront property was owned by the doctor who'd allowed Lucas to use his clinic for his covert meetings with Victoria's people. But not even the good doctor knew that Victoria and Lucas were here now. He'd long ago given Lucas a standing invitation as well as a key to the property.

Complete secrecy was essential.

He hated like hell to think that there was a leak of some sort or, worse yet, a mole in either his or Victoria's agency. But there were far too many factors weighing in at the moment to deny that possibility.

Leberman was all too aware of Victoria's every move, as well as Lucas's.

As soon as the bastard was taken care of, looking for that inadvertent leak or, God forbid, mole would be Lucas's next order of business.

No, that wasn't right.

His next order of business had to be the assassin.

He had already briefed their security detail. Logan, Ferrelli, Callahan and Drake already knew that the assassin was Victoria's son. No one had questioned the announcement, they'd merely nodded gravely. Ian and Simon knew, as well, both were keeping watch on things at the Colby Agency.

Maverick and Ramon were still searching for North.

Lucas hoped like hell that little girl kept herself alive. For the first time in his career, he wasn't quite sure he could live with the weight of her death on his shoulders.

And then there was Victoria. How was he supposed to tell her the truth? She had finally accepted the past for what it was—the past. She was ready to move on, to love him. Now that very past threatened not only that love, but also their very lives. How could fate be so cruel? How was he supposed to tell her that her own son wanted her dead?

That he was a brutal, relentless assassin who cared nothing for human life.

Lucas remembered the small boy…had kicked himself over and over for not recognizing him as a man. He'd felt there was something familiar about him, but hadn't been able to nail down just what it was.

Now he knew.

And he had to figure out some way to tell Victoria.

More important, however, he had to keep her safe. Her son wanted her dead, would likely stop at nothing to see his mission to fruition.

Lucas had recanted his previous order and had issued a new one, that his and Victoria's people were to maintain visual contact but not to engage the assassin unless absolutely necessary if they located him. As much as he wanted to stop him, he wanted him alive. He couldn't imagine having to tell Victoria that one of his people had killed her son.

He shuddered at the thought…told himself it was the cool breeze wafting in off the water, but he knew better.

The quake he'd felt was one of uncertainty…of fear. Fear for the woman he loved. Fear of losing her.

There was no way to even guess how this would end.

As much as he loved Victoria and wanted to ensure her safety, he knew with complete certainty that she would not survive losing her son a second time.

For one fleeting moment the possibility that he could conceal that truth from her flashed through his mind. If keeping her safe meant killing her son, was there any real reason to tell her the truth? What would it accomplish, other than to bring her more pain?

"Lucas."

The sound of her voice tugged him from his troubling thoughts, and one look into those dark, caring eyes gave him the answer he sought. He would tell her because he couldn't lie to Victoria. There had never been a lie between them; he wouldn't start now.

"Are you coming inside?" she ventured hesitantly.

She looked so lovely with the gentle breeze lifting those loose tendrils of hair around her throat. He longed to see it down again. Longed to touch her…to kiss her. This was the first time he'd seen her dressed so casually. Petal-soft, pale yellow slacks and matching sweater and low-heeled slip-on shoes made her look like a fragile flower.

This was the Victoria he had yearned to know for so very long. The vulnerable, soft side that lacked the tough professional veneer she wore at the office.

Yet he loved both personas more than life itself.

"The bread is warm and the wine has had plenty of time to breathe. Everything's ready."

She'd insisted on cooking, swore it would take her mind off things. He'd offered to help, but she'd wanted to do it alone. She'd been right. She looked more relaxed than he'd seen her in months. Since before those horrifying hours on that island when Leberman had been close on that last occasion. The total change, considering all that had happened the past few days, abruptly unsettled him. Had she resigned herself to some fate she'd decided inescapable? Had the presumption that her son had suffered a violent death pushed her over some unseen precipice? Should he tell her right now that her son was alive?

If only he knew the right words to say....

"I won't let you down, Victoria," he felt compelled to say as he reached for her, unable to restrain any longer the need to touch her. "I swear to you that I won't let him harm you in any way."

The smile that spread across her lips warmed his heart despite his seemingly overwhelming concerns. "I'm not afraid, Lucas," she said quietly, patiently. "I'm not resigned, either, if that's what you're thinking. I have complete faith in your people as well as my own. Leberman won't win." She took his hands in hers. "What I am at this moment, more than anything else, is determined." She let that sink in for a moment, then continued, "Determined to get on with my life. To put the past firmly behind me. I can't live with it anymore." She looked deeply into his eyes, the hurt there evolving into need. "Now, come inside, Lucas. We're going to eat and then we're going to make love."

"But—" he began, his body already racing full steam ahead on the very course she'd drawn in his active imagination.

She shook her head, cutting him off. "No buts tonight nothing else in this world matters except us."

VICTORIA BRIMMED with nervous anticipation, so much so she'd scarcely eaten the meal she'd gone to so much trouble to prepare. When Lucas had offered to make coffee, she hadn't been sure she would be able to contain herself. Finally she'd simply had to spell it out for him.

"We'll have coffee later," she'd said simply, then she'd taken him by the hand and led him to the cabin's spacious bedroom.

Now he stood waiting for her to make the first move as she'd known he would. Lucas had spent half a lifetime being patient...waiting for her to come to terms with the tragedies fate had dropped like bombs into her life.

But that was all behind her. She would not look back. Lucas had highly skilled people who would take care of Leberman and his hired killer. Her own people would see to the agency. This—here and now—was going to be their time. She didn't want anything else to get in the way of this precious moment. Here they were safe.

She stepped out of her shoes and scooted them aside. Next she removed her sweater. She loved the feel of it, so soft and warm. She'd known when she packed it that she wanted to be wearing it at this moment. The pastel-yellow color looked good against her skin, and the fit was flattering.

For just one moment as the exquisite fabric drifted to the floor, she suffered a pang of panic. What if her body failed to please Lucas? She was not so young anymore. Almost fifty.

She forced the thought away. She'd been down that road, had considered what he might think, and she knew there was only one way to find out. Youthful beauty only went skin-deep. What she and Lucas shared went far deeper than that.

Far, far deeper.

She reached behind her and unzipped her slacks, then slid them down and off in one, smooth motion. She stepped forward, out of the confines of the garment puddled around her ankles.

His cane propped against the night table, Lucas watched her intently, his breathing visibly more ragged. Was he half

as worried about pleasing her as she was about pleasing
him? She smiled, realizing that he likely was. Even men
suffered that plight…to some degree.

As she tugged at the pins restraining her hair, he shouldered out of his jacket. Anticipation soared through her. He
wasn't going to keep her waiting.

She watched his capable movements as he tossed the
jacket into the nearby chair. While he removed his tie she
freed the length of her hair, allowing it to fall down and
sway around her shoulders, the feel of it against her bare
skin making her shiver. She blinked, nearly certain she'd
seen him shiver, as well. Could he have waited for
this…allowed himself no other as she had? The mere idea
made her tremble again.

Moving closer to him, she watched as he slowly released
one button after the other along the front of his shirt. She
moved more quickly now, wanting—needing—to be close
enough to touch him. The final button was scarcely freed
before she boldly pushed the starched cotton from his broad
shoulders. Her heart pounded hard at the sight of his well-
defined chest. A twinge of trepidation plagued her at the
thought that her body was not nearly so nicely toned.

"You're beautiful," he whispered, as if reading her
mind.

She took a deep breath and met that hungry gray gaze.
Though she'd carefully selected delicate, feminine under-
garments, she still felt like an old woman dressed in pastel-
yellow designer lace and satin.

"So are you," she whispered back, unable to resist
touching him a moment longer. Her palms smoothed over
the masculine contours, tingled at the raspy feel of his chest
hair. She traced every line and ridge, reveled in the powerful muscles that felt so hard and smooth. He had such an
amazing torso. She wanted to see more.

She reached for his belt and he stayed her hands. "There

are some things that you might not find so appealing," he reminded gently.

Her heart thumped hard. The prosthesis. All those years ago as a prisoner of war, he'd saved her husband's life, but he'd lost his right leg from the knee down while doing so. She'd forgotten all about that. Lucas Camp was the kind of man who exuded power and strength, obliterating any doubt in his physical prowess. She'd completely forgotten the matter of his prosthesis.

She looked up into his eyes and said the words she knew he needed to hear. "I love you, Lucas. I can't imagine a man more appealing in every way."

He removed his shoes, then unfastened his belt and his trousers. He sat down on the side of the bed and removed the trousers as well as the prosthesis. He sat there a few moments, wearing nothing but his boxers, before meeting her eyes.

"You sure about that?" he asked, looking more vulnerable than she could ever have anticipated. Lucas Camp was not a man one associated with any sort of vulnerability.

She sat down beside him and took his hand, his unguarded fragility leveling the playing ground more than he could possibly know. "Positive."

He touched her hair, his expression reverent. "I've wanted to touch you this way for so very long."

Her pulse leaped at his words. "I know. I'm sorry I've kept you waiting."

His fingers trailed down her back and she turned to give him better access to the closure of her bra. He released the hooks and she shed the bra without hesitation, allowing him to see her slightly less-than-firm breasts.

His deep, satisfied sigh made her head spin just a little. "If you were any more beautiful I'm not sure my heart could take it." Moving slowly, giving her ample time to stop him, he reached up and cupped one breast.

A surge of longing made her gasp. The feel of his palm against her nipple, his strong fingers around her made her inner muscles quake with renewed anticipation. No one had touched her like this in more than fifteen years. How she had missed knowing a man this way.

She reached for him, taking her time, exploring his body more fully, careful of the bandages, while he acquainted himself with hers. He leaned closer and kissed her, his mouth hungry, his desperation undeniable. She drew away from him, scooted back onto the bed and lay down in invitation.

He slid off his boxers, revealing well-formed buttocks and muscled thighs. He eased down next to her and gently tugged her panties down her legs and off. He tossed the lacy scrap of fabric across the bed.

When he'd stretched out beside her once more she felt complete just feeling his warm body along the length of hers. "It feels so good just lying next to you," she admitted.

He played with her hair, allowing it to slip through his fingers and feather down against her skin. "You truly are beautiful, Victoria," he told her. He caressed her cheek. "Right now, before we take the next step, I want you to know that I love you and I will never allow anything to hurt you again. No matter what it takes."

His eyes were far too solemn…that worried her. "Lucas, is something wrong?" Was he having second thoughts? Had he learned news that he hesitated to share with her?

He shook his head. "Everything is perfect." With that he kissed her. Kissed her softly at first. His firm lips moving skillfully over hers, the taste of wine making her want to drink him in. His hand moved down her abdomen, and her entire body quivered with need. He tangled his fingers in the curls between her thighs and her breath caught harshly.

"It's been a long time," he whispered between kisses. "We need to take this slowly."

His touch was as skilled as his kisses. His fingers magical. He knew just how to touch her...how to draw out the desire. And then his mouth moved downward until those masterful lips had latched on to her breast.

Her fingers plunged into his silky hair, urging him on as her body built toward an almost forgotten crescendo. Every draw of his mouth, every dip of his fingers and she edged closer and closer to release. The heel of his hand rubbed firmly against her clitoris, making her writhe with longing. How much longer could she stand this building tension? It coiled harder, deeper until...her senses erupted. Her feminine muscles throbbed with climax...her whole body shuddered with it.

He parted her thighs and nestled himself there. The feel of his hardened length made her whimper his name. Her arms went around his waist as he slowly, carefully nudged inside. They both cried out as he sank deeply inside her. And for one long beat neither of them moved. They could only lie there, gasping for breath, caught in the sweet, sensual trap of pure desire.

He started to rock, gently at first, allowing her body to adjust. Eventually the pace and depth increased and then all else was forgotten.

He took her back to that place of sensual bliss before he plunged over the edge himself.

But Lucas Camp had never been a selfish man. He pleasured her well before taking his own and that only made her love him more.

When they lay side by side, still panting, and utterly sated, she hugged him tight to her side. "Lucas," she whispered.

"Hmmm," he murmured, his voice still rough with desire.

"I've made a decision."

"That we should have an encore?" he teased, then kissed her forehead.

"Well, that, too," she agreed. "But no, I was just thinking. I believe it's time you made an honest woman out of me."

CHAPTER THIRTY-SIX

THE GUN DANGLED from his fingers as Leberman stared down at the hole in his chest. Blood spread quickly across the front of his shirt, like the center of an ever-expanding bull's-eye.

He lifted that beady gaze and stared at the man who'd shot him. "Why?" The single word came out more a hiss of disbelief than pain.

Seth took aim again. "I told you if you came near me again I'd kill you."

"You swore you would fulfill this promise to me. You owe it to me," Leberman snarled with more strength than a man already dead should possess.

Seth made that sound that wasn't quite a laugh. "You're right. I do owe it to you and I won't fail to deliver."

"I was supposed...to see it...for myself," Leberman shouted the words between frantic gasps for breath.

"Use your imagination." The next shot split Leberman's skull right between the eyes. Blood and brain matter sprayed across the wall behind him like a bad Impressionist painting. He crumpled to the floor, and the girl he'd kidnapped screamed hysterically.

Tasha looked from Leberman's body to Seth. He stood in the doorway, his weapon still leveled, ready to fire, his face a blank canvas, devoid of any emotion whatsoever.

He had shoved her to the floor and fired a fatal shot in Leberman's direction before she could depress her own trigger. As she stared at the aftermath, she felt frozen by emotion. Not quite fear…not quite relief and confusion. Something in between.

Before she could gather her wits, Seth had snatched her weapon from her hand and stalked over to the girl cowering in the corner. She shook uncontrollably as he jerked her to her feet and pulled her arms away from her face. He surveyed her wound, which, to the best Tasha could tell, was superficial.

He pushed the girl toward the back door. "Get out."

The girl didn't hesitate, nor did she look back.

Tasha dove for the gun Leberman had dropped a split second before Seth's attention swung back to her.

She grabbed the weapon and lunged to her feet, shoving the barrel into Seth's face when he took a step in her direction. "Stop right there," she ordered.

He tucked the weapon he'd taken from her into the waistband of his jeans. As he did so she noticed the blood streaking his hands. She blinked, uncertain where it had come from. Then she knew. He'd ripped open his flesh while freeing himself.

Maybe she tied a better knot that she'd realized.

"Give me the weapons," she demanded. She tried to calm her racing heart and her whirling thoughts, but she kept seeing Leberman's head explode and wondering what had made Seth decide to kill him. And the girl…? He'd looked to see that she wasn't hurt that badly before he sent her scurrying away. Where had this sudden burst of compassion come from? It was like that first day when he'd taken her home and told her to warn her roommate that she'd better not hurt her again. How could this killer care what happened to anyone?

But somehow he did. On some level, anyway.

"Hand over the weapons," she repeated, her aim steady.

He looked at her with that impassive face and those ice-cold eyes. "You decide I wasn't worth saving after all."

If he'd uttered the words with any emotion whatsoever she might have felt a pang of regret. "I just don't want to end up dead like your friend over there." She jerked her head in Leberman's direction. "Why did you do that?" She had to know. The analytical part of her screamed for answers.

"Why I didn't let him kill you or why I killed him?" he asked, seemingly oblivious to the inhumanity of his own words.

"Why you...both," she demanded, annoyed at her inability to keep perspective here.

He glanced at the weapon in her hand then settled that arctic gaze on hers. "I warned him. He just kept coming back."

She swallowed, moistened her lips. "And what about me? Why am I still breathing?" As if to emphasize her words, a little soblike mewl escaped her lungs. She steeled herself, tightened her grip on her weapon. She might have to kill him yet. He didn't need to know how his actions had affected her.

But God, he was Victoria Colby's son.

Did Lucas know by now? Had the DNA test told him that?

And could she...could she actually do *it* if necessary?

He didn't answer her question, just turned his back on her. The move startled her from her worrisome quandary.

"Where are you going?" she demanded, altering the aim of her weapon to keep a bead on him.

He hesitated at the door just long enough to glance back at her. "I have a job to finish."

She followed him onto the rear deck of the house. "Wait," she shouted. "He's dead. What does it matter now? Don't you understand what this all means? Victoria Colby is your mother."

Even in the moonlight she could plainly see his savage

glare when he spun around to face her. "She's nothing to me," he ground out. "I hate her more than I hated Leberman."

She had to stop him—distract him—and she wasn't sure, knowing what she knew, that shooting him was actually an option. "Because you think she abandoned you," she called out after him, "left you to be rescued by the likes of Leberman. She loved you, Seth. He stole you away from her. This isn't her fault. They both loved you."

He turned around again but this time instead of just glowering at her he strode straight toward her. The murderous look on his face had her backing toward the house. He pinned her to the wall with his free hand. The light from inside the house cut across his face highlighting the fury contorting his features.

"If she loved me so damned much then why didn't she stop him?"

And there it was…the tiniest, almost imperceptible crack in his impervious armor. The little boy who'd been praying for a savior all these years peeked out.

"Because she couldn't find you," Tasha said softly. "She tried…but Leberman kept you hidden from her."

"I was right here," Seth snarled. "Right here in Chicago all that time. She didn't want me. Neither of them did. He told me that every day of my life. Every time he punished me, he reminded me that I would be nothing without him. So you tell me, Tasha, why the hell didn't she stop him?"

Pain flickered in his eyes for just one second before he banished it, but he couldn't erase the memory of what she'd seen. The emotion had been so achingly profound that her lips trembled with the empathy welling in her chest.

"You can't believe anything Leberman told you," she urged. "He did this to you to get back at the Colbys. He—"

"Just shut up!" Seth roared. "I know what I lived

through. What *she* let me live through. And now she's going to pay for that. I've waited a long time to have her look me in the eye and know.'' A muscle jumped in his tightly clenched jaw as he struggled to restrain the emotions she sensed were raging inside him. ''I want her to know what he did to me and then I want to watch her die.''

Tasha blinked back the tears that brimmed behind her lashes and glared right back at him. A part of her wanted desperately to hold him and make him see that it would be all right now, but part of her just wanted to kick the shit out of him and tell him what a jerk he was. ''Then I guess you'd better go ahead and kill me now because I'm not going to let you do this.'' She was betting that he wouldn't kill her. That he couldn't. She hoped like hell her instincts were on the money this time.

He pressed the muzzle of his weapon beneath her chin. She tensed. ''Do you really want to die? Is Lucas paying you enough to die for him?''

''This isn't about Lucas,'' she said, her voice shaking despite her best efforts to keep it steady. ''This is about you and your mother.''

The weapon bored painfully into the soft flesh. She winced. ''I don't have a mother,'' he said softly, lethally. ''I have a target.''

The sound of sirens in the distance snagged his attention. He swore. The girl had probably made it to the closest neighbor, which was quite a distance, and called the cops. A smidgen of Tasha's tension eddied away.

He snatched Leberman's weapon from her hand and tossed it into the grass. ''I guess you got yourself another reprieve. Just remember that you might not be so lucky next time.'' He released her and bounded across the deck and down the steps.

''You're not leaving me here to straighten out your mess,'' she yelled at his back as he headed toward the woods. She followed. If she planned to keep him in sight, she didn't have time to search for the weapon he'd tossed.

As hard as it was she managed to stay within a few meters of him. Thank God she'd kept in shape. At one point he tried to lose her, but she didn't take the bait. She just kept dogging his steps. When they reached the clearing where he'd originally brought her, to kill her she imagined, he stopped abruptly and turned around.

"Why are you following me?"

She took a moment to catch her breath. "Because I have to stop you."

He charged up to her, didn't even bother to draw his weapon from his shoulder holster. But then, he was a lot bigger than her. She held her ground, refused to let him see her uneasiness.

"That's not going to happen. Don't try to pretend you're not afraid of me," he murmured. "I know you are."

"I've had sufficient training to give you a run for your money if you want to go hand-to-hand," she shot right back, hoping like hell she wouldn't have to back that up.

He laughed softly. "I can see your pulse fluttering. You're definitely scared."

She touched her throat, had forgotten how well he could see in the dark. She parked her hands on her hips. "How do you know it's fear?" She couldn't be sure of the exact timing of Lucas's and Victoria's departure. Keeping him away from Victoria's private residence for as long as possible was essential. Not to mention it would keep him alive. The last word she'd heard, Lucas's men had been ordered to take him out.

A beat of silence passed. Her tension escalated to an unbearable level in that one moment.

"Your cover is blown, Agent North," he taunted. "No need to keep up the precept. You don't have to pretend to be attracted to me any longer."

"Who says I was pretending?" Her heart was racing all over again, only this time it had nothing to do with having to run like hell to keep up with him. It was hard to believe that she'd just watched him kill a man—lowlife bastard though he was—and still he could make her respond to him this way.

She couldn't see his face clearly, but she knew she'd given him pause. She could sense his hesitation...his need to pursue the issue. But he never catered to his own needs.

"Stay away from me," he growled. "If you know what's good for you, stay away from me."

She didn't hesitate. When he walked away this time, she followed him again. How else was she supposed to get out of here, anyway?

When they reached his SUV, he glared at her once more before climbing inside. Not about to back off now, she glared right back and climbed in herself.

She stared at the vacant house while he shoved the keys into the ignition.

"Last chance," he said quietly. "Get out while you still can."

She looked at the digital clock on his dash—11:00 p.m. Surely Lucas and Victoria were gone by now. She could very well get out...she'd done the only thing necessary to fulfill her mission. She'd kept him out of the way while they escaped. Though she hadn't been able to lead Lucas to...

Leberman was dead.

The realization penetrated the confusing layers of emotion that had wrapped around her good sense. He was dead. She had to get word to Lucas. That bastard was dead... would never bother them again.

But then there was Seth. He was hell-bent on killing Victoria for her part in what happened to him. A part of Tasha understood what he felt...but she knew the truth.

How could she make him see that truth? What could she do to ensure a safe conclusion to this assignment?

Victoria's son was alive.

She should have the opportunity to know him...to make everything right.

But if he had his way that would never happen.

His mother would die.

Somehow she had to keep that from happening.

Since she made no move to get out, he started the vehicle and backed out into the street.

He drove in silence until he pulled into the parking lot of a gas station not unlike the one Martin had lured her to. That felt like a lifetime ago. Would he want her back, knowing she'd screwed up so badly here? Then again, Lucas had told her she had a job. She pushed away the thoughts. All she could think about right now was the moment.

The gas station was closed, ruling out the possibility of a fueling stop, since the pumps were the old-fashioned kind that didn't accept credit cards.

"Why are we stopping here?"

He didn't answer. He simply got out and walked around to her door. He opened it and barked an order. "Get out."

With a roll of her eyes and a huff of disgust, she obeyed. Somebody needed to teach this guy some manners. He opened the door to the men's room and ushered her inside.

Even in the dark she imagined the worst about the place. The smell wasn't as bad as she'd expected, but bleach would camouflage most anything and the bleach smell was damn strong. He flipped on the light and she was relieved to see that the bathroom was actually halfway clean, which was so not what she needed to worry about right now.

When he unzipped his jeans she cursed under her breath and gave him her back. He couldn't have taken a leak in the woods where it was dark? She huffed in frustration. Maybe not…the police had been headed their way.

He ignored her sounds of protest, simply did his business. She tried to block the sound of him taking a piss, but it just didn't work.

She knew this wasn't right. Why hadn't he just disposed of her? Gotten her out of his way? He knew her intentions and yet he allowed her to live. No matter how he denied it, there was some kind of weird connection between them, and it wasn't just the sex. She wished she could understand it. The toilet flushed and the water in the basin came on. She turned around and watched as he washed the blood from his wrists and hands. The cuts her bindings had made were nasty, but he didn't even flinch. She wondered if he'd learned to ignore the pain when Leberman punished him. Had he ignored all the other atrocities he'd suffered in much the same way?

She blocked the vivid mental images the words echoing inside her head evoked. Just the thought of all that he'd suffered made her insides quake with emotion. Victoria would be devastated when she learned the truth. No matter how this ended, both of them would suffer. But there could be light at the end of the tunnel…if he'd only listen to her, open up fully to her. Trust her.

He tossed the paper towel he'd used to dry his hands into the trash, then gestured to the toilet. "It might be a while before we see another one."

"No, thanks."

She studied his eyes, his face. How could she get through to him? Could anything touch him at this point?

He reached for the door but she snagged his hand, her pulse leaping at the contact. "Does it hurt?" She turned his hand over, inspecting the damage he'd done freeing himself. "Must have hurt like hell," she murmured. If he hadn't gotten free, Leberman might have killed her before she could kill him.

He pulled his hand away. "Don't start anything you're not prepared to finish."

Did her touch have that effect on him? She definitely felt something when he touched her…. What difference did it make? She would never be able to get through to him. She definitely wasn't qualified to analyze this guy. She had to stop thinking that way.

She turned her back on him and reached for the door herself. There was nothing she could say to that remark. She wasn't prepared to go there again…didn't trust herself to hold on to any semblance of perspective and go there.

"I guess reality dampened your case of the hots for me," he accused. She didn't miss the edge in his voice. She'd hurt him somehow by turning away.

She did an immediate about-face. "Do you want to know the truth? Do you think you can handle the truth?" she challenged.

Anger slashed across his face, but he tamped it down. "Don't play with me, Tasha."

She couldn't stop the shiver that trembled through her at the sound of her name on his lips. "The truth is that hearing about your past made me sad for the little boy you used to be. Made me wish I could do something to change it. But I can't. Nothing I could say or do is going to change how twisted you are. But none of that has anything to do with how I feel about the man standing in front of me."

She watched that wall go up as he went on guard.

"I hate what you do," she told him bluntly. "You're a cold-blooded killer. But there's still something decent inside you, and that part cries out to me. I can feel it." She peered into those ice-cold eyes. "I can almost touch it. Don't bother denying it, I know it's there…just waiting to break free."

He forked the fingers of his left hand into her hair and pulled her close. "The only thing crying out for you is right here." He pressed her hand against his crotch. "Can you handle that truth?"

She lifted her chin in defiance of his challenge. He needed the contact. Had just killed his long-term caretaker. He needed her even if he would never admit it. "I can handle it, but we do it my way this time." As much as she knew she shouldn't let this happen, it would delay his discovery that Victoria was now out of his reach. It would... help him forget.

He shrugged. "As long as your way is right now." His mouth claimed hers. He kissed her so hard it hurt.

She pushed him away and shook her head. "Not like that." She tiptoed and kissed him softly. "Like this." She kissed him again and again, feather-soft kisses. He resisted at first, hating the very idea of doing things her way. But then he relented, gave himself up to the temptation she offered.

Forcing all else from her mind, she put everything she had into kissing him. She wanted him to know how it felt to really be kissed, sweetly, passionately...tenderly.

He responded in kind, gentling the pressure of his lips, moving more slowly, mimicking her moves. His hands moved under her blouse...found her breasts and squeezed hard. She drew back and murmured, "Not so rough."

He tensed briefly, then lightened his touch. She let him hear how much his touching her that way pleased her. He released the buttons of her blouse quickly, fumbling once or twice, and then he laved her bare breasts with his mouth. She closed her eyes and groaned with the pleasure of it. He sucked urgently, but not to the point of pain as he had before. He dropped to his knees and unfastened her jeans and dragged them downward, along with her panties. She toed off her shoes and kicked free of the garments he'd peeled down to her ankles.

He tongued her navel, then lapped her skin. Slowly, surely driving her out of her mind and making a path to her sex, spreading her legs until his mouth was centered where he could thrust his tongue inside. Every thrust grew stronger, more impatient as her legs quivered beneath her. She plunged her fingers into his hair and urged on his ministrations.

Her whole body verged on climax. She couldn't stop panting…couldn't catch her breath… Then he stopped. Sat back on his heels and just.looked at her.

She made a desperate sound. "You can't stop now," she pleaded. She closed her eyes. Damn, she was so close. Her heart pounded even harder in protest.

He dragged her hand to where she was burning up with slick heat for him. "Finish it. I want to watch you come."

She laughed, a breathless sound. "I…need you to—"

"Finish it," he ordered, his eyes aglow with blue heat.

She flattened her spine against the cool metal of the door and groaned. She was so close…and he was watching her so intently. A ghost of a smile tipped one corner of his mouth, and victory claimed his expression. "Can't do it, huh?"

He thought he'd won…had turned the tide.

No way.

She touched herself and gasped at the sensitivity. He had her so close that any contact would likely set her off. Oh, yes, she could do this. She squeezed her eyes shut and slid her fingers into the heated flesh…lost herself to the rhythm. Her free hand fisted in the cotton of her blouse as she strained to reach that elusive pinnacle he'd brought her to the very crest of. And then she flew over the edge. Her body stiffened then quivered as wave after wave of sensation washed over her.

When the last of the release had shuddered through her, her eyes opened to find him still watching.

She sighed and shook her head. "You bastard, now you're going to pay."

He pushed upward to his full height, going for intimidation, but she was way past being intimidated.

She unbuttoned his shirt, revealed his scarred chest and relished the feel of his warm flesh beneath her palms. "Sit down," she ordered. She pushed him back toward the toilet.

He sat without much persuasion, his curiosity piqued.

She straddled his lap and pressed herself intimately to him. The bulge in his jeans told her he was doing a little suffering of his own.

Carefully tracing every line and mark on his flesh, she kissed him repeatedly. His mouth, his eyes, his chiseled jaw. Too many places to remember, all the while she rocked against his hardened sex. Finally, when he'd had all he could take, he drew her back to look him in the eyes.

"This isn't enough," he said breathlessly.

"It'll have to be enough," she threatened. "Or maybe you want to finish it yourself."

Those blue eyes closed as she pressed against him yet again. "No," he growled, the sound strangled. He reached beneath her and unfastened his jeans, pulled his throbbing penis from its confines. "I need..." He lost his voice... groaned as she lightly rubbed herself against his tip.

"You need what?"

"You," he confessed in desperation.

She smiled. "That's all I wanted to hear."

That hot, hard flesh touched her, and a ripple of pleasure went through her. She lifted her hips slightly, while he positioned himself. She let her weight down just a fraction, bringing him inside an inch or two. She moaned with the exquisite feel of him, but she held on to control, resisting the urge to sink down fully onto that incredibly hot length.

He arched upward but she reacted too quickly, not allowing him additional penetration. A ragged breath hissed from between his clenched teeth.

She kept up the game a while longer, easing down an inch, then lifting until she couldn't stand it any longer... until he visibly shook with need. Then she plunged downward, sheathing him fully inside her. His startled gasp almost sent her over the edge again.

She kissed him...softly, as she set a slow, steady pace of rising and falling...of squeezing and tugging. When he came, his whole body jerked with the force of it and he cried out her name. She followed him over that edge, her climax so powerful her chest ached with the gravity of it.

He held her for a long while after that, the feel of his heart beating bringing a new rush of tears to her eyes.

Somehow she knew that this moment was a first for him. The way he held her...awkwardly almost. He didn't know how to do this...how to relate on this level.

It would be morning soon, and then he'd know that Victoria and Lucas were gone.

That moment was one she had no idea how to control.

She just hoped they all survived it.

CHAPTER THIRTY-SEVEN

TASHA WATCHED the sun rise from the darkness of the SUV. Seth had parked in a position where he could watch Victoria Colby's private residence from the neighboring residential area. A few more minutes, an hour tops, and he would realize that something was wrong. How fitting that it was Halloween. A holiday celebrating the dead. A group they would both likely join before the day was up.

She glanced at his profile now. A fresh wave of emotion flooded her. Each time she thought of what he'd experienced as a child she wanted to weep.

Lucas had shown her that grainy photograph in the beginning, had estimated his age at thirty, but that was wrong. Seth, James Colby Jr., was a mere twenty-five years old. But he looked several years older. The cruelty Leberman had dealt him was engrained in his very flesh. The scars, the memories he carried of each one, the damage to his state of mind were unfathomable. There were ways, she knew, to deal with that kind of damage, but it would be a long, drawn-out process. Leberman had likely used a form of intensive brainwashing. He'd instilled a certainty in Seth that his parents didn't love or want him. That they were evil. The little boy had forgotten any memories he'd made with his family; those memories had been replaced with sheer hatred and terror. He'd been punished every day of his life for his parents' perceived sins.

Was it possible to overcome such abuse? Years and years of physical and mental torture that accumulated like the dust on an air filter, eventually, if unchecked, clogging the system, shutting it down. She now understood why he had killed Leberman. Though the man had held immense power over him as a child and even to some extent as he became a man, Seth reached a point where Leberman no longer controlled him. The two men had simply shared a common goal—the destruction of the Colbys. That common goal had dragged out the relationship when it would have otherwise ended.

If the house at Oak Park was, as she suspected, the one Leberman had used to hold him hostage as a child, the memories it evoked in Seth might have pushed him closer to the edge. Might have given him the necessary determination to end Leberman's control once and for all.

The part she couldn't begin to comprehend was how to awaken those old memories of his seven years with his family before Leberman. If she could just reach that place somehow. Make him see how much they'd loved him, maybe—just maybe—some emotion would surface and strike a chord of recognition…alter his course.

Every bit of it was nothing but speculation. She was not a psychiatrist just a psychology major. She understood to a degree the workings of the human psyche, but there was a lot more involved than her minimal understanding could encompass. What she did know with complete certainty was that she had to find a way to let Lucas know that Leberman was dead. To make sure he knew who Seth really was.

The police. She suddenly remembered the sirens at the lake house. They would have found Leberman's body. Lucas would know by now, she felt certain.

She could only imagine how this turn of events would affect Victoria Colby. When she learned how Leberman had treated her child and how very close he had been—

literally hidden in plain sight—it would devastate her. But he had to know.

The past was here…right in front of her.

"Something's wrong."

The sound of his deep voice startled her back to attention. Tasha folded her arms over her chest to hide her trembling fingers.

"What do you mean? It's still early." Only 5:00 a.m. But he'd likely watched Victoria long enough to know her routine. He would spot an inconsistency in a heartbeat.

"She's usually up by now." He started the engine. "I'm going to take a closer look."

The guards at the gate didn't arrive until 6:00…that could only mean that he had the access code to the small supposedly secure community.

"How will we get in?" she ventured.

"The same way you got into the lake house," he answered, tossing a look that said "don't yank my chain" at her.

She nodded. "Right." She might as well chill out and follow his lead.

Seth's instincts were humming. Tasha knew something. He could feel it.

He drove to the gate, braking long enough to enter the access code. The gate opened and he drove into the small *secure* community Victoria Colby called home.

He stole another covert glance at Tasha. She'd been strangely quiet all morning. Nothing at all like the sassy girl he'd met that first night, but then, that had been an act. Just as, he felt certain, was her physical responses to him. Though some of her reactions couldn't be faked, the tenderness she displayed…the compassion, that was likely part of her job. She wanted him to believe she'd fallen for him. But he knew better.

No one would want him. He was nothing.

Less than nothing.

And that didn't matter…all that mattered was accomplishing his goal.

His jaw hardened instantly at the memory of Leberman aiming that gun at her. Had the bastard really believed that he would allow him to continue to interfere with his plans? Seth would follow through with the commitment he'd made, but doing so was no longer for Leberman. It was for him. He *wanted* to watch Victoria die. Had waited for years to experience that climatic moment.

Leberman had told him over and over how his parents hadn't wanted him. He'd only been in the way. They had only cared about the Colby Agency and he had been left to fend for himself. The memories twisted in his gut, burned in his brain. He'd been alone and helpless… vulnerable. But no one had given a damn. All that he had suffered had been because she had allowed it. She didn't deserve to live.

Leberman hadn't deserved to live either. He had punished him one time too many. He would never touch him again. Would never gloat about how he'd created him… saved him. Seth owed him nothing. He only owed himself. He felt no guilt, no regret, no nothing for what he'd done.

Leberman had trained him too well.

Seth blocked the thoughts from his mind. Focus and absolute control were essential to the success of his mission. Lucas would want him dead…would be guarding Victoria closely. But that wouldn't change the outcome.

Victoria Colby would die.

And so would anyone else who got in the way.

His gut clenched when his gaze shifted to Tasha for one fleeting second. She was not important, he reminded that part of him that hesitated. The fact that she had brought him to his knees, in a manner of speaking, last night in that rest room, made no difference this morning. It was true that sex had never affected him that way and that no woman had ever reached so deep inside him. But, ultimately, it meant nothing. He'd learned the hard way never to trust a single emotion...only his instincts.

He parked across the street from the Colby house and waited. Watched. The sun climbed above the treetops and poured its warming rays down on the small cul-de-sac and still nothing changed. No lights came on inside. No movement anywhere on the grounds.

There was no one here.

He opened the vehicle door and climbed out.

"What're you doing? You shouldn't—"

He shut the door, cutting her off.

Moving slowly, scanning continuously for any movement, he walked across the street, up the sidewalk and to her front door without encountering resistance.

Fury started to simmer deep in his gut.

Tasha moved up behind him. "We should get out of here before Lucas's men spot us," she urged.

He turned on her, then, his patience at an end. "There's no one here." He reached into his pocket and retrieved the key and unlocked the door and then disarmed the security system. They'd changed the code but he already had the new one. Leberman had never failed to provide the essential details.

"You have a key?" She stared at him, slack-jawed with surprise and still standing on the outside of the threshold.

"Close the door," he ordered. The last thing he needed was a neighbor calling the police to report an unknown intruder. He needed time to assess the situation. When she obeyed, he locked the door and reset the alarm.

Seth moved through the house, checking room after room. Nothing. He went back to her bedroom and checked the walk-in closet. He had memorized exactly how it looked before. Several items were missing. She'd packed light, but she was gone. Her scent still lingered in the air making his jaw clench and his gut tie in knots.

He spun around and pointed the rage building inside him directly at his only connection to Lucas. "Where is she?"

Tasha shook her head. "I don't know."

He grabbed her by the shoulders and shook her, control slipping away. Leberman always provided the details... gave him the orders. Confusion slowed his ability to think but he quickly regained control. He was in charge now. He didn't need Leberman. "Tell me where she is."

"I swear I don't know."

She was telling the truth. He could see it in her eyes. He could also see the fear. She didn't want to be afraid of him but she was.

He gritted his teeth.

She should be. He could not fail.

The telephone on the table next to Victoria's bed rang. Seth released her and glanced at it.

"Answer it," he ordered, turning back to her. "It'll be for you." They were watching. He didn't need to recognize the number on the caller ID or make visual contact with the enemy to confirm it. He knew they would be.

She moistened her lips. "What should I say?"

"Tell him to give me Victoria's location or you die. That if he comes near this house, you'll die."

To her credit she didn't flinch. "That won't matter."

"Just answer it!" he roared as he drew his weapon. He had to know where she was! He swallowed hard, fought the dizzying sensations clawing at his composure.

Tasha nodded reluctantly. When she reached for the receiver he moved closer, put his head next to hers so that he could hear the other end of the conversation, as well.

"Hello." Her voice sounded shaky.

He didn't give a damn. He just needed that location. He

had allowed her to distract him last night and now they were one step ahead of him.

"North, are you all right?"

Male. Not Lucas.

"Yes," she said. "We're fine."

With those two words she'd just let the caller know that he was listening. She was no fool.

Maybe he was the fool.

"He wants to know where Victoria is," she said bluntly. "If you don't tell him he says he'll kill me. If you come near the house, he'll kill me."

"I understand. I can't give you that information because I don't have it," the man explained. "But I'll contact Lucas for further instructions. I'll call you back at this number in a few minutes. Stay calm, North. We've got your back."

Seth wondered if the man was stupid enough to believe he could stop him.

"Leberman is dead," she blurted as he snatched the receiver from her to hang it up. Seth didn't miss the other man's response. "We know." He slammed the receiver back into its cradle and glared at her.

"Don't do this, Seth. They'll kill you. When I told you I thought you were worth saving, I meant it. Don't let this happen. Leberman is gone. He was the one who caused you all this pain. Let it go."

"Shut up." He didn't want to hear about how the woman who called herself his mother really loved him and still grieved for him. He didn't want to hear any of it.

"Please listen to me." She touched his arm. He jerked away from her. Hurt glimmered in those brown eyes. A ploy, he told himself. She wanted him to believe she cared.

No one cared if he lived or died.

He didn't even care. He existed for one purpose only. For vengeance.

He dragged her from the room and down the hall. He

needed to set up surveillance around the perimeter. Lucas's men would be moving in for the kill, if they hadn't already.

He hesitated outside the door to the guest room and glanced inside. Victoria's house was always meticulously neat. The box and its scattered contents on the bed didn't fit. He moved in that direction to investigate. What he found had him dropping down on the mattress for a closer look.

Tasha eased onto the bed and picked up first one item and then the next. The shuffling of photographs and papers echoed in the stark silence that followed.

His heart rate steadily increased as one alien sensation after the other bombarded him.

"This is you," she murmured, pointing to a picture of him as a small boy, James Colby kneeling beside him, smiles beaming from both their faces.

"This, too."

She picked up picture after picture of little Jimmy Colby. His father showing him how to ride a bike. His mother playing in the sand on a beach with him. The whole family, all smiles, in front of the castle at Disney World.

He didn't remember any of it. It was like looking at pictures of strangers. But somehow the images affected him…confused him.

Then there were stuffed animals, a baseball with some famous player's autograph, tiny race cars…childish artwork. But none of it gripped his insides like the newspaper articles he looked at next. He scanned headline after headline. All focused on the massive search for one missing boy. He read the quotes from James and Victoria Colby. The pleas for the return of their son. The million-dollar reward they'd offered.

His hands started to shake and it was hard to see.

He scrubbed at his eyes and his hand came away wet. It

had to be a trick...couldn't be real. Leberman had told him over and over...

Tasha peered up at him from the article she'd been reading, tears streaming down her cheeks. "Would people who didn't want you...who didn't love you...have done all this?"

He lunged to his feet, a new fury building inside him burning away the other sensations. It was meant to confuse him. All of it. This box had been left here to throw him off course and make him second-guess what he knew.

"Let's go."

"But Maverick's going to call back with word from Lucas," she protested as she got up, some of the yellowed-with-age clippings still in her hand.

"We're not waiting."

She retreated when he reached for her. "But how are you going to find her if you don't wait for the call?"

He grabbed Tasha by the arm and jerked her close, staring into those emotion-filled eyes with all the savage rage burning inside him, searing away the lingering remnants of those alien feelings he'd experienced only moments before. "If she loves me so damned much, she'll find me."

CHAPTER THIRTY-EIGHT

THEY SAT ON THE DECK and enjoyed coffee, with the morning sun sparkling across the still water. Lucas knew without doubt that he could spend the rest of his life doing nothing but looking at Victoria. Making love with her had completed the bond he'd felt for her all these years. Had sealed his fate.

She'd been right when she said it was time he made an honest woman out of her. They'd laughed about it afterward. But it was no laughing matter. They were no longer young with a lifetime ahead of them. He wanted to share the rest of his years on this earth with her…like this.

But first he had to tell her the truth. He could not hold back that knowledge any longer.

"Victoria, I've made a decision of my own this morning," he announced with as much cheer as he could summon.

She sat down her mug of warm coffee and peered across the table at him. "Oh, really. And what decision is that?" She smiled, and all those years of pain and suffering etched on her face disappeared.

God, how he hated to resurrect this part of her past.

But he had no choice.

Maverick had called. "He" wanted a face-to-face with Victoria. Or Tasha would die.

Lucas would ensure Tasha's safety, one way or another, even if it meant exchanging himself for her. There was no way he was letting this man anywhere near Victoria. But he couldn't make this move without Victoria's full understanding of what might happen in the course of protecting her. Her son might have to die.

"You were right last night," he said, delaying the inevitable. "You know I would have asked you to marry me long ago had I felt you were ready." Her little comment last night was her way of letting him know she was ready. Warmth spread through his chest. She wanted to be his wife. Whether he lived to see that happen or not, simply knowing gave him more joy than she could imagine.

"Lucas." She placed her hand on his. "I made you wait a very long time. I'm so thankful for your patience, but it's time now. Our time."

He nodded. "You're more right than you know. I have news."

She sat up a little straighter. "What news?"

"Leberman is dead." He'd learned this information hours earlier, but he'd waited until morning to tell her, not wanting to spoil their night. Now he was glad he had. At least this news would temper the rest.

Her breath caught, then she released it in a sigh filled with equal parts confusion and relief. "How?"

Now for the hard part. "The assassin he hired, or coerced into stalking you, killed him."

Her hand went to her chest. "My God. What does this mean?" She shook her head. "Other than the obvious. I mean, you're sure it's Leberman. The bastard is really dead."

Lucas nodded. "It's him."

"But the assassin still poses a threat?" she guessed.

He nodded again. "He has his own ax to grind with you."

She frowned. "Should I know this man?"

Lucas took the hand she'd placed over his and held it firmly. "I want you to know up front that I've confirmed his identification through DNA. There is no question as to who he is. But you also have to understand that he's not the same. It's him, but…it isn't really. I don't know all the details just yet but I suspect brainwashing at the very least.''

"You're scaring me, Lucas," she said softly.

He felt a fine tremor go through her. Saw the tension turn her posture more rigid, tighten the features of her face.

"There's no other way to tell you this, Victoria. This assassin is your son.''

For several seconds she simply stared at him. Shock, disbelief, horror, all danced like frantic shadows across her face.

"That's impossible,'' she finally said, her voice as thin and fragile as handblown glass.

"It's difficult to comprehend, but it's true.''

She blinked back the tears shining in her dark eyes. "Well, that's…insane. Why would my son want to kill me? Why would he be following Leberman's orders? The shirt…''

"Victoria." Lucas leaned forward, wrapped his other hand over hers as well. She started to shake…the shock, he knew. "He's been brainwashed. He's not the same. He doesn't understand what really happened.''

Victoria stiffened, fury sent a flush up her neck and across her face. "What did that monster do to him?''

Her breathing became labored, and Lucas knew she was about to break down. He shoved out of his chair and moved beside her. "We don't know all the details yet.''

She snatched her hand away. "How long have you known?''

"Not very long," he hedged.

"I want to see him.'' She pushed to her feet, knocking over her chair. "I want to see him now.''

Lucas stood, reached for her, but she retreated too

quickly. "You have to understand that he's still a danger to you."

"My own son wants to kill me," she lashed out. "Why is that? What did Leberman do to him? Tell me, Lucas!"

He dropped his hands to his sides. There was no point in trying to do this rationally. There was nothing rational about it. He couldn't spare her feelings. There was no lighter side...no saving grace to any of this.

"We only know that there are lots of scars. He doesn't appear to feel any kind of emotion. He killed Leberman last night." Lucas looked directly into her eyes, hoping he could reassure her as he told her the rest. "His intentions are to kill you next."

She closed her eyes as the import of those words rocked through her. Lucas's chest squeezed painfully. What he would give not to have to put her through this.

When she looked at him again, she said the last thing he wanted to hear. "Arrange a meeting." She squared her shoulders and struggled to put a stop to the visible shaking. "I want to see my son...even if it kills me."

CHAPTER THIRTY-NINE

"YOU HAVE TO BE RESONABLE, Victoria," Lucas argued.

"Reasonable?" She looked directly at him, those dark eyes clear and crackling with determination. "What's reasonable about any of this?"

Lucas wanted to throw up his hands. Wanted to hog-tie her and throw her over his shoulder and carry her away to safety. All reason had fled from her the moment he'd told her the truth about the assassin.

Lucas couldn't bring himself to consider this man bent on killing Victoria as her son. He supposed, to a degree, he was being irrational, as well. The only difference was he was trying to save her life.

"You've ordered my men to leave," he argued. "You want to just let this man—this killer, need I remind you—waltz in here and do whatever he pleases."

"That killer," she said pointedly, "is my child."

"Yes, I understand that he's your child," he half shouted, exasperated. "I understand it well."

She shook her head, tears welling in her eyes once more. "You can't possibly. Lucas, I know you love me, but you can't possibly even fathom how this feels." She moved closer to him, her hands clasped together in front of her. "I carried him inside me for nine months...held him close to my heart as a baby, then taught him how to tie his shoes...how to brush his teeth properly. I tucked him into bed at night, read stories with him. He felt safe with me." A single teardrop slipped down her cheek. "And I let him down. I let that monster steal him from me and I couldn't save him. Can you honestly say that you…'' She paused a moment to compose herself. ''You can't know how that feels.''

He pulled her into his arms, held on tight when she resisted. ''You're right,'' he confessed softly. ''I can't possibly know how it feels. But, dear God, I can't let him harm you. Can you understand that?''

She nodded. ''I know it's because you love me. But I have to do this, Lucas. I have to. Because he's my son, and I love him.''

He did understand that. But he would do this his way. She didn't have to know that his people had taken up sniper positions all around the cabin. He'd insisted the meeting take place on the deck just for that reason. Inside, his people couldn't put a bullet in the assassin's head. He suppressed a shudder at the too-vivid image that accompanied that thought.

Killing her son was the last thing he wanted to have to do, but he had ordered his men to trust their instincts. His Specialists would not shoot to kill unless it was absolutely necessary.

Back at the Colby Agency Ian and Simon had been put on alert. Victoria had insisted that they merely stand by. Neither of the men liked it, but would obey her orders, just as Lucas's would obey his.

He held the woman in his arms more firmly for a few seconds more, then drew back to look into her eyes. ''As much as I hate to admit it, I do understand that you feel compelled to do this. But you must understand also that I will do whatever I have to in order to protect you.''

She smiled faintly. ''That's a given, Lucas.'' She took his hands in hers and held them close to her heart. ''I only wish I could protect you, but you won't go, as I've asked you to. I'd rather you were safe from whatever is going to take place.''

Asked? She'd demanded that he leave her here alone. She could forget that one. He gave her an answering smile. ''Well, I guess we'll just have to face this together.''

Tears glimmered in her eyes once more. ''Then so be it.''

He desperately hoped it wouldn't be the last thing they did together.

SETH BRAKED TO A STOP at the entrance to the long drive that would take them to the cabin where Lucas and Victoria waited.

Tasha watched Seth survey their surroundings. The woods were dense, most of the brilliant fall foliage still clinging to their limbs. Vivid hues of orange and gold and rust against the varying shades of gray bark formed an ironically natural backdrop for the wholly unnatural scene about to play out.

Seth was intent on killing his mother. She knew his plan. Lucas, no doubt, had estimated what he had in mind, as well. Though they might sit here now and see nothing but the lovely forest landscape, danger lurked in every direction. Lucas's Specialists would have taken careful positions to protect their leader and the woman he loved.

''They're going to kill you, you know,'' Tasha murmured as much to herself as to him. He knew exactly what was going to happen and he didn't care. But she did...she cared far more than she should.

''Not before I accomplish my goal,'' he said without reservation. And she didn't doubt his certainty.

He intended to tell Victoria Colby what Leberman had done to him and then he fully intended to kill her.

There would be no happy ending.

Dread and fear and regret all churned in Tasha's stomach. Whatever happened this afternoon, no one would walk away untouched by the horror of Errol Leberman.

The bastard had won.

The SUV rolled forward, slowly making its way down the long, narrow dirt-and-gravel road that led to certain death.

Though Maverick had given her specific orders along with the time and place of the meeting when Seth finally allowed her to call him back, she had no intention of obeying those orders. He'd told her to stay out of the line of fire, not to get involved.

She knew what that meant. They had it covered. Every possible scenario had been run. Every precaution taken. As far as they were concerned, if anyone died today it would not be Victoria Colby or Lucas Camp. Tasha was to stay out of the way. Seth would be terminated if they couldn't control the situation. She didn't need anyone to spell it out for her.

Seth had to know this. He was far too smart to believe he would get away with what he had planned. Simply walking in and shooting Victoria wasn't going to happen. But something inside him had changed after he'd looked at those photographs and newspaper clippings. The rage was still there but it was different somehow.

He stopped in front of the cabin and turned off the engine. He took out his 9mm and faced her. "Slide over the console and get out on my side."

"Wait." She grabbed him by the shirtsleeve when he would have opened his door. "It's not too late to just drive away." She searched that icy gaze for any flicker of uncertainty and found none.

"It's been too late for eighteen years."

There was something in his voice…some emotion that she'd never heard before. "Seth, I don't want you to die."

For one fleeting instant she thought she'd reached him.

He looked at her with an intensity that made her believe he felt something for her...something beyond the physical attraction.

"I'm already dead."

With that simple yet profound statement he got out of the vehicle and she had no choice but to follow. She blinked back the tears and cursed herself for loss of all professionalism. What the hell kind of field operative would she make if she couldn't keep it together any better than this?

His weapon resting against the back of her skull, she led the way around the cabin to the back deck, just as Lucas had ordered. Other than the occasional seagull and the lapping of water against the shoreline, absolute silence crushed in around them. She felt the weight of it directly on her chest, making each breath difficult.

When they rounded the rear corner of the cabin, the deck came into view.

Tasha tried to slow her step, but he urged her forward with the muzzle of his 9mm. Victoria waited on the deck, Lucas at her side. Neither of them appeared armed.

As they moved up the steps, Tasha could see the devastation and the anticipation cluttering Victoria's weary face. She drank in the sight of her son as if he were the answer to her prayers rather than an assassin determined to end her life. And he was. She had likely prayed ceaselessly for his return. Did it have to end like this?

"Jimmy?" she offered, her expression so hopeful it made Tasha's heart ache to look at her.

Seth pushed Tasha aside, leaving nothing between him and Victoria except a six-foot span of thick-with-tension air and aged wooden deck.

"That's right," he said tightly. "Your long-lost son has returned."

His every feature was set in stone. His eyes as cold as

ice as he stared at the woman who had given birth to him…who'd loved him and cared for him for the first seven years of his life. But he didn't remember that time… Leberman had erased it. Had tortured him until he forgot all else but the pain. Until he knew nothing but the lies.

"Don't do this, Seth," Tasha pleaded, praying somehow her voice would get through to him. The hand holding his weapon hung loosely at his side. If he lifted it, even a fraction, she was certain he would be terminated.

"Listen to her," Lucas urged. "Leberman is dead. Let the past die with him. You've got a chance for a new beginning here. We know he did this to you. We—"

Fury erupted across Seth's face and he aimed all that rage at Lucas then. "You don't know anything." He ripped open his shirt with his free hand, displaying the hideous scars like badges of honor. "You have no idea what I've endured. What *he* did to me." He turned back to Victoria. "What he paid others to do to me."

Victoria drew in a shuddering breath. "I would give anything to change that." Tears spilled past her lashes, and Tasha's heart squeezed so hard for her and this man who could not bear what life had done to him that she lost her breath.

"Please," Victoria urged, "please, let me help you."

Seth shook his head. "It's too late. I've waited a long time for this moment. To be able to look into your eyes and see the horror when you learned the truth…when you realized what your precious son had suffered because of your negligence. I wanted to be certain that you took that knowledge to hell with you. So watch closely."

At the same instant that he lifted his weapon Tasha suddenly understood what he intended to do.

She hurled her body at his. *"No-o-o-o-o!"*

The sharp *crack* of a high-powered rifle rent the air.

The impact knocked her off her feet.

Slammed her against the wooden deck.

She blinked at the sun, confused, numb.

Seth stared down at her…blocking the bright light like a sudden eclipse.

The weapon slipped from his fingers.

Frantic voices.

Hurried footsteps.

He dropped to his knees beside her. His lips moved… called her name…. His voice followed her into the darkness.

CHAPTER FORTY

THERE WAS HOPE.

Victoria sat very still in the private visitation room and recalled those moments after the gunshot rang out.

Tasha had realized his intentions and shoved him out of the line of fire. She'd taken the bullet intended for him.

Thankfully the result had merely been a shoulder injury, but it had required immediate surgery. She was fine now. It could have been so much worse. She and Victoria both had learned something about the men in their lives. Lucas, contrary to her specific orders, had stationed his people around the cabin. Blue Callahan had taken the shot which had been intended only to disarm the man wielding the handgun.

But he hadn't come there to kill Victoria, they now knew. He'd decided to destroy her in a completely different manner. She was to have acknowledged that her son was indeed alive and the extent of what he'd suffered, then she would witness his assassination, ordered by the man she loved. That was to have been her final punishment, her destruction, for having allowed her son to fall into Leberman's hands. He had assumed Lucas's orders were to shoot to kill. She might never know precisely what had altered his course...the discovery of the mementos she'd left on the bed, possibly. The old newspaper clippings and keepsakes from his childhood. Perhaps fate had been on her side for once.

Despite the turmoil of those frantic moments when the

gun had slipped from his hand and half a dozen Specialists had swarmed onto the deck, she had watched this would-be assassin…her son…fall to his knees next to Tasha. She'd seen the pained expression of helplessness on his hard, unyielding face as he'd watched the blood soak into Tasha's blouse.

That's when Victoria had known there was hope.

He wasn't completely without emotion…he could still feel. He'd felt something at that moment. And some basic human compassion had rendered him unable to execute her or maybe he'd simply thought that watching him die would be more devastating to her. She couldn't be sure. Despite the horrors he'd suffered she was so thankful he was alive…to have him back. As selfish as that was, she couldn't help herself.

If only the doctors could get through to him. The team of medical experts working on his case had insisted that he could have no contact with anyone for a period of thirty days while they evaluated his condition. Victoria had waited impatiently for the time to pass. Tasha had waited with similar anticipation.

The day had finally arrived.

Victoria, of course, being immediate family would go first.

She didn't know what to expect. The doctors had warned her that he was uncooperative, even violent at times, but those moments had lessened in frequency the past couple of weeks. Despite his decision to allow one of Lucas's people to kill him in front of her, he wasn't considered suicidal, just determined to wield the ultimate blow. He refused medication, resisted hypnosis and outright defied their attempts to analyze him. The one thing he had done that even hinted at cooperation was to study the photo albums and other mementos Victoria provided. That was the only thing he really appeared to respond to. The doctors were amazed he even accepted the suggestion to view them. He'd adamantly refused to give them up since.

She couldn't help but smile. He'd definitely inherited his father's stubborn determination. Well, admittedly, he'd gotten some of that from her. Being exposed to the moments they had shared before he was kidnapped might not change anything, but maybe, just maybe, it would tear down that wall Leberman had erected. If Seth…Jimmy, remembered even one moment they'd spent together as a family, he would know without question how very much he'd been loved. Still was.

For that very reason, Victoria knew what she had to do. It had to be done today.

SETH STARED beyond the bars that obscured his view from the window of his room. He watched the people moving about outside. It was colder now, forcing them to wear coats and hats. He touched the glass and wondered if he would ever be free again.

He didn't actually care about his freedom, but he did want to find Tasha. To see with his own eyes that she was all right. That bullet she'd taken had been intended for him. He could no longer deny that she felt something for him. Anyone who took a bullet for another person definitely cared. But no one would give him any significant information, only that she had survived and was fine. He banged his fist against the glass in futility. He hated being trapped in this mental institution.

No matter how they prettied it up or how much it cost to be here, that's what it was. A frown tugged at his mouth. He didn't like the questions they asked him…the way they made him remember too many details of the past. He preferred to forget. But they just kept digging, kept prodding for more. What the hell did it matter? He was screwed up. It didn't take a whole damned team of shrinks to figure that out. And until one month ago he hadn't really given a damn.

But things were different now. He lived and breathed for one thing, to see Tasha again.

Nothing else mattered.

Leberman was a ghost who only haunted him in his dreams. The past couldn't hurt him anymore, except when those mind excavators started their digging. He blocked it out the rest of the time. He glanced at the table across the room and the photo albums there.

She had sent those.

Victoria…his mother.

She wanted him to remember…like he had for that one instant when Tasha had first shown him those newspaper clippings. A hundred memories had come flooding into his head, overwhelming him. But he'd tried to push them away, the same way he always had. It was easier not to remember. But the knowledge that his parents had searched for him had somehow changed something inside him. Made it difficult to keep the memories at bay. Had rendered him unable to execute his original plan. He'd told himself that watching him die would wield much more devastation, but he wasn't so sure of his motives now. He simply hadn't been able to kill her. Hadn't been able to strike.

And now, *she* wouldn't go away.

The doctors said that she required daily briefings on his progress. That she was coming to see him today. The frown that had been annoying his mouth worked its up and across his forehead. He wasn't sure he wanted to see her. What she'd shown him with her old photos confused him.

He heard the lock on his door being disengaged and he knew she was here. Lunch was over, and he didn't have any appointments this afternoon. It had to be her.

Two orderlies stepped into the room. The tallest one said

to him when he turned around, "Okay, Mr. Colby, let's make this easy, shall we?"

He didn't like being referred to as Mr. Colby, but they all called him that. Like it would change who he really was. But then...he didn't even know who he was. Little Jimmy Colby had died in a cold, dark basement a long time ago. And Seth, the man he had become, was missing in action in a lot of ways. They'd even removed the tattoo that Leberman had used to mark him as a beast.

He allowed the two men to restrain his hands in front of him with transparent nylon bands. This place was too ritzy to use iron shackles, but the effect was the same. They led him to the visitation area. Not the one the rest of the residents used, but one especially for him since he was considered *dangerous*.

He didn't miss the relief on the two men's faces when they'd reached their destination.

"Behave yourself now," the tall one said as he opened the door. "We'll be waiting right outside."

Seth smiled at him, and every ounce of assurance drained from the man's expression. Maybe he really was a monster. It definitely had its advantages.

Inside the room he hesitated a moment before turning to face his visitor. The subtle scent of her flowery perfume reminded him of her home. Her room had smelled that way. He hadn't been able to put the scent out of his mind the past few weeks.

"It's good to see you," she said, hoping to garner his attention.

He executed a slow, deliberate 180-degree turn, more to control his reaction than to intimidate her. He wasn't sure how he would respond to her presence. He was unsure of a lot of things lately. He'd been ready to die to hurt her, hadn't he? His brow creased into a frown. He didn't know anymore.

Forcing the disturbing thoughts away, his gaze settled on her. It felt strange to look at her and not feel the hatred that had been his constant companion for so long. He wasn't sure where it had gone. It was simply gone. Maybe it was the medication they sneaked into his food. He was reasonably certain that's what they were doing since he refused to take it. He'd eventually had to eat. They had known he would. Which provided the opportunity they needed.

She sat stiffly at the table provided. The bland room hadn't been designed for comfort. Only one barred window. A table with four chairs. Nothing else. All white, no pictures on the walls, no rug on the floor, plain old commercial-grade tan tile.

But she was anything but bland. She wore a pink suit that looked tailored for her. Her dark hair was up in its usual smooth bun. Her makeup, what little she wore, was applied expertly. She was a woman of means who wore her position in society proudly.

She was too strong to give up on him…or too stubborn. Seth hadn't decided which yet.

He approached the table and sat down, his scrutiny continuing as he observed her every response to his movements. She wasn't afraid…resigned maybe, but definitely not afraid. She looked troubled and he knew he was the reason.

"I want to know more about Tasha," he said, careful to keep the alien emotions he'd experienced of late out of his tone.

Victoria nodded. "She's fine. In fact, she's here to see you."

Anticipation surged through him, but he suppressed the urgency that welled up in his chest. "She wants to see me?"

"Yes. She's wanted to see you from the moment they

released her from the hospital, but the doctors wouldn't allow you visitors until now.''

He didn't like those damned doctors.

''I'd like to see her now.'' Anything Victoria Colby had to say to him could wait. He wanted to see Tasha. His heart kicked into a faster rhythm as his mind recalled the moments they had shared together. He tried to control how the memories affected him, but he couldn't manage the feat anymore.

''I'd like to spend a few moments with you first,'' Victoria said, dragging his attention back to her.

He had endured endless beatings and worse in the past to earn the right to a meal or a few hours' sleep, he supposed he could endure a few minutes of her company. Though he couldn't understand why she would want to see him. He'd spent a great deal of time thinking about killing her. She was well aware of that. And still she came to see him.

''The doctors have told me that you've experienced a few breakthrough memories about your life before…''

Before Leberman, she didn't say. He didn't like thinking about Leberman. ''That's right.'' He resisted the urge to tap his foot as his agitation began to build. There was something about her demeanor now that made him uneasy. He couldn't quite put his finger on it…but something wasn't right.

''You must know, then, that your father and I loved you very much. We were a happy family.''

The tears he expected to see in her eyes weren't there, just a dullness that made him curious to know what was going on inside her head.

''What do you want me to say to that?'' The question came out bluntly. What did she expect from him? A sudden return to life the way it was before? Was he supposed to hug her and tell her that he loved her? He didn't know how to love. Leberman had made sure of that. Hell, he'd never even missed another human until Tasha.

Victoria looked away for a moment, then settled her gaze back on his. "I don't know what I expect you to say," she admitted, her fingers clasping the clutch purse she carried even tighter. "This is difficult for both of us."

She was upset. The doctors would be watching and analyzing his ability to interact with her. Shit. He'd never get out of here if he didn't do better. Did it matter? He thought of Tasha and decided it did.

"The photo albums have been useful," he offered, hoping to placate her.

Her whole expression seemed to brighten at his words. The reaction confused him. Increased that uneasiness twisting inside him.

"I've done a lot of thinking since I learned that you were still alive," she said quietly. "And I've decided that you're right."

His instincts went on alert.

"If I had been a better mother I would have found you before your father came home that day. Then you wouldn't have slipped through the gate and hidden in the forest. I would have found you…before."

The doctors had told her the things he'd remembered. She had been playing with him in the backyard. She'd gone inside to answer the phone and he'd hidden in the bushes near the entry gate to the lake house property. The security measures had been to protect him from the water…and other things he'd been too young to understand. While she was looking for him in the backyard his father had come home. He'd sneaked out as the gate closed behind his father's car. He'd thought it would be so funny to hide in the woods. He and his mother had taken walks there before, he wasn't afraid.

But night had come too fast for her to find him. Then

he'd gotten scared…had tried to find his way out…but he'd found Leberman instead. Leberman had had someone watching the house for just that moment. Under hypnosis, Seth had remembered another man but couldn't identify him.

"I should have watched you more carefully. I didn't protect you…it was my fault." She looked into his eyes, and the pain he saw there was hard to look at. "All of this was my fault. You're right to hate me. I should have protected you."

His apprehension escalated, making him increasingly uncomfortable. She didn't seem to want answers…she just wanted to talk…to say the words.

"I would have gladly traded places with you if I could have found you. But he was too elusive…too smart for me, so I failed. Now the decision is yours. Where do you want this to go, or do you want it to end here and now? I need to know how you feel. If you still wish me dead. I, for one, can't live another day with this guilt. With the not knowing."

He thought of the strong woman he'd watched for months, waiting until the time came. Leberman had wanted him to kill her as well as Lucas Camp. He'd planned for it from day one. But Seth hadn't been able to follow through…he'd decided to simply destroy her from the inside out. To make her suffer as he had. At least, he thought that's what he'd decided. She would see him die and that would be worse than death.

As he stared into her dull, hollow eyes, he knew he had accomplished that goal.

Oddly, it gave him no satisfaction.

All he'd ever seen of Victoria Colby was her strength…her stoicism no matter what was thrown her way. Where was that woman now?

"I've decided to give you the opportunity to have your vengeance."

He stilled, his instincts rushing to a higher state of alert.

"You realize, of course," she went on, "that they're watching us, so there won't be time for second thoughts or deliberation. But I have to know that I've done everything within my power to make the past up to you. If taking my life will give you even one moment's peace, I'll gladly surrender it."

Before he could string together a response, she reached into her purse and withdrew a small-caliber handgun. A .32. She placed it on the table in front of him and said, "The decision is yours."

He stared at the gun for about three seconds then looked directly at her. She was dead serious. Willing to do anything to give him peace, even if only for one fleeting moment. Could anyone really be that selfless? Could he possibly mean that much to her? His gaze dropped to the weapon once more. For his whole life a weapon had been the one thing he could rely on. The one thing he trusted. But now, staring at the cold, black steel, he felt nothing. No desire. No urgency.

He heard the scuffle of running feet in the corridor outside.

"They're coming," she warned.

He didn't know how the hell she'd gotten in this place with that weapon, but he had to hand it to her, she didn't make idle boasts. She was willing to die for him.

Two guards rushed into the room. He didn't move. Knew if he did that he'd get an injection that would put him out for about six hours. Like all his lessons, he'd learned that one the hard way.

The .32 was snatched off the table by one of the guards. "Mrs. Colby, we'll have to ask you to come with us now."

She looked confused...startled.

They needed more time.

Seth glared up at the burly guard and said, "We're not finished yet."

If the widening of the man's eyes was any indication, he didn't want to argue. "I'll need your purse," he said to Victoria. She handed it over. The guard glanced at Seth. "We'll be right outside with your orderlies."

Seth said nothing. There was no need.

For a couple of minutes after the guards left, he and Victoria simply looked at each other. He wasn't sure what he wanted to say and he imagined she felt the same way.

But there was one thing he had to know. "Did you have that much faith in those few years we spent together to believe that I wouldn't take you up on your offer?"

She smiled sadly. "Yes, I did. But I had to know for sure."

He shook his head. There she was. The superwoman he'd watched from a distance. The woman who visited him every single day through the memories her photo albums evoked.

He exhaled a mighty breath. "I guess we have a long ways to go in a lot of respects."

"Does that mean we have a truce?" she asked, that hope springing to life in her eyes once more.

He stared at his bound hands for a moment and tried to think above all the lies and ugliness he'd been force-fed all those years. "Yeah." He met her gaze once more. "I guess it does."

She stood, seemingly satisfied. "I've taken enough of your time. I'll send in Tasha."

He wasn't sure he could let her go without saying more, but he wasn't even sure what he needed to say. "Wait." He grappled for the right words.

When she hesitated and turned back to him, he stood, towered over her by nearly a foot. But she didn't look intimidated, she just looked hopeful. That undying hope affected something in his chest. "I don't know where things will go from here. I don't know how to be what you probably want me to be." She shouldn't get her hopes up. He might never be able to live up to her expectations.

A tremulous smile peeked past the emotions cluttering her face. "For the record, I only want you to be happy." She laid her hand against his arm, a gesture of comfort. Remarkably, he didn't feel compelled to flinch. "I'll be back tomorrow."

He nodded, then watched her go.

His heart started to beat faster at the thought of seeing Tasha. He was so damned thankful that she was here.

The orderly came in, looking annoyed. Seth tensed. Were they taking him back now? Had someone decided he wasn't allowed to see Tasha?

"I'm going to let your hands loose," the orderly said gruffly, "but if you give us any trouble, they'll go back on. Got it?"

Seth nodded, relieved that they weren't taking him away. Victoria had to be behind this. She must have insisted they release his restraints. He could see her making that happen. Something like respect nudged at him. It was going to take time to get used to all these unfamiliar feelings.

When the orderly had exited the room, the door opened again. Tasha stepped inside. She looked great. But a whole month had passed. Her injury had obviously healed.

He started to shake, and he didn't understand the reaction…couldn't stop it. He had to look away. Didn't want her to see the weakness.

She moved in close to him, took his trembling hand. "Hey."

Despite the way his body shook and his gut clenched, he had to look at her, had to hold her. He pulled her into his arms, and his breath caught at the feel of her.

"They wouldn't tell me what I wanted to know," he managed to say without his voice quavering. "Wouldn't let me see you."

"It's okay," she murmured as she held him tight in her arms. "Everything's okay now."

They held each other that way for a long time. He couldn't say for sure just how long.

She finally pulled back far enough to press a soft kiss to his lips. "It's good to see you. I've missed you."

He cupped her face in his hands and tried to think of how to tell her what he was feeling but couldn't find the words. "It's good to see you," he echoed.

"Victoria says they're moving you to a different room now. You'll be able to have visitors every day."

He liked watching her lips move…liked the way she smelled. He wanted to taste her. "Will you come every day?"

She smiled and nodded. "If you want me to."

He tasted her lips and she kissed him back. "Yes," he whispered between kisses. "I want you to."

She kissed him again and he shivered. He wondered vaguely if the guards would come running if he stripped off her clothes and took her right here on the table.

Maybe he'd just see.

EPILOGUE

"I'LL BE READY in a moment!" Victoria called from the bedroom of their penthouse suite.

Lucas loosened his bow tie and pulled it free of his neck. The wedding was behind them. The champagne was on ice. And Victoria was getting "comfortable." He still shuddered when he thought of her taking that weapon into that clinic, but she'd been determined to do something to break the ice between her and her son. When Lucas had learned about her bold move he'd gone ballistic. But she'd insisted that she'd known going in how it would end.

He opened the French doors and stepped out onto the grand balcony. All the suites on the empress deck had balconies and he'd wanted the best for their honeymoon. The crisp December breeze sent a chill across his skin, but the knowledge that the woman in the other room was now his lawful wife kept him plenty warm.

If he squinted he could just make out the wedding party still waving from the pier as the ship moved farther and farther from shore. Every single member of the Colby Agency was there, as were a number of his Specialists.

A nice long cruise was in order.

He and Victoria deserved it.

Ian and Simon could take care of things at the agency.

Director Casey had Mission Recovery under control.

And Tasha would keep Jim company.

He still considered himself Seth, the name Leberman had given him long ago. He'd never had a social security number or driver's license. Leberman had provided the essentials he'd wanted him to possess to go along with any number of aliases as necessary. For all intents and purposes, the persona Seth had never existed on paper or in any other "legitimate" capacity. He tolerated Victoria's constant use of the name that had belonged to the boy he once was. He had a long way to go. The doctors weren't sure he would fully recover his early memories, but he would learn to cope with his newly developing emotions. His sessions had gone well enough that he was allowed to leave the clinic for weekends. All of which were spent with Tasha, except for Sunday brunch with Victoria, of course.

All in all, Lucas felt good about the way things had worked out. Leberman was dead, the evil bastard, and Victoria had her son back, for the most part anyway.

Tasha had given Lucas notice that she'd decided to join the Colby Agency rather than his team. Well, he couldn't fault her there. She wanted to be close to Jim. A job in research at the firm would keep her out of harm's way, as well. Making a life with Jim was going to take a lot of patience and understanding. Tasha was the right woman.

His cell phone rang, and Lucas fished it from his jacket pocket. He'd taken care to mute it during the service or risk facing Victoria's, as well as the minister's, wrath.

He smiled at the thought as he flipped open his phone. Victoria Colby-Camp. It had a hell of a nice ring to it.

"Camp," he said by way of greeting.

"I'm not interrupting anything, am I?"

Director Casey. "Not yet," Lucas warned. He glanced back into the room to see if Victoria had appeared.

"There might not be a better time for us to talk later."

"Now is fine," Lucas insisted. He knew his director wouldn't call unless it was important.

"I spoke with the doctor at the clinic this morning. Since they started hypnosis there hasn't been much real progress.

According to his conclusions, Jim is still resisting, subconsciously he believes.''

Lucas rubbed his forehead and considered the ramifications of that information. He'd asked Casey to personally look into the situation with Victoria's son since he couldn't do so without her knowledge. No one at the Colby Agency could know about his growing suspicions. It wasn't that he didn't trust Victoria, she simply had enough on her plate right now with sorting out the fledgling relationship with her son. She didn't need this added worry. But he was certain that there was, at the very least, someone in the agency who'd leaked information, quite possibly without realizing it. Leberman had known too much. According to Tasha, he had known who she was from the beginning. He'd known the security codes to both Victoria's properties. The very thought of a mole made him extremely nervous. Lucas had to be certain.

''We need to know how he got his information,'' Lucas said on a sigh, well aware that he was preaching to the choir. ''With Leberman dead I guess we have no choice but to wait it out. See if Jim knows something. With the brainwashing technique Leberman used he could know all sorts of things and be completely oblivious to the information. Like the identity of the other man involved in his kidnapping eighteen years ago.'' Not to mention certain aspects of his neurological programming could be in sleep mode. God only knew what Leberman may have programmed him to do at some unknown future date. Just another reason why he needed Tasha by his side. But Casey was already well aware of those possibilities. He'd sought out an expert to work with Jim, but there were no guarantees he would learn anything.

''I agree. I'll keep you up to date,'' Casey assured him before ending the call.

Lucas dropped the phone back into his pocket and looked

out over the water. Although there were still outstanding questions and concerns where Leberman was concerned, most especially with regards to the Colby Agency, life was good.

Scratch that, he amended, life was excellent.

"I'm ready, Lucas."

He turned in time to see his lovely bride exit the bedroom wearing the sexiest, most beautiful white silk negligee he'd ever laid eyes on.

The only thing he could imagine being more beautiful was her out of it.

"So am I," he murmured as he moved toward the woman he loved and their future together. *So am I.*

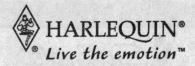

A brand-new adventure featuring California's most talked-about family, The Coltons!

SWEET CHILD
OF MINE

by bestselling author
Jean Brashear

When Mayor Michael Longstreet and social worker Suzanne Jorgensen both find themselves in need of a spouse, they agree to a short-term marriage of convenience. But neither plans on their "arrangement" heating up into an all-out, passionate affair!

Coming in February 2004.

THE COLTONS
FAMILY. PRIVILEGE. POWER.

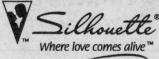

Where love comes alive™

Visit Silhouette at www.eHarlequin.com   PSSCOM

**Return to the sexy Lone Star state
with *Trueblood, Texas*!**

Her Protector

by

LIZ IRELAND

Partially blind singer Jolene Daniels is being stalked,
and Texas Ranger Bobby Garcia is determined to
help the vulnerable beauty—and to recapture
a love they both thought was lost.

Finders Keepers: Bringing families together.

Available wherever books are sold in March 2004.

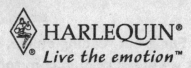

HARLEQUIN®

Live the emotion™

Visit us at www.eHarlequin.com

CPHP

If you enjoyed what you just read,
then we've got an offer you can't resist!

Take 2
bestselling novels FREE!
Plus get a FREE surprise gift!

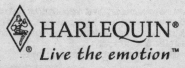